'What's that

Belatedly, Sullivan
asked his lawyer to
man to show it to him first, not mail it. 'You weren't supposed to get this now.'

'Then when?' she demanded. 'Just when is a good time to tell me that you intend to rip this child out of my arms no matter what?'

'Marlene,' he began, then stopped. Given the situation, he would have expected her to be turning red. But she was a very deathly shade of white. 'You're turning pale.' Sullivan grabbed her arm as Marlene's knees suddenly buckled beneath her. 'What is it?' he demanded.

'I don't know.' She was bewildered. 'I—' Her eyes flew open. 'Oh, my God.'

And then he saw what had caused her to gasp. 'Marlene...I think your water broke.'

Dear Reader,

Welcome to Special Edition®! This month we get the holidays off to a fine start with the newest novel from Marie Ferrarella, *Baby's First Christmas*; it's the first of five in a cross-line series called THE BABY OF THE MONTH CLUB. The other books appear in Sensation™ and Desire™ and, of course, there are babies in all of them...eventually!

There's also a special Christmassy HOMETOWN HEARTBREAKER from Susan Mallery and a new PARENTHOOD novel from Diana Whitney. The last of the stories set over the holidays is Karen Rose Smith's *The Sheriff's Proposal*, where Meg Dawson's whirlwind romance had an unexpected result...

CUPID'S LITTLE HELPERS by Tracy Sinclair finishes this month and there's a really strong story of reunited lovers from Janis Reams Hudson, too. Don't miss any of them!

Merry Christmas!

The Editors

Baby's First Christmas

MARIE FERRARELLA

All the characters in this book have no existence outside the imagination of the author, and have no relation whatsoever to anyone bearing the same name or names. They are not even distantly inspired by any individual known or unknown to the author, and all the incidents are pure invention.

First published in Great Britain 1997
Silhouette Books, Eton House, 18-24 Paradise Road, Richmond, Surrey TW9 1SR

ISBN 0 373 23997 1

23-9712

Printed and bound in Great Britain by Mackays of Chatham PLC, Chatham

To Isabel Swift, Leslie Wainger, Tara Gavin,
Anne Canadeo, Lucia Macro & Melissa Senate.
Thank you for letting me do this.
Love, Marie

MARIE FERRARELLA

lives in Southern California. This award-winning author describes herself as the tired mother of two over-energetic children and the contented wife of one wonderful man. She is thrilled to be following her dream of writing full-time.

Other novels by Marie Ferrarella

Silhouette Special Edition®

It Happened One Night
A Girl's Best Friend
Blessing in Disguise
Someone To Talk To
World's Greatest Dad
Family Matters
She Got Her Man
Baby in the Middle
Husband: Some Assembly Required
Brooding Angel
†Baby's First Christmas

Silhouette Sensation®

*Holding Out for a Hero
*Heroes Great and Small
*Christmas Every Day
Callaghan's Way
*Caitlin's Guardian Angel

* *Those Sinclairs*
† *The Baby of the Month Club*

Silhouette Desire®

Father in the Making

Books by Marie Ferrarella writing as Marie Nicole

Silhouette Desire

Tried and True
Buyer Beware
Through Laughter and Tears
Grand Theft: Heart
A Woman of Integrity
Country Blue
Last Year's Hunk
Foxy Lady
Chocolate Dreams
No Laughing Matter

Marlene Bailey
Proudly
Announces
The Birth Of
Her Long-Awaited
Baby:

Robert Travis
Bailey

Chapter One

"What do you mean, you don't have it?"

Sullivan Travis's voice thundered off the small office's glass walls, filtering out into the stark white reception area of the Hawley-Richman Institute. All sorts of horrifying ramifications occurred to him as he looked at the lab coat clad technician. There had to be some mistake.

"If you don't have it, where is it? Is it lost?" If it was lost, no one could use it, he reasoned. He began to relax. Lost. All right, that would be the end of it, then.

The young woman looked up at him, torn between being annoyed and being intimidated. The tall, dark-haired man on the other side of her desk had a commanding presence that unnerved her. She eyed the security buzzer on the underside of her desk. They didn't get many irate people at the sperm bank. At least, none since she'd been there, but there was a guard on duty just in case. She wondered if this was going to be that kind of "case."

He was literally leaning over her desk. In an effort to keep things calm, she rose, shoving her hands deep into her pockets so he wouldn't notice that they were shaking. Martha Riley cleared her voice and tried to sound official.

"It's been used, Mr. Travis." What had he thought they would do with his "donation"? After all, he had been paid for his contribution. It was the Institute's property now, not his.

One look at his face told her that he wasn't ready to accept that line of reasoning.

"Great, just great." He blew out a breath, momentarily stumped. *Now what?*

Sullivan ran his hand through his hair as he sighed. He looked up toward the ceiling, metaphorically seeking heavenly guidance. It seemed rather ironic when he thought of it. Heaven had never figured into the path that his older brother had chosen. A rebel from the moment he formed his first words, Derek Travis had been one of a kind. He had been the epitome of the prodigal son, except that he had never returned home to make amends.

He'd reveled in discord for discord's sake, and the pieces that were left in his wake were something that Sullivan was always required to reconstruct. Or, when that failed, to sweep away.

But this latest stunt defied description. It was outrageous, even for Derek. How could he have done this? What could he possibly have been thinking?

Sullivan had still been reeling from his brother's sudden death when he had come across the letter from the sperm bank among Derek's possessions. He'd stared at it for several minutes, stunned. What made it all the more bewildering was that the letter hadn't been addressed to Derek. It had been addressed to *him,* care of Derek.

Reading it, Sullivan had sunk down on the lumpy mattress in his brother's meager studio apartment, his knees buckling beneath him. He read and reread the letter several times, but the words remained the same each time.

Derek had sold his connection to the future, his potential offspring, for what amounted to a few dollars. Sullivan assumed he'd done it to buy art supplies. Getting back at his father was only an added bonus.

Derek and Oliver Travis had never been on the same side of a conversation. It seemed to Sullivan that Derek had always gone out of his way to upset their father.

But this . . . this was beyond understanding.

Though Derek had pulled some really stupid stunts in his time, Sullivan hadn't thought for one moment that he had actually sold his genes when he had thrown that up to their father in what amounted to their last argument. Sullivan had assumed that Derek only said it because family heritage and image had always been important to their father. It was easy enough to believe that, like everything else, he'd said what he had only to annoy the old man.

But Derek had not only done it, he had put Sullivan's name to it, compounding the embarrassment.

Pocketing the letter, Sullivan had lost no time in locating the sperm bank. He'd gone there, determined to pay whatever amount that it took to undo Derek's reckless folly.

Now it looked as if he'd arrived too late. He stared unseeingly at a commemorative plaque on the wall behind the woman.

Well, it looks like you've really gone and done it this time, Derek. You finally made a mess that's impossible for me to clean up.

The technician touched his arm hesitantly. "Are you all right? I mean, that *is* why you donated the sperm, isn't it? So it could be used?"

Sullivan thought of saying that *he* hadn't donated any part of himself to this high-tech, antiseptic recycling institute, that it was his brother who had done it and then, to add insult to injury, or perhaps to give vent to some macabre sense of humor, signed *his* name to the form.

But that would be making a stranger privy to his own inner turmoil and the tensions that existed within his family. That just wasn't Sullivan's style. He had always handled his brother's transgressions with a minimum of fanfare.

Sullivan searched for patience. Somehow the situation had to be salvaged, no matter what sort of damage control he had to exercise. There had to be a way.

"That's just it. I've changed my mind. I want to buy it back." He paused significantly. Maybe she'd made a mistake and confused his file with someone else's. "At any cost."

The woman keyed in something on the computer. A moment later she shook her head, looking sincerely regretful. "According to my records, your..."

Raising her eyes to his, Martha blushed, then flustered, began again. "It was implanted March twenty-fifth." Her fingers slipped from the keyboard. "I'm afraid that it really is too late."

Yes, it certainly is.

Sullivan scrubbed his hand over his face, wondering how many paramedics it would take to revive his father once Oliver Travis learned the extent of his oldest son's latest sin. Since he had suffered a stroke last year, his father had become a shadow of the man he had once been, bound to a wheelchair and the past. Sullivan sighed. Dead and gone, and Derek was still getting back at the family.

Nice work, Derek.

Sullivan looked at the technician, his expression softening. It wasn't her fault that the Travis family had given birth to a black sheep. "All right, who was the recipient?"

The woman shook her head. "I'm afraid I really can't tell you that. It's against our confidentiality policy."

He could appreciate her dilemma, but he had a larger one to consider. There was still such a thing as family honor, even in this day and age. And obligations. "I realize that there are rules and regulations—"

She looked at him apologetically. Her hands were tied. Sullivan took out his wallet, his eyes on hers.

"Very strict rules and regulations," she breathed watching him absently sort through a large wad of bills.

He nodded. "But these are extenuating circumstances, and— "

Her eyes were glued to the hundred dollar bill Sullivan carefully laid out on her desk. She wavered, then looked around to see if anyone was within eyeshot. They were alone, but that didn't seem to put her at ease.

She chewed on her lower lip. "It would mean my job if I showed you."

He added a second hundred to the first, carefully flattening a curled edge. "I'm not asking you to show me the name," he assured her. His eyes shifted to the computer. "You could, however, pull up the right screen, and then perhaps..."

He glanced around the room as if he were searching for the right word. He did it for effect. Words had never been a problem for Sullivan. He always knew exactly what he was going to say, exactly what he needed to do. His life had been mapped out for him at an early age by a father who had been filled with great dreams. Dreams that had flourished. The Travis Corporation was the leading land development company in the state. A fourth-generation family business, it had risen to the top of its field due largely to his father's efforts in the early years. He ran it now. The mantle Sullivan wore had been intended for Derek's shoulders, but Derek had refused even to try it on.

"Drop your pencil on the floor," he finally suggested. "If it rolled under the desk, it might take you a few seconds to locate it."

He discreetly moved the hundred dollar bills toward her, separating them from his fingers as if they had never been there at all.

The woman stared at the bills, tempted. Debating. The debate was summarily terminated when a third bill joined the first two.

She moved her swivel chair around and typed out a few words on the keyboard. The keys clicked quickly, accentuated by the sound of her agitated breathing.

On the monitor, screens blinked, scrolled and finally came to a halt at the right one. She glanced around once more. There was no one passing by her office. It was now or never. Eyes hooded, Martha leaned an elbow on her desk and sent a pen tumbling to the carpet.

This was one woman who would never qualify for high-tech espionage, Sullivan thought with a grim smile. He leaned forward, tucking the three bills under the corner of the woman's blotter as he scanned the screen.

Within moments he had a name, an address and a telephone number, as well as a sick feeling in the pit of his stomach. Marlene Bailey, whoever she was, was now carrying his brother's child. If the offspring turned out anything like its father, Sullivan could almost feel sorry for the faceless Marlene.

The feeling passed quickly, though, replaced by annoyance. Annoyance at his brother, at the burden now placed on him, and at Marlene Bailey. What kind of woman went to a sperm bank to get impregnated, anyway? It sounded so cold, so calculating. Like ordering a child from a menu.

Maybe that would make his job easier in the long run.

Marlene Bailey's personality and peculiarities were not his concern, he reminded himself. The Travis name, and his father's health, were. The sooner he got this cleared up, the better.

Martha, her runaway pen in her hand, sat up and nervously looked at Sullivan. With an almost imperceptible nod of his head, he rose.

"Thank you, Ms.—" Sullivan glanced down at the nameplate on the woman's desk "—Riley. You've been a great help."

Her sweaty palm curved over the bills, and she looked at him uncertainly. "You won't tell . . . ?"

"Tell what?" he asked, the soul of innocence. "As far as I'm concerned, you were the unshakable pinnacle of integrity."

With that he walked out of the office. He heard her sigh of relief in the background.

Too many people could be bought, he thought, as he hurried out of the building. The fact saddened him even though it did make his life easier. At times it seemed as if there was no honor left in the world, no principles. But then, he supposed, that was a given.

What was also a given, he decided as he got into his car, was that he intended to have Ms. Marlene Bailey sign over custody of her unborn child.

There was no other option open to him. His brother's death last month had hit his father very hard. It had sent the already infirm man into a spiraling depression. Having a grandchild, Derek's child, around might help fill the gaping hole he was carrying around in his heart.

At least he could hope that it might, Sullivan thought. Besides, he'd been taught that family always came first. He only wished that Derek had remembered that once in a while.

No use dwelling on what was in the past, he told himself, pulling out of the lot. He needed to concentrate on the present. The child would be a Travis, entitled to everything that went with the name.

He wondered just how much Marlene Bailey would hold out for before caving in.

Sally clutched her chest, her spidery fingers spread over her heart. Her crepe soles squeaked as she took a step back on the gray-and-white glazed tile in the foyer. Squinting, she looked up at the person she had known for thirty years, acting as if she didn't recognize her.

"My God, you're home, and it's not even dark out yet. Did the office burn down?" The biting sarcasm abated as her expression suddenly grew serious, making her withered cheeks sink in even further. "Or are you...?" Her eyes darted to the pronounced outline of Marlene's abdomen.

"No, I am not." Mimicking Sally, Marlene deliberately left the end of the sentence hanging. "I'm home because I'm meeting someone here."

Sally closed the door and followed Marlene into the living room. She moved very quickly for a woman who only shuffled. "A man?"

Marlene ignored the incredulous yet hopeful note in her housekeeper's voice. "Yes."

Sally sniffed, as if to hide what Marlene knew was her secret wish that Marlene would find someone to settle down with, someone who could finally take care of her the way she deserved to be cared for. After all, she wasn't getting any younger, as Sally frequently told her.

Sally stared at Marlene's protruding silhouette. "Should have thought of that before—"

Obviously Sally wasn't going to give this up until she told her. "No romantic assignations, Sally. I'm expecting a private investigator."

Sally's brows knit together in a wiggly line of confusion. "What do you need a private investigator for?"

Marlene knew that it would never occur to Sally that the answer to that question was none of her business. Sally had been in the family's employ since before Marlene was born, and had become even more integral in their lives after Marlene's mother had walked out on them. For years Sally had been the only maternal influence she and her sister Nicole had had in their lives. She was their buffer against James Bailey's paternal demands. If the woman was a little rough around the edges, that could be forgiven. After all, love didn't always come neatly packaged in shiny gold foil.

"I've decided to try to find out who the baby's father is."

Marlene placed a protective hand over her belly, the way she did each time she and Sally discussed the baby. Sally had very vocally disapproved of her method of entering into the state of motherhood, but then, Sally hadn't been the one to experience the yearnings that insistently battered her.

Her father's untimely death thirteen months before had caused Marlene to stop and take stock of her life. At a juncture where most women already had families, Marlene stood barren and alone. The life she had was meaningless unless there was someone to be shaping her legacy for. Unless there was someone to come home to. But since she'd never had time for relationships, that left her decidedly short of one would-be father.

Never one to hang back and leave things to fate, Marlene had taken matters into her own hands. She had remedied the situation the best way she knew how. And she had no regrets.

Sally's frown deepened. "You would have known that if you had gone about it the way God had intended you to."

Marlene sighed. She felt especially tired today. She'd pushed hard to wrap up an ad campaign before taking the rest of the day off. When she had originally made up her mind to become pregnant, she had sworn to herself that she wasn't going to let her condition slow her down or change her life beyond weight gain and the sweet satisfaction of knowing she was carrying another life within her body. Pregnancy, like everything else, became a challenge for her to overcome. Each day was business as usual.

To that end, she made certain that her makeup was meticulously applied each morning without fail. And she still wore the same three-inch heels she had always favored. God, in his infinite kindness, hadn't sent down an onslaught of varicose veins to plague her or puffy ankles to slow her down.

The only plague she had to deal with was on the home front: Sally and her disapproval.

"We've been through this, Sally. That's all behind us," she said patiently.

The smirk took years off Sally's age. "No, that's all in front of us, especially you."

Marlene raised an eyebrow and simultaneously lowered her voice. "Sally—"

The housekeeper threw up her hands, not so much in surrender as in disgust. Marlene knew just what she was thinking. If only the girls had had a normal upbringing, Marlene would have a husband in the picture by now. And Nicole wouldn't have run off with that worthless bum.

"I know, I know, butt out." A smile that would have made the Mona Lisa envious graced the old woman's thin lips. "You should be so lucky." Sally cocked her head, studying Marlene, reminding her of a gray-haired sparrow. "What brought this on? I thought you told Nicole that it didn't matter to you who the baby's father was?"

That had been true in the beginning, Marlene acknowledged. But curiosity had nibbled at her incessantly until it had worn a hole right through her. Besides, there were other reasons to know.

"It doesn't," Marlene insisted. "But someday my baby might want to know who its father is. I want to be able to offer a name, a history. A picture. He—or she—deserves that."

Sally snorted. "You don't deliberately start out being a one-parent family if you can help it. That baby deserves a father who isn't just a resumé or an eight by ten glossy."

With anyone else, Marlene would have been defensive. But Sally knew the story. She'd been there as it was unfolding.

"I never have the time to meet anyone, Sally. You know that."

"You would have if you hadn't spent all your time trying to please your father." She shook her head, remembering. "Sooner get blood from a stone than win that man's respect and affection."

Marlene sank down in the wing chair, the firmest one in the room. She was bone weary and didn't have the stamina to go into this now. Whatever James Bailey had been didn't change the fact that he was her father and that she loved him.

"If you felt that way about him, why did you work for him all those years?"

"Same reason I'm still here. You. And your sister, when she lived here. I figured that you two needed someone in your corner, and that I'd do until someone better came along."

Touched, Marlene rose and kissed her wrinkled cheek. "No one better than you will ever come along."

Sally shrugged self-consciously. Having worked for James Bailey all these years, she had little experience dealing with praise. She shuffled out of the room. There was still dinner to deal with.

"Don't think that means you're getting out of buying me a Christmas present," Sally huffed over her narrow shoulder.

Marlene laughed. Sally was one of a kind. Probably by popular demand. "I've got it picked out already," she called after the woman.

Sally stopped in the doorway and turned toward Marlene. Maternal concern softened the harsher contours of her thin face. "Can I get you anything? Tea? Sandwich?"

Marlene shook her head. "I'm fine, Sally."

Sally smiled to herself. "Yeah, I guess you are at that," she murmured under her breath.

The doorbell rang just as she was about to disappear into the kitchen. With a sigh, she turned on her heel.

Marlene glanced at her watch. The private investigator was early, though not by much.

He had said that he might be late because of the traffic. The infamous El Toro Y, located south of her home, tended to knot up between the hours of three-thirty and seven.

Since he had to come from that general direction, he'd obviously allotted extra time.

Or maybe all the holiday shoppers were out at the malls and not on the freeway today, she mused. She waved Sally back to the kitchen.

"Don't bother. I'll get it," she told her as she passed Sally on the way to the door.

Bony shoulders rose and fell. "Suit yourself. My pay's the same whether I answer doors or not." Sally moved back toward the kitchen, then stopped, hovering on the threshold between the two rooms as Marlene opened the front door.

He wasn't at all what she'd been expecting, Marlene thought. As far as she knew, detectives weren't supposed to arrive wearing expensive three-piece suits, but then, she thought ruefully, she'd been raised on TV detectives. Endearingly mussed PI's who were filled with snappy patter and caught their man, half the time by accident, before the last commercial aired.

Marlene put out her hand. "Hello, I'm Marlene Bailey. You're early."

As if in a trance, Sullivan took her hand. Whatever he'd been going to say flew out of his head. Her words had caught him completely off guard.

As did her appearance. She was the most pregnant woman he had ever seen. At least, the most pregnant woman he had ever seen from such a close vantage point. But that wasn't what had words curling up on his tongue. The woman was gorgeous.

Not only that, but she had class written all over her, from her tilted cleft chin to her tailored, pale blue suit. It was the kind of class that came from bloodlines, from pampering and from never having to worry about paying bills, no matter how large they were.

Why would a beautiful woman have to resort to a sperm bank in order to conceive a child?

"I am?" he finally said, mystified by her reaction. How could she have been expecting him?

Unless, he suddenly realized, the woman at the Institute had had a change of heart and called her, warning her that he was coming.

Marlene had made up her mind not to feel awkward about this. All the way home from the office, she had rehearsed what she was going to say to the investigator. Though she suspected that her request did not exactly run along the lines of the mundane, she was certain that he probably dealt with a great many strange requests. And successfully, if his clothes were any reflection of his track record.

She glanced expectantly over her shoulder at Sally. Muttering, the older woman withdrew. Marlene led the man into her living room.

"Yes, I didn't expect you for a while."

She *did* know, he thought. The Riley woman must have told her he was coming. Dollar signs were probably dancing in her head.

His eyes narrowed as he looked at the woman before him. Unaccountable disappointment washed over him. He'd thought himself securely jaded by now, but this situation generated a really bad taste in his mouth. She looked honest, genuine and, despite her very obvious condition, pure. So much for first impressions.

"Then this isn't a surprise?" he asked darkly.

He was acting very odd, Marlene thought. "No, why should it be?" she asked. She gestured toward the sofa. The entire room was done in light pastels, complementing the airy effect created by the cathedral ceilings.

Following her lead, Sullivan sat down, waiting for her to continue.

They hadn't talked about his fee on the telephone, and she thought it best to get that out of the way first. "Perhaps we should get the financial end of things cleared up first. I'm sure we can come to an arrangement that you would find to your liking."

She knew who he was, all right, he thought. The woman had nerve, he would give her that. She didn't look like an operator, but then, maybe that was how she had acquired this house to begin with. You just never knew.

"To my liking," he repeated.

Every word tasted like acid on his tongue. If his brother hadn't already been dead, he would have wrung Derek's neck for putting him through this. It was beyond him how he could have ever worshiped Derek when they were both younger, how he had actually envied him his freedom. It was only later that he had recognized that desire for freedom for what it was. Pure, selfish recklessness.

Marlene was beginning to have second thoughts about hiring this man. Maybe she should have researched his credentials a little more thoroughly. He really was behaving very oddly.

"Well, yes," she said slowly. "It's only fair that we both get something from this arrangement."

He leaned back, his arms crossed before him. "And just what do you expect out of this arrangement, Ms. Bailey?"

Was he kidding? "I expect you to deliver, of course."

She was referring to the money. Didn't waste any time, did she? Sullivan pressed his lips together grimly. "Of course."

She had the definite impression that he was mocking her. The man had to be doing very well indeed to be so high-handed. Still, he did have an impressive track record, according to one of the VPs at her company.

"I mean, I realize that these things can't be guaranteed, but you do have a reputation."

Now they were getting down to it. "Yes, I do."

Why was he scowling at her like that? He was a very handsome man, but he looked like Zeus about to unleash a thunderbolt on a group of mortals who had displeased him.

She squared her shoulders. "And I assume that there is some amount of truth in it."

He nodded, prepared to concede very little. "To a degree."

He was being awfully cagey. She wondered if this was his normal mode of operation, or if the fact that she was the head of a very successful ad agency had something to do with it. "Why don't you give me a price, and then I'll tell you what I think of it?"

He wanted to tell her exactly what he thought of her, but he managed to maintain his control.

"Why don't you start the bidding?" he suggested genially, but his smile fell short of his eyes.

"Bidding?" Marlene repeated. What was he talking about? Didn't he have set rates? She was beginning to smell a setup. Her doubts about him continued to escalate.

But he was here, and she might as well see this thing through. "All right, how does a hundred dollars a day sound?"

Was she serious? Did she really intend to sell her child for a daily fee? Just what kind of a monster was she?

"A hundred dollars a day," he repeated grimly.

Was that too little? It would help if he gave her some kind of a ballpark figure to work with. "Plus expenses."

"Expenses?" This was getting worse and worse. Just how long did she intend to bilk them? "And for how long?"

Boy, talk about wanting to play a good thing out. "As long as it takes." Her eyes narrowed. "Within reason, of course."

"Reason?" He'd heard of unmitigated gall, but the worst offender he had dealt with was a humble saint in comparison to her. The burden of years of cleaning up after Derek finally took its toll, and he shouted, "I don't think the word *reason* has anything to do with this."

He had completely lost her. She had no idea what he was talking about, or why he had suddenly raised his voice to her, but she wasn't about to take it.

"Why are you yelling?" she shouted back at him.

It was completely out of character for him. Generally he was the calm within the stormy family. Sullivan paused, but he couldn't regain the control he sought. "I don't know. Maybe it's because I always yell when someone is trying to sell me a baby."

Marlene's lips formed a perfect circle as her eyes grew wide. She stared at him, utterly speechless for what was possibly the first time in her life.

Chapter Two

"What are you talking about?" Marlene demanded.

This whole conversation was taking on surrealistic overtones. Sell her baby? She'd moved heaven and earth and endured censure from people close to her to have this child. She would sooner sell her soul than sell her baby.

He could almost believe that the shocked indignation on Marlene's face was genuine. But he had been privy to some elaborate double-dealing in his career, and he wasn't about to let himself be taken in by a pair of wide indigo eyes and a full mouth.

His look cut her dead. "Don't play innocent with me now, Ms. Bailey. It's a little late for that." His eyes narrowed. This had to be the dirtiest scam he'd ever come across. "I've seen some cool customers in my time, but you really take the cake."

How dare he stand there, pontificating about some delusional thought that was floating through his head? She knew all she had to do was let out one scream and Sally would be punching out the numbers to the police on the telephone in the next heartbeat. But she didn't want it to come to that. She was going to handle this hustler on her own.

"Listen, mister, if I had a cake, you'd be wearing it right now. I have no idea what you're talking about. Aren't you Mr. Spencer?"

Sullivan suddenly had an inkling that a horrible mistake had been made, and that he had been the one to make it. Some of his anger abated. He stared at her like someone who had opened the wrong door and found the tiger, not the lady, waiting for him.

"No, I'm not. Who's Mr. Spencer?"

"John Spencer. He's a private investigator—" Marlene stopped abruptly. "Why am I explaining this to you?" She certainly didn't owe him an explanation. She didn't even know who he was. All she did know was that he had to be deranged. Taking a step back, she raised her voice. "Sally—"

The woman had never gone more than a few steps into the next room. "I'm already calling 911," Sally assured her as she hurried to the phone.

"No, wait," Sullivan called out. It was an order, not a protest.

Like a feisty bantam rooster, Sally bobbed into the doorway. "Why should I?" she demanded. "The way I see it, you could be dangerous."

Men had called him that, but the description had been issued across a bargaining table. It had never been applied to him in the sense that this small troll of a woman meant it.

He leveled a look at Sally that was meant to freeze her in her tracks. "Hardly."

"I don't know about that." Marlene folded her arms before her as she regarded him coldly. "Most deranged people are dangerous to some degree."

"I am not deranged." Although after years of having to deal with Derek's indiscretions, he probably had a right to be. Sullivan looked at Sally expectantly, waiting for the woman to go. "Ms. Bailey and I have some business to discuss, so if you don't mind leaving..."

"Stay where you are, Sally," Marlene ordered. Her eyes flashed as she looked at Sullivan. "We have nothing at all to discuss. How could I have any business with you? I don't even know who you are."

His eyes swept over her form. "In a manner of speaking, you do."

If she hadn't been waiting for Spencer, if overwhelming curiosity hadn't kept her up at night and wiggled its way into the structure of her workday like a tenacious gopher burrowing its way through the ground, the thought wouldn't have occurred to her. But it did, coming to her riding a lightning bolt.

Marlene's mouth dropped open. Her hand splayed across her abdomen as if that could somehow protect the baby from this. In the last month she'd imagined the baby's father over and over again. At times he was tall, dark and handsome, just like the man standing in her living room. But never once had she envisioned a ranting madman.

"You don't mean that you're...?" Her voice trailed away. She was unable, unwilling, to complete the thought and give it credence.

The last bit of doubt that she had in any way known the name of the donor disappeared. "No, my brother is."

She didn't understand how he could have known that, or what he was doing here. The Institute prided itself on secrecy and discretion. That was why she had chosen it in the first place, and why, eight months later, she'd been forced to hire a private investigator to uncover the information she now wanted. They had refused, politely but firmly, to give a name to her.

Marlene struggled to pull together the scattered pieces of information into the semblance of a whole. "Do you want to start this at the beginning?"

Sally drew closer until she was at Marlene's elbow, an old, protective pit bull whose teeth were still sharp enough to be reckoned with. "Why don't I just make myself comfortable here?" she suggested to Marlene.

Instinctively Marlene knew she had nothing to fear from the stranger, at least not physically. Emotionally might be a completely different story, but she needed to get to the bottom of this. "It's all right, Sally."

But Sally stubbornly remained where she was, unconvinced. "He looks shifty to me."

Despite the situation, Sullivan couldn't help laughing. Now that was a new adjective for him. He was hard and tough when he had to be, but no one had ever accused him of being shifty.

"I assure you that you have nothing to worry about from me."

Marlene wasn't altogether sure about that. Fear worked on many levels, and there was something in the man's eyes that made her feel uneasy, although she couldn't quite say why. Still, she knew that she wasn't going to find out anything more as long as Sally remained in the room like a hovering harpy. His bearing made that clear.

"I can take care of this, Sally."

Reluctantly, Sally withdrew for the second time. "All right, but I'll be within earshot if you decide that you need me."

Marlene's eyes remained fixed on the stranger's. Never let your opponent know that he had intimidated you. That had been one of her father's prime rules of thumb. And whatever else this man was, he was her opponent. It was written all over him.

"Fine," she told Sally.

"With the dogs," Sally added as a postscript. Her small eyes narrowed to slits as she looked at the man standing in the living room. "Hungry dogs." With that, she shuffled out of sight.

Marlene saw what appeared to be amusement flicker across the stranger's face. "We don't have any dogs," she said. But she had a feeling he already knew that.

A hint of a smile curved his mouth. The old woman was as protective of her as Osborne was of his father. It was nice to know that there were still people like that out there, even if it was getting in his way now. "I didn't think so."

Marlene silently indicated the sofa again. He sat down, waiting for her to do the same. Rather than join him, she took a seat in the wing chair opposite him. He noticed that she was gripping the arms.

First things first. She couldn't keep thinking of him as "the stranger." "You seem to know my name, but I still don't have a clue as to who you are, or why you're here in my house, ranting at me."

"I am not ranting." Sullivan caught himself before his voice had an opportunity to rise again. Taking a breath, he started over. "My name is Sullivan Travis." He paused, waiting. There was no recognition in her eyes.

He obviously thought that piece of information was supposed to create an impression on her. "Should that mean something to me?"

"It should if you're involved in land development or know anything about it."

The company's acquisitions and developments periodically made the newspaper columns. Among other accomplishments, they had all but single-handedly developed an entire city in Orange County.

Marlene looked at him in surprise. He couldn't be *that* Travis. "I'm involved in advertising," she informed him. She glanced down at her stomach before continuing. *Oh baby, if this is true, what roots I've inadvertently given you.* "Are you by any chance related to Oliver Travis?"

He tried to read her expression and couldn't. He nodded. "About as closely as possible. Oliver Travis is my father."

Though his tone was formal, there was warmth in the words. Marlene couldn't help wondering what that had to feel like, to feel warmth when you spoke of your father instead of just experiencing an incredible void.

Though she'd never stopped trying until the end, Marlene had long ago come to terms with the fact that she would never really get through to her father.

She was under no illusion that James Bailey had ever felt anything for her or her sister. The only thing that had ever mattered to him was his company, his work. After Robby had died, the advertising company her father had built up had become his legacy. Thirteen months ago he had died at his desk, while crossing out lines in a report she had just sweated over. He'd died just the way he wanted to, working and trying to make her feel inferior.

She collected herself and looked at Sullivan squarely. "I'm impressed, but I still don't see what that has to do with me."

She was telling the truth. Sullivan flattered himself that he could see through a ruse, even one executed by someone as apparently sophisticated as the woman sitting opposite him.

Because caution was second nature to him, he qualified his statement. "If my information is correct, and I see no reason to doubt that it is," his eyes dipped toward her stomach, "you're carrying his grandchild. My brother Derek's child."

None of this was making any sense. Though they were somewhat out of her league, it was a known fact that the Travis family was exceptionally well off. She had only his word that he was who he said he was. She began to wonder if this was a scam of some sort. Or an elaborate joke. Nicole had a warped sense of humor at times. If this was Nicole's handiwork, she was going to kill her.

"Forgive me, but your father's company—"

He'd worked long and hard to earn his place within the company. Nothing had been handed to him. Oliver Travis didn't believe in being soft. You had to earn his respect. In the last year, Sullivan had almost completely taken over the reins.

"Our company," Sullivan corrected her.

Touchy. She knew how that could be. Her father hadn't allowed her her true place within the firm until after he was dead. Then it had been accorded her via the will. One "well done" or a single "thank you" would have done far more for her.

"Your company," she amended, "is written up in *Fortune 500.* Why would your brother donate his—" she searched for a delicate way to put it "—genes—to a sperm bank for money?"

Sullivan couldn't fault her for the incredulous look on her face. It was hard for him to believe, and he had been there to watch the circumstances of his brother's unorthodox life unfold.

"It's a long, involved story."

Holding on to the arms of the chair for support, Marlene crossed her legs. The action drew Sullivan's eyes to them. He was surprised that they weren't puffy, and that she was wearing such high heels. She probably had the greatest pair of legs he'd ever seen, he realized. He forced himself to raise his eyes to her face again.

Marlene smiled to herself at the silent compliment his eyes had accorded her. "I usually don't have any time, but today you're in luck. Tell me," she urged. "I'm curious." She was more than curious, given that her baby's father was the topic under discussion.

A private person by nature, Sullivan didn't believe in baring his soul or airing his family's problems in public, especially not to a stranger. Not to mention that he was still trying to figure out a way to break this news to his father.

Sullivan shook his head. "I'm afraid that's a private matter."

Fine, she didn't have to know. But neither did she have to suffer his being in her house if he wasn't going to tell her anything. "So why are you here?"

The quicker he resolved this, the better. He hoped that it might help to ease his father's shock if he had good news to counterbalance the bad. "To make you an offer."

Marlene had a feeling that she wasn't going to like what she was about to hear. Instinctively defensive, she stood up, as if height could somehow give her the added leverage she felt she needed.

"It had better be a nice one, Mr. Travis," she said guardedly. There was no smile on her lips.

Sullivan had the distinct feeling that he was picking his way through a minefield. It wouldn't be the first time. "That all depends on your point of view."

"Go on," she said quietly.

Had he known her, he would have been able to recognize the Approaching Gale signs going up. But the bulk of Sullivan's dealings took place in the corporate world. Socializing or, more to the point, women, was predominately Derek's domain. His own relationships never lasted long enough for arguments to break out.

Though the consequences were more important, for Sullivan the matter was almost routine. He was cleaning up after his brother. It was nothing he hadn't done countless times before. He proceeded the way he always did, honestly, straight from the shoulder.

"My brother, Derek, fancied himself an artist. He enjoyed having the sort of reputation that went with his chosen life-style. He especially enjoyed it when it irritated my father. I think he hit a new high, or low, with this last trick."

Sullivan saw Marlene raise one eyebrow and knew that he'd chosen the wrong word. But he pressed on to the crux of his visit.

"I went to the sperm bank to buy back my brother's 'donation,' if you will." He looked at her pointedly. God, he hoped she would be cooperative, although he didn't see why she shouldn't be. It wasn't as if the child Marlene was carrying was a love child created in the heat of passion. She'd gone to an institute and ordered a baby. There couldn't be very much emotion involved in that. "They informed me that I was too late."

Her expression remained unchanged. "Obviously."

For a reason he couldn't quite fathom, he felt himself flinching inwardly. "Now there seems to be an heir in the offing."

So that was it. He was afraid that she was going to try to make money off them. Perhaps sue them for a share of their fortune. This really *was* becoming surreal.

"Let me set your mind at ease, Mr. Travis. Until you descended on my doorstep, I had no idea who the father of my baby was, although I have to confess that I was going to try to find out." She saw a look she couldn't read entering Sullivan's eyes. "Purely for academic reasons," she hastened to add. "I had no intention of getting in contact with him."

Right, and he was really Elvis. Everyone wanted something. It was a sad fact of human nature. "Then why did you want to know who the father was?" he challenged mildly.

She thought of telling him that it was none of his business. But maybe it was. Since he had told her the baby's genealogy, saving her the trouble and the expense of finding out, she supposed she owed him one.

"It's very simple. So that if someday my child asked, I could give him an answer." She saw the dubious look on his face. "But until that day arrived—if ever—there would have been no mention of the 'donor' and certainly no contact with him. Believe me, your brother has nothing to worry about. He can rest in peace."

It was an ironic choice of words, Sullivan thought. "My brother is going to be resting for all eternity, Ms. Bailey. He's dead."

He said it entirely without emotion, as if he were reading a stock market report out loud. But she saw something flicker in his eyes, something that told her he was human after all. You couldn't have something like that happen without it leaving an indelible mark.

"I'm sorry. I lost a brother, too. Years ago." And it still hurt, she thought.

Sullivan hadn't expected Marlene to share anything so personal with him. It took him aback for a moment.

"I'm sorry for your loss," he muttered awkwardly, echoing her sentiment. He wasn't any good at condolences, not when the need to express them was sprung on him without warning. He took a breath. "My brother isn't the reason I'm here."

"He's not?" No, this was definitely not Nicole's handiwork. This was real. Marlene felt nervous. Where was this all leading?

"No, my father is."

Oh, the seat of power and money. She thought of her own father and the way his mind had worked. Blackmail would have been the first word on his lips.

"I have no intention of bothering him, either. I'm very comfortable, thank you, and this baby is all I want."

She expected him to terminate the visit at that point. When he didn't, she wondered if he wanted her assurance in writing. Some sort of prenatal agreement to hand over to his lawyer would probably satisfy him.

He began to get an inkling that this wasn't going to go as smoothly as he had hoped. He spoke as earnestly as he could.

"My father has no grandchildren, Ms. Bailey. My brother's death hit him very hard. They were two very different people and had a great deal of difficulty getting along. Periodically, they were estranged. They were in one of those periods when my brother was killed in a drive-by shooting.''

He saw the genuine horror spring to her eyes. Maybe this wasn't going to be so difficult after all. Clearly she could empathize with the situation.

''My father never got to make his peace with Derek.''

She thought of Nicole and their father. Their differences hadn't been resolved at the time of his death, either.

''I'm very sorry to hear that.''

She really was, he thought. Why should it make any difference to her? He found himself wanting to know. ''Why?''

She shrugged. Why did he need it explained when it was self-evident?

''Because it's sad. Because unresolved conflicts always remain with you if the other person dies.'' But he hadn't come here to discuss any of this. He was obviously uncomfortable with the topic. So why *was* he here? ''What is it you want from me, Mr. Travis?''

It was time to stop beating around the bush. ''Your son. Or daughter.''

She stared at him. There had to be some mistake. He couldn't be saying what she thought he was saying. That sort of thing only happened on movies of the week. ''What?''

She was making this very difficult for him. He couldn't shake the feeling that he was an ogre. ''I want your child.''

Marlene leaned forward. There had to be a different meaning to his words. ''Want it how? To visit your father?''

Damn, but this felt awkward. He was only doing what was right. What would ultimately be right for everyone, especially the baby.

''To stay. To be legally adopted.'' Sullivan supposed that was the way to go. He would have to consult with his lawyer, of course, but since the child was a documented Travis, he didn't foresee any difficulties cropping up in that area.

But then, he hadn't foreseen Marlene.

Her eyes lost their sheen and grew hard. "That means I would have to give up custody."

Now she understood. "Exactly."

She felt like pacing to rid herself of the sudden edginess that had seized her. But pacing seemed too much like running, and that would let him see that he was unnerving her. She remained where she was.

"I don't know if you're crazy, or if the air here is a little too clean for you after all this L.A. smog and it's clouded your brain. Either way, I have no intention of giving up this baby." She glared at him. "It wasn't easy for me to make up my mind to go this route, but I've done it. This baby is *mine.*"

She was still young, there would be other babies for her. But there would never be another piece of Derek, and his legacy would mean the world to his father. "You would be compensated."

If he had tried, he couldn't have come up with a worse thing to say. Her expression turned stony as she pressed her lips together. "I think you'd better go."

He had to try again and make her see reason. "Ms. Bailey—"

She was through being nice. "Go, or I swear I'll have Sally borrow some hungry dogs and have them satisfy their appetite on your carcass."

She was babbling. He chalked it up to her condition. "There's no reason to get nasty—"

Her mouth went dry. "No reason? *No reason?*" With the flat of her hand planted on his chest, she caught him off guard and pushed him toward the door. "Have you been paying attention to your end of the conversation, Mr. Travis?" Marlene's voice went up an octave as she pushed him again. "You've just asked me to make a profit on my baby. Not even my father was that unfeeling, and he pretty much set the standard for being cold-blooded."

He had to make her understand. He wasn't being cold-blooded. He was being the exact opposite. He was attempting to prevent his father's heartbreak and give the child a heritage. "This grandchild will mean a great deal to my father."

She wanted him out. Now. "Fine, we'll visit. Often, if necessary." Her hand on the doorknob, she conceded one small point. "The baby could use a grandfather. Now get out of here before I forget that I am a lady—a very large lady, but a lady nonetheless."

He had no intention of leaving yet. He examined the situation. His resolution to gain custody didn't waiver, but there were more things to be gotten with honey than with vinegar, and no one appreciated that more than he did. His agitation over the situation had made him temporarily lose sight of that.

Sullivan tried again. "Look, maybe we got off on the wrong foot—"

Maybe? "That wouldn't be an understatement even if you were a centipede." Her expression remained cold. "I'd like you to leave my house."

He couldn't leave, not until he felt certain they at least were making some headway. Sullivan damned his brother from the bottom of his soul for placing him in this miserable position. "Perhaps—"

There was no "perhaps" about it. Her hand tightened around the knob as she prepared to yank the door open. If she could have, she would have booted him out.

"Now!"

The doorbell rang just then, an answer to a silent prayer. Marlene swung the door open, ready to enlist the aid of anyone on the other side.

The tall, slender man in the black turtleneck sweater, black slacks and blue-gray windbreaker looked from Travis to Marlene. From his expression, he was accustomed to domestic discord. His eyes rested on Marlene.

"Mrs. Bailey?"

"Ms.," she corrected with more verve than she customarily would have. It was men like Travis who made her grateful that she'd never married. "But you have the surname right." She looked pointedly at Sullivan. "It's Bailey." She said the name with emphasis. "And it's going to remain that way."

She wasn't talking about herself, she was talking about the baby, Sullivan knew. He wasn't going to get anywhere today. Resigned, he took his wallet out of his breast pocket and extracted a pearl gray business card. He held it out to her. "This is my number."

Marlene took the card and folded it in half without looking at it.

The action piqued his temper, but hc held on to it. Flaring tempers were for children. People in his position didn't have the luxury of losing their tempers, and he knew that the harder he pushed, the more it would make her dig in. She needed time to think this over; he could appreciate that. In time, he felt confident she would arrive at the right choice.

"We'll get together and discuss this further when you're feeling more rational."

The pompous ass. Did he think that money entitled him to destroy lives? "I'm afraid that day will never come, Travis. This is about as rational as I get with people who want to buy my baby."

Spencer scowled. "Problem?" he asked Marlene.

"It was just leaving," Marlene said sweetly. "Weren't you, Mr. Travis?"

There was nothing to be gained at the moment by remaining. "For the time being."

"I think the lady means forever," Spencer observed mildly.

Marlene looked at the man on her doorstep. Travis had made her so angry, she'd nearly forgotten about her meeting with the private investigator. "John Spencer, I presume?"

A smile brought out the creases around his mouth. "At your service."

Murphy's law. All these years, nothing. Now suddenly the house was overflowing with men. Why hadn't this happened nine months ago, when she had made up her mind that her life wasn't going to be an empty shell any longer?

She turned toward the private investigator. She no longer needed him to discover the identity of her baby's father, but there might be a few things she did want him to look into. "You're just in time to help me show Mr. Travis out."

Spencer smiled. "My pleasure."

"That won't be necessary," Sullivan told him. He crossed the threshold, then turned and looked at Marlene. "Keep the card, Ms. Bailey, and call me. We really do need to talk."

With an exaggerated motion, Marlene tore the card in half as Spencer obligingly closed the door on Sullivan for her.

"I wouldn't sit by the telephone waiting if I were you," she called through the door.

This definitely did not have the earmarks of something that was going to shape up well, Sullivan thought as he exited the freeway. Marlene Bailey was not going to be easy to win over. More than likely, she would be downright impossible.

The difficult we do immediately; the impossible takes a little longer. He should really have those words branded somewhere on his anatomy after a life of being Derek's guardian angel.

Derek. Damn, but he was going to miss that heartless son of a bitch.

Sullivan brushed a tear from his cheek as if it were an uninvited intruder. He tried not to think what a waste it all was, dying at thirty-two in a neighborhood his brother had no business living.

Damn you, Derek.

He had another errand to see to before he finally went home.

Sullivan had put off talking to his father as long as possible, hoping that he could temper the bad with the good when he finally told the old man what he'd discovered. Now he was going to have to give it to his father straight.

He wasn't looking forward to it.

When Sullivan entered the living room, Oliver Travis appeared to be dozing over his side of a chess board. Sullivan arched an inquiring eyebrow toward Osborne, his father's housekeeper. The thin man shrugged.

Tomorrow, Sullivan thought. This could definitely keep until tomorrow. Maybe by tomorrow, Marlene would have a change of heart. He turned quietly on his heel.

"Don't skulk away." His father's voice stopped him just as Sullivan reached the threshold. "I'm just meditating. Can't a man close his eyes without everyone thinking he's asleep, or dead?" Oliver pressed the controls on his armrest and brought the motorized wheelchair around. "Well, you certainly took your time coming to me." He didn't wait for Sullivan's reply. "So, did you go through Derek's effects?"

"Yes." Damn, this was hard. He knew how his father was going to take the news, and he dreaded what it would do to him.

"And it was just another one of his cruel jokes, right?" Watery green eyes looked up at him hopefully, charging him to give an affirmative answer. "He didn't sell himself, did he?"

It would be a great deal easier to lie and say it had all been a cruel hoax. But then he would have to eat those words should the information ever come to light. Sullivan exchanged looks with Osborne.

The old man knew, he thought. Somehow, he knew. But then, he'd always had an uncanny ability to see through them all.

"No, it wasn't a joke, Dad. Derek really did go to a sperm bank."

Oliver's jaw slackened, and anger colored his shallow cheeks. "Buy it back!" he thundered. "Hang the cost, just buy it back."

Sullivan shook his head. "It's too late for that."

"Too late?" Oliver uttered the question as if air were leaking out of him. "What do you mean, it's too late? *How* late?"

"A woman's already been impregnated."

For a moment Sullivan was afraid that his father was suffering another stroke. The old man's face turned red, and he looked as if he were struggling to breathe. But he waved both men back when they approached him.

"Who is she? What kind of woman would do that? No, never mind who she is. I don't care. The less I know, the better." Oliver seemed to make up his mind instantly. "I want that child, Sullivan. Do what you have to do. Offer her the moon, whatever she wants, but I want that child."

Momentarily energized, he swung his chair around to face Osborne. "We can turn Derek's old room into a nursery."

Sullivan knew it wasn't going to be as easy as that. He didn't want his father riding for a fall.

"Dad—" he began.

Oliver didn't want to hear any protests. He was old and had earned the right to have things his way. His oldest son was gone, and now here was another chance to make things right, to do things for Derek's child the way he hadn't been able to do for Derek.

It was as if Providence had smiled down on him again, giving him a second opportunity.

"Just do it," Oliver ordered, turning his piercing gaze to the chess board. "I don't want to play that silly game any more, Osborne. I'm tired. Take me to my room."

The pencil-thin man in the black livery rose. "Very good, sir." The look Osborne gave Sullivan was one filled with compassion.

Sullivan was left standing in the living room, feeling bone tired.

Chapter Three

It had been one of those extremely long days that felt as if it would never end. Marlene sighed as she kicked off her high heels and entered the living room. The thick rug felt good beneath her stockinged feet, and she allowed herself to absorb the sensation, letting it settle over her. It always took her a while to unwind.

She had thought, once she had gotten through her fourth month, that she would cease to feel so tired. But she supposed she hadn't taken into account marathon days that began at six and lasted until seven in the evening. Tonight she felt like the rag that had been used to wipe the benches at Dodger Stadium.

Sinking down in the wing chair, she raised her feet onto the ottoman. Even that little movement was a tremendous effort.

She knew she really should make more of an attempt to cut back on her hours. Dr. Pollack had been pretty adamant about it, saying that if she wasn't careful, she ran the risk of coming down with toxemia. Then she would really be out of commission. That warning had put the fear of God into her. Temporarily. Marlene had compromised by restructuring her work day—down to ten hours from sixteen.

Except for today.

A rueful smile lifted the corners of her mouth. God knew she tried, but in reality she didn't know how *not* to work. And she had completely forgotten how to actually relax for more than a few minutes at a time. Her usual pattern was to work until she was numb and then collapse into bed.

Just like Father, she remembered ruefully. The comparison didn't please her.

Marlene lifted her hair from her neck. It was the end of November, but she felt uncomfortably warm. She hoped it wasn't a warning sign that something was wrong.

Her thoughts returned to her father, making her frown. She liked to think that she was different from James Bailey. Yet here she was, working long hours and still living in the family house, just as he had continued to do after her mother had left.

The house was hers now, just as the business was. She hadn't been able to convince him to divide it equally between Nicole and herself in his will. He'd hung on to the feud with Nicole until the day he died.

After his death, Marlene had tried to persuade Nicole to move in with her, especially after Craig had been killed in a race car accident. But, widowed and pregnant, Nicole had remained stubbornly against it. To this day she wanted nothing to do with her father's things and insisted on going it alone. There were times when Nicole could be maddeningly independent, Marlene mused.

Just as she was.

It was a Bailey trait, Marlene supposed. But it did tend to get in the way when the Baileys' dealt with each other. It would have been better for Nicole to have moved back in.

Just as it would have been better if she had never run off to marry Craig in the first place.

Marlene let her head drop back against the padded chair. That was all in the past, she thought. Her hand rested on her abdomen. And this was her future, at least a very important part of it.

The house was almost eerily quiet. Sally had gone to bed after straightening up the kitchen, complaining about the meager dinner Marlene had consumed.

"You're doing harm to the baby, see if you're not," Sally had announced, her dark brows forming a single accusing line over the bridge of her hawklike nose.

Marlene had let her grumble. She knew Sally enjoyed fussing over her. The old woman anticipated the birth of the baby almost more than she did. Sally liked to boast that after the baby's arrival, she was going to add nanny to her résumé, right after housekeeper.

Sally didn't need a résumé, Marlene thought. She intended to keep the woman on forever. Without Sally, she would be lost.

She passed her hand over her eyes. The beginning of a headache was taking hold. It did nothing to improve her mood. She hated these mood swings that insisted on battering her. Something else she had been unprepared for in this pregnancy.

One more month to go, she promised herself. It seemed endless when she thought of it in single minutes.

The phone rang, startling her. Habit had her glancing at her watch before answering. Nine o'clock. She wondered if it was Harris calling from London. She'd sent him there a week ago to handle the final negotiations of their first transatlantic account.

She preferred handling everything on her own and had wanted to make the trip herself. But her due date was less than a month away, and she didn't want to take any unnecessary chances. She wanted nothing to ruin this precious opportunity she had at becoming a mother.

If that meant trusting someone else to take care of the negotiations for the agency, so be it. If this deal fell through, then there would be other contracts. But there was never going to be another child for her. This one was it.

That feeling alone, she thought, separated her from her father. Nothing had ever gotten in the way of negotiations for James Bailey. Not his children, not his wife, not the death of his father. It was always business—first, last and always.

If Robby had lived, perhaps things would have been different.

She was getting maudlin. This had to stop. Marlene jerked up the receiver on the third ring, shaking off her mood. "Yes?"

She snapped out greetings like a commando. He wondered if it was going to set the tone of their conversation. "Ms. Bailey?"

The rich voice that filled the receiver didn't belong to Harris. His was higher with an undertone of nervousness that never left him. She knew instantly who it was. The man whose calls she'd refused to return at the office.

Marlene tensed. "Why are you calling me at home?"

"I would think that would be obvious. You won't return my calls during office hours." He had left a dozen messages in the last three days. She hadn't returned any of them.

She had hoped that he would get the point and tire of calling her. Wishful thinking. "How did you get this number?" she demanded.

He laughed and the sound was oddly warming, like wine drunk too quickly on an empty stomach. Marlene pressed her hand to her forehead. She was more tired than she'd thought.

Getting her number had been relatively easy with his connections. "To quote a cliché," *which might be more than apt here,* he thought, "Where there's a will, there's a way, Ms. Bailey."

"Not always," she snapped. Why didn't he just go away?

Charming to the end, he mused. And yet, there was something about her that was compelling.

He read the message in her voice loud and clear, then disregarded it. "You've had a few days to think about our conversation. I'd like the opportunity to discuss it further with you. How about lunch tomorrow?"

When hell freezes over. "Sorry, I'm busy."

"All right, dinner then." He had a previous engagement, but this was more important than attending one of Alan and Cynthia Breckinridge's parties.

She smiled smugly. Usually, her evenings were free, but not tomorrow night. It spared her the trouble of lying. She'd accepted the invitation to the party over a month ago. "I'm sorry, I have a social function I have to attend tomorrow evening."

"Black tie?" he guessed.

She didn't see why that would make a difference to him. "Yes."

"Lucky for you I own one."

Marlene sat upright, removing her feet from the ottoman. Was he actually inviting himself along? "What you have in your closet doesn't interest me, Travis. You're not invited."

He could easily swing an invitation, too, if necessary. Almost anyone throwing what Marlene termed a social function had to be on his list of acquaintances. If not his, then his father's.

"You need an escort, don't you?"

There was no end to this man's gall. "What makes you think I don't have one?"

He laughed. This time, the sound annoyed the hell out of her. "You went to a sperm bank to become pregnant, Marlene. I think it's safe to assume that you do a lot of things by yourself. So, when do I pick you up?"

He'd called her Marlene, not Ms. Bailey. He was getting way too personal.

"You don't." With that, she broke the connection and left the receiver off the hook. She let out a long breath. That should stop him from annoying her tonight.

Tomorrow was something she would deal with when the time came—and it would come all too soon. Right now, she didn't want to think about it.

Nicole eased the door open and slipped quietly across the threshold into the office. Marlene's secretary, Wanda, had momentarily stepped away from her desk, so there was no one to announce her. She liked it that way.

She observed her older sister for a moment before she greeted her. Marlene was so immersed in her work, she was oblivious to the fact that there was anyone else in the office with her.

Marlene worked too hard, Nicole thought reprovingly. She'd always worked too hard. There'd never been a financial need to do so, but Nicole knew that for Marlene there had been an emotional one.

As if James Bailey had ever noticed.

Nicole remained in the doorway and crossed her arms over the swell of her abdomen. It'd been a little over a year since their father had died, but it still felt odd seeing Marlene sitting behind that desk.

The few times that she had been ushered into this office along with her brother and sister, her father had been sitting in that very chair. Like as not, he would be bent over his work, just as Marlene was now. He would ignore their presence until the last possible moment, even when one of them made a noise to catch his attention.

Whether it was to put them in their place or because he really was so absorbed in what he was doing that he didn't notice them, Nicole never knew. But even as a child, she'd been aware of being angry. Angry because he was making all of them feel so insignificant.

Or trying to.

And now Marlene was sitting there in his place, frowning over a report just the way their father had done countless times before.

Nicole felt like taking her sister and shaking some sense into her, forcing her to realize what she was in danger of becoming. Making her stop before it was too late. Before Marlene traveled down the same road their father had.

Nicole sighed quietly. Maybe things would change once the baby finally arrived.

At least she hoped so.

Nicole closed the door behind her and walked over to the desk. She cleared her throat loudly. "You realize, of course, that you are going to have to stop working long enough to give birth. Two, three hours might be forever lost."

Marlene looked up, startled. She hadn't heard her sister come in. Nodding a greeting to Nicole, Marlene straightened, pressing her back against the chair's padded upholstery. She flexed her shoulders slightly. There was a crick in them that traveled down the entire length of her spine.

"I'm trying to work that into my schedule." Marlene smiled fondly at her sister. She blinked, clearing her mind of statistics. It wasn't easy. They seemed to cram her head just like the baby crammed her body. "What are you doing here?"

Nicole glanced at Marlene's desk. The surface was an ode to compulsive organization, folders all neatly piled and placed parallel to the edge of the desk. No flurry of papers the way there would have been if she was working here instead.

But advertising campaigns weren't her forte. Neither was neatness. They would have clashed inside of a day. It was better this way.

Nicole moved a folder with the tip of her index finger, her eyes on Marlene's. "Well, I thought that since Mohammed wouldn't come to the mountain, the mountain would come to Mohammed."

Very carefully, Marlene returned the folder to its original position. It made her feel better to have things exactly where she wanted them. Where she could easily put her hands on them when she needed them. It was comforting. The reason the company ran so smoothly was due to creativity, but it also owed its success in no small part to organization. Her organization. That meant a great deal to her.

Marlene nodded at her sister's widened waist. "More like the mountain coming to the mountain and forming a huge range."

Holding on to the armrests, Nicole lowered herself into the chair before Marlene's desk. Due roughly a couple of weeks after her sister, she was larger and appeared even more so because she was almost three inches shorter.

She let out a long sigh of relief as she sat back. "I'm on my lunch break, and since you haven't taken one in five years unless it involved a client, the odds were that I'd find you in, so I decided to pop by."

That still didn't explain what Nicole was doing here. Marlene knew firsthand that these days it was difficult for Nicole to just "pop by" anywhere. There had to be a reason behind this so-called spontaneous visit.

Marlene rose from her desk and rounded it until she was beside her sister. Only concern about Nicole's welfare ever managed to get her mind off her ever increasing mound of work. "Is anything wrong?"

Nicole shrugged casually, shifting the point of focus back to her sister. "I was going to ask you the same question."

Marlene looked at her, puzzled. "What do you mean?"

It wasn't actually the main reason she'd stopped by, but now that she'd thought of it, Nicole followed up. "You didn't make any sense on the telephone when I talked to you yesterday. I thought maybe things might sound a little clearer if I watched your lips while you talked."

Marlene laughed shortly. She supposed she had sounded a little distraught when she told Nicole about Travis's appearance. She'd meant to keep the whole thing to herself, but Nicole's call had caught her at a bad time and part of the story had tumbled out. Not wanting to upset Nicole, she had glossed over the rest of it.

"Believe me, it won't sound any clearer now." She thought of Travis and the annoying phone call last night. "All I know is that my unborn child's uncle is an ass."

"He just appeared out of the blue? For no reason?"

"Oh, there's a reason, all right. I told you, he wants custody." Just talking about it had her throat tightening. "The bastard is willing to make 'compensations.' As if I'd sell my baby."

Nicole knew that look in Marlene's eyes and could almost feel sorry for Sullivan Travis. She had no doubts that Marlene had put him in his place royally. "Do you think he'll try to bother you again?"

"I don't think, I know." She sighed, exasperated. "I've been refusing his phone calls, but he got through last night at the house and wanted to meet with me again now that I've had 'time to think it over.'"

"Did you tell him to go to hell?"

"I think he got the message." Marlene rested her bottom against the top of the desk. She tried very hard not to let pregnancy slow her down, but there were times when it seemed to hit her right between the eyes. Or a little lower, she thought in momentary amusement.

"Do you think you should get in contact with Monty?" Nicole asked, referring to their family lawyer.

"Not yet, but I will if I have to. Right now, I'm not going to think about Travis. The holidays are coming. I'm pregnant, and I've got a social function to attend tonight." Her mouth curved as she remembered. "One he wanted to 'escort' me to. That's when I hung up on him."

"That sounds like you." Nicole looked at her sister's face. "You look tired, Marlene. Why don't you stay home tonight instead of going out?"

Marlene knew exactly what Nicole thought of the social get-togethers she attended. Her sister felt that they were full of pompous people who liked to hear themselves talk. Who liked to have other people hear them talk. She thought the assessment unfair. But whether it was true or not, business was business. She had to attend. Besides, she had promised Cynthia.

"It's the best place to make connections, Nic," she reminded her.

Nicole rolled her eyes. "Oh yes, those almighty connections. Where would we be without them?"

A wall materialized between them, the one that always rose when their diverse approaches to life came up. "Don't use that tone with me, Nicole. You sound just the way you did when you talked to Father."

Nicole's eyes held her sister's. James Bailey had been heartless; Marlene wasn't. She couldn't stand to see her sister waste her life away in some office. There were more important things than work. Marlene had to know that, or why else would she have gone to the trouble of getting pregnant?

She frowned. "Maybe that's because sometimes you sound just like Father. Like now."

Marlene retreated behind the desk. Splaying her hands across the chair's high leather back, she drew herself up. "You're pregnant and your hormones are running havoc on your judgment, so I'll overlook that remark."

"Don't overlook it, take it to heart." It was a frustrated plea.

And then she relented. Nicole rarely employed retreat, but she knew its value. Because Marlene was her sister and she hadn't come by to antagonize her, she dropped the subject.

Nicole rose slowly from her chair. Another couple of minutes and she wouldn't be able to get up at all. Her leg felt as though it had fallen asleep. The baby, ever restless, had apparently shifted its elephantine weight over a nerve.

"Maybe I'd better get going and let you do what you do best."

Marlene frowned as the buzzer sounded on her desk. She depressed the speaker button. "Yes, Wanda?"

Her secretary's crisp British accent filled the air. "You wanted me to remind you of your twelve-thirty meeting, Ms. Bailey."

Marlene mechanically reached for the folder she'd been reviewing earlier. Where had the morning gone? She'd meant to finish up the idea she was working on before joining the others for a brainstorming session to revamp a car manufacturer's stodgy image. She'd always liked being prepared, but it still wasn't completed.

"I'm already on my way." Marlene's finger slipped from the small key, and Wanda's presence instantly vanished. Marlene could feel Nicole's eyes on her, studying her critically.

"Slow down, Marlene, or this baby you're about to have isn't going to have a mother to help him or her celebrate a first birthday."

Marlene opened her mouth, then closed it again, reshuffling the words that were on the tip of her tongue. Nicole was only being concerned. And sometimes, it did feel good to have someone care if she ran herself into the ground.

"You're right, I am doing too much. It's just that—"

"You can't let go." Their father had always said that. Nicole's mouth twisted in a bitter smile. "Correct me if I'm wrong, but those aren't original words."

Marlene had been at the office since six, and she wasn't in the mood to argue. "Stop hinting that I'm Father."

"Who's hinting? Aren't you listening? I'm stating it outright."

The baby kicked hard, hitting something that felt very vital. Marlene winced. "We'll talk about this later, okay?"

Nicole merely nodded as she began walking toward the door. Almost there, she stopped and turned around. "Oh, and by the way..."

Her tone was far too nonchalant for Marlene to be fooled. Now they were getting down to it, she thought, crossing to where she stood. Now they were getting to the real reason that Nicole had come by.

"Yes?"

Nicole dug into her purse and produced an envelope. "This came yesterday." She held it up to her sister. "I'm sure it was sent in error."

Marlene didn't have to look at the contents to know what her sister was talking about. She'd mailed the envelope herself the day before yesterday. It contained a single piece of paper. A check against Nicole's trust fund.

Exasperation shimmied through her. Nicole could be so damn stubborn. Marlene made no move to take the envelope from her. "So that's why you're here?"

"That's why I'm here." Crossing to the desk, Nicole dropped the envelope on top of a folder.

Marlene struggled not to lose her temper. "Nic, grandmother's money must be gone by now."

Nicole shook her head. "Not yet," she answered mildly. "There's still some left."

Nicole's tone belied the feelings of frustration churning within her. She hadn't wanted to wind up in these circumstances, pregnant and widowed, on the threshold of the rest of her life but caught in a holding pattern. But she would be damned if she was going to take handouts. She had always wanted to earn her own way, and she was going to do just that. Very soon.

"I stretched it," she told Marlene. An ironic smile curved her soft mouth. "Some things I did pick up while living under James T. Bailey's reign of terror."

It felt right referring to her father by his given name, more so than calling him Father. He'd never been that to any of them. Only biology had made him a father, not love. Never love.

Nicole shrugged. "Being frugal comes in handy these days. And," she added needlessly, "I do work at the art gallery."

That wasn't earning her anything and they both knew it. "A few days a week."

Nicole remained unfazed by her sister's sharp tone. "The holidays are here. I'm almost full-time. It all adds up."

Marlene felt her temper sharpening. Lately, it took very little to set her off. "Why will you accept the art gallery owner's money and not that?" She waved a hand at her desk to where the check lay. "It's rightfully yours, you know."

The money was part of a trust fund that had taken all of Marlene's best negotiating skills to set up. Initially her father had staunchly refused to allow it. He'd wanted to cut Nicole off without a penny after she'd run off. But Marlene had finally convinced him, utilizing his vanity as a tool. How would it look, his cutting off his penniless daughter? He had always been concerned with what others thought of him. In that light, he'd thought of his children as extensions of himself. So he had agreed, and Nicole had benefited—if she would only accept the money.

"Answer to question one..." Nicole said, holding up a finger. "Because I work for Lawrence, and what I get from him is a paycheck, not charity. Answer to question two..." A second finger joined the first. "It's rightfully mine when I'm thirty, not now. I can get by, Marlene. And I really don't want his money."

It always came back to that. The feud. "He's dead, Nicole, can't you forgive him?"

"No." Nicole snapped, then relented. "Not yet."

Marlene felt the clock ticking away the minutes between her and the pending meeting. Still, she couldn't let this matter go just yet. "At least come live at the house."

Nicole smiled at Marlene, but she remained adamant on that point as well, even though the invitation was extended to her almost weekly. "No way."

For all intents and purposes, their parents were gone. Their father was dead and their mother had disappeared out of their lives years ago. There was no one in the house but her and Sally. Marlene's voice lowered. She didn't hear the trace of wistfulness in it. But Nicole did. "I'm not that bad company."

Nicole didn't want to hurt Marlene, but she couldn't turn her back on what she felt was right, either. "You have nothing to do with it. Call it stubborn pride. Call it not wanting to encounter the ghost of our 'beloved father,' whispering, 'I told you you'd come crawling back.'"

"Nic—" Marlene reached out to touch Nicole's shoulder, but Nicole moved aside.

"Call it whatever you want," she continued, "but I want to do this on my own—financially." She tempered her voice and looked at her sister. "Just let me lean on you emotionally once in a while and I'll be fine."

Marlene smiled at Nicole. This was what she wanted, to have Nicole turn to her. If they did it in degrees, that didn't change things. For now, they were all the family they had. Until the babies were born.

She shook her head at Nicole, her expression a fond one. "God, but you are stubborn."

Nicole agreed readily. "Also learned at Ye Old Inn of Sadness. Besides," she said, nodding at Marlene's desk, "I wouldn't throw any rocks if I were you."

The buzzer sounded again like an angry goose that had been ignored. Nicole sighed.

"Try to enjoy yourself tonight, Marlene." She patted Marlene's arm as she slipped by her into the hall.

Marlene thought of the hours she would be on her feet and sighed inwardly. "I'll do my best."

Marlene slowly slipped on her black pumps.

She really didn't want to go to this party. She felt tired and heavy tonight.

If she could, she would have just collapsed onto the bed and closed her eyes. But even as the idea suggested itself, she knew it was impossible. She had responsibilities. Clients to socialize with and new ones to garner.

She looked into the mirror, slowly running her hands along the outline of her stomach, trying to visualize the occupant housed within. The one who made her so tired all the time.

Never had eight months taken so long to drag by. Part of her couldn't wait for the baby to be born, and part of her, the part that secretly feared the unknown, could hang on just a while longer until she was more prepared.

She sighed. It felt as if she had been pregnant forever.

Marlene focused on her reflection. Her hair was piled up high on her head, with tendrils curling along her neck. She knew she looked attractive, but that didn't change things. She still didn't feel like attending the party. The prospect of talking about nothing but business wearied her before the night had even begun.

Not that she wasn't good at networking. Despite what her father had implied, she had a flair for it. It was a gift. She was good at dreaming up campaigns that could take a flagging product and boost its sales until the manufacturer made an exceptional showing on the market. Schooled at her father's unbending knee, Marlene had a knack of tuning in to the right buzz words, the right attributes to showcase a product and capture the public's attention.

She supposed that it might seem odd to some that with a knack like that, she couldn't manage to transfer it directly to people. But she couldn't.

She'd never had time to relate to people and their natural foibles. Whatever friendships she had were all work related.

Marlene curled one stubborn wisp until it fell like the others along her neck. Maybe if she had succeeded in getting her father's approval just once, she wouldn't have been so intensely involved in work.

Marlene smiled to herself. It was a sad, knowing smile. If she *had* succeeded once, she probably would have tried even harder, hoping lightning would strike twice.

In the privacy of her own room, in the shadows of her own mind, there was no denying the hunger she had always had to win his approval. To win his love. She had believed—hoped really—that there was more to him than he outwardly showed. That was why she had tried so hard to relate to him on his own territory.

Marlene glanced one last time at her image in the full-length mirror. The flared black velvet evening jacket gracefully camouflaged the fact that she was bordering on something that Greenpeace was taking under its protective wing. Beneath the jacket she wore a wide, floor-length black velvet skirt and a crimson camisole that flowed over it. It was flattering and made her feel a little less like a Sherman tank.

But not by much.

Sally looked up as Marlene descended the stairs. "You look like a knockout," she told her matter-of-factly, and Marlene knew she meant the compliment.

Sally never wasted time with words she didn't mean. She was more like a drill sergeant than a housekeeper, but she had her soft edges. Marlene loved her because she felt that Sally always told her the truth, whether it was good or bad.

"You're wasting it on those bozos tonight."

Leave it to Sally to take everyone down to a common denominator. "I don't think the head of Acme Oil sees himself as a bozo."

Sally grinned as she handed Marlene her purse. "That makes the title all the more fitting. I sure hope you're not going to be doing this once the baby's here."

Once the baby was here, everything would change. "No, I promise you, the pace will lessen." She smiled. "You sound like Nicole."

"The girl makes sense. Well, if you're determined to go, go." Sally shooed Marlene to the door. "Have a good time."

Marlene leaned over to brush her lips over the old woman's wrinkled cheek. "Just for you, Sally."

She grinned as she heard the woman muttering under her breath as she closed the door behind her.

Chapter Four

She had barely crossed the threshold to Breckinridge's ballroom when she saw him.

Sullivan Travis, looking suave in the black tie he had told her about. Even from across the crowded room, she could appreciate the figure he cut in his suit, black, like his hair. There was a strawberry blonde wearing a dress one size too small who appeared to be hanging on to his every word.

Probably mesmerized by his blue eyes.

God, listen to her. She was writing an ode to a man who was out to cold-bloodedly separate her from her child. What was the matter with her?

A combination of being overworked and pregnant, she decided, watching Sullivan. By his bearing, he reminded her of someone who, as the old expression went, was "to the manor born."

Well, she wasn't planning on being some peasant he could just plow under.

For a moment Marlene wavered, undecided whether or not to just leave. It certainly would be the easier way out, just beg off because of her condition. But that would mean hiding behind it, something she swore never to do, and besides, it was tantamount to running. Also something she refused to do.

Instead, she crossed the floor, coming at Sullivan like an arrow intent on a target. Bull's-eye.

Sullivan looked in her direction a moment before she reached him. He was as surprised to see her as she was him, but he hid it better. He'd learned to allow very little to register on his face. It made for better negotiations when the time came.

With a swift, gentle movement, he extracted his arm from the woman beside him.

"If you'll excuse me, I have someone I need to talk to," he murmured.

Sullivan welcomed the reprieve. Janice DuBarry seemed to have her sights set on acquiring a piece of the Travis Corporation, namely him. It was something he was accustomed to and never cared for. Every woman he had ever met saw him only as part of the Travis dynasty, never as Sullivan.

"What are you doing here?" Marlene demanded in a hushed, angry whisper.

She looked loaded for bear, he thought. All in all, the lady was some piece of goods. He felt sorry for any man who would become involved with her. Fortunately, that man wouldn't be him.

He took her arm, turning her away from Janice, who was very obviously trying to eavesdrop. "I was invited. How about you?"

Marlene was tempted to say "Like hell you were," but given his position, he probably had been. Just her luck that she hadn't thought to obtain a guest list from Cynthia beforehand.

He didn't look as if he was smirking at her, but she knew that beneath that smooth exterior, that was exactly what he was doing.

"I suppose who Cynthia and Alan want to socialize with is their own business." Now that she knew he wasn't merely stalking her, she wanted to get away from him. It was a large room, a large party. If she was careful, she didn't have to cross his path again. "Have a nice time," she told him icily.

With that, she began to turn away, but Sullivan took her arm. She stopped, unwilling to cause a scene.

Somewhere in the back of his mind, he wondered if her anger ever rechanneled itself into passion. If it did, she would be more than a handful for that same unfortunate man he'd pitied earlier.

"Since opportunity seems to have knocked on my door, I'd be remiss in not opening it." He waited for her to contradict him.

"Open any door you please, as long as it's not near me." If she was forced to pull her arm away from him in order to get away, she would. She didn't want to spoil the evening by getting into a discussion with him.

From out of nowhere, Cynthia Breckinridge swooped down on them with the unerring instinct of a woman who had been bred to be a hostess from early on.

"Hello, darling." She kissed the air near Marlene's cheek. "I'm so glad you could make it, given your situation and all."

Her eyes swept over Marlene in a quick appraisal, before turning her attention to Sullivan.

"I didn't know that you two knew each other." She hooked an arm through Marlene's, simultaneously slipping the other through Sullivan's.

"Not really," Marlene politely corrected. "We've only just met." She saw that the information somehow pleased Cynthia rather than deterred her.

Very carefully, Marlene extricated her arm and turned her back on Sullivan, cutting him out of her range. "Cynthia, I was wondering—"

"—If I could have a word with Ms. Bailey," Sullivan concluded the sentence. Very smoothly, he moved to Marlene's side. Marlene gave him a murderous look.

With a look that bordered on elation, Cynthia spread her hands benevolently.

"That's what parties are for. Talk away." Her eyes almost danced with gleeful anticipation. "Go forth, mingle. I'd say 'be fruitful,' but our Marlene already seems to have covered that area."

If she didn't like Cynthia so much, Marlene would have been tempted to strangle her. She redirected her anger to the man beside her. She turned on him as soon as Cynthia was out of earshot, fluttering away to tend to her other guests.

Marlene struggled to keep her voice low as she allowed Sullivan to usher her off to the side. "Is that how you and your father built up your company? By strong-arming people?"

"Only if they refuse to return my calls and won't meet with me." She was wearing some sort of heady perfume that managed, even in this crowd, to be distinctive. He felt it subtly surrounding him and struggled to block out its effect.

Marlene disengaged her arm from his grasp. "I've already told you, we have nothing to discuss—especially if you take that tone with me."

Maybe he did sound a little high-handed. It happened when his temper became frayed. But that didn't change matters between them. "You're carrying my brother's child."

"We've already established that—according to you," she said pointedly.

She didn't add that she had retained Spencer to look into Sullivan's background for her. Though there seemed to be no real reason to doubt Travis, she wanted verification that he was who he claimed to be and that the situation was exactly the way he presented it.

Why in heaven's name would he make any of this up? "What does that mean?"

Marlene shrugged. "What proof do I have that you're not conducting some elaborate ruse?"

She knew it sounded as if she were fishing, but stranger things had happened. Not all uncanny situations took place in the pages of a book.

Now she was being absurd. He took a small step backward. Anything more would have caused him to bump into the wall. "Do I honestly look like a man conducting a ruse?"

Marlene strove to look bored. In truth, she was growing uneasy. She looked around for someone to rescue her from Travis.

"I don't know. People don't come with labels stuck to their foreheads." She thought of a newspaper story she'd read recently about the breakup of a black market that dealt in selling stolen babies to desperate, childless couples. "You might not be who you say you are. For all I know, you might be involved in some sort of blackmail scheme."

"And what is Cynthia?" he asked mildly. "My front woman?"

He made her feel like an idiot. He had managed to rattle her so that she wasn't making any sense. Something else to hold against him.

"I have to admit," she said primly, silently damning him to hell, "your knowing Cynthia does verify your identity."

"Thank you." With Marlene, it was going to be one small step at a time. He had no other choice if he wanted to settle this without publicity. "So now are you willing to listen to my proposition?"

She raised her chin, a cool smile on her lips. She would be willing to bet that he was just as averse to a scene as she was. Escape would be simple as long as she kept her head.

"I wouldn't go that far. Now if you'll excuse me, I have work to do."

"Work?" He looked around the room with its elegantly dressed people and tastefully arranged Christmas decorations. Cynthia Breckinridge had been determined to throw the first holiday party of the season, and she had succeeded royally. "But this is a party."

"Exactly." Marlene began to move away from him and was annoyed when he followed. "And I'm here to see and be seen."

The comment made him smile as he surveyed her silhouette. "I'd say there was no missing you."

That sounded like sarcasm. She turned to look at his expression, but she couldn't read it. "You're not married, are you?"

He had no idea where that had come from. In light of Cynthia's effort to pair them together, he would have thought the answer was obvious. "No."

Marlene saw Tim Sakiota standing by the huge Christmas tree in the center of the room and decided he would be her first target. She began making her way toward him. "I didn't think so."

Sullivan managed to sidestep a waiter with a full tray of champagne glasses and followed her. "Meaning?"

She looked over her shoulder at him. It wasn't crowded enough to lose him, she realized. "You're just a little too blunt around the edges to make it in the romance department."

What was she talking about? "I wasn't aware that I was trying to do anything of the sort."

"Good," she said with finality. "Because you weren't succeeding."

He shook his head as if to clear it. The momentary pause allowed her to move further away from him. "I hope your ad campaigns are clearer than you are. Otherwise, I'd advise selling your agency. Quickly."

"I'll keep that in mind." Her voice drifted back to him as she began to make her way toward Sakiota.

Sullivan took hold of her wrist before she had managed to take two steps. She turned and looked at him accusingly. "You have my wrist."

He was beginning to see why she'd had to resort to artificial insemination. "You can have it back if you tell me when I can talk to you."

"If you want to discuss advertising, I'll listen to anything you have to say. Otherwise, I've already told you twice that we have nothing to talk about."

Sullivan struggled to contain his annoyance. "At the risk of sounding like a broken record, there is the matter of my brother's unborn child."

His father had called him just before he'd left for the party, demanding to know what headway he had made with securing custody. Sullivan didn't want to continue putting him off with platitudes. Besides, he heartily felt that the child belonged in their family.

She was about to tell Travis that his brother had given up all claim to a child when he was paid his fee, but she refrained. That would only be opening up an argument, and she wasn't here to argue.

With a sigh, she nodded. "All right. Let me mingle a little and pay my respects. Afterward, we'll talk."

And probably not resolve a damn thing, she added silently. She was beginning to think that Nicole was right. She was going to have to get in contact with their family lawyer. Travis wasn't going to back down the way she'd hoped.

And it went without saying that neither was she. She hadn't gone to all this trouble just to act as a vessel for some pompous family's benefit.

"I can wait. It's a deal." What choice did he have, really. Maybe if he was gracious, she would reciprocate and give him a chance to sway her mind. It was still his hope that all this could be handled privately, without coverage on the eleven o'clock news.

In a moment of whimsy, she placed her hand in his and shook it, sealing the bargain. With that, she turned away and began to do what she had come to do.

Her lips barely seemed to move when she talked. It was an interesting trick, Sullivan thought a few hours later. He wondered if they did when she kissed.

He had to stop allowing himself to be sidetracked this way.

But looking at her, it was difficult not to be. She was, what his grandfather would have termed, a handsome woman. Derek's appraisal of Marlene would have been summed up in a single word: *Wow.*

She deserved that reaction and more. Which made the mystery of why she had opted to do what she had done even more mystifying. Her sharp tongue notwithstanding, she wasn't the type of woman he would have thought lacked admirers. Observing the way men looked at her even now told him that. The woman at the Institute had said that Marlene was impregnated March 25th, making her eight months pregnant.

It didn't seem to put a crimp in her style, though. He wondered what she would look like approximately twenty-five pounds lighter.

That, he reminded himself, was totally irrelevant.

Deciding that he had been patient enough, Sullivan made his move, disrupting the circle of men around Marlene. He knew several of them and nodded a greeting as he took Marlene's hand. "Excuse me, gentlemen, but I believe that this is our dance."

Holding her hand tightly in his, Sullivan led Marlene away.

Stunned, Marlene was rendered temporarily speechless by his intrusion.

"Our dance?" she finally echoed.

She hadn't been dancing since...she couldn't remember when.

The Mulcahy account, she suddenly recalled. Dave Mulcahy had been very heavy on his feet. The weight was only outdone by the size of his wallet when it came to the account. All things considered, it had been worth a few squashed toes. This wasn't going to be.

"We don't *have* a dance."

He looked at her innocently as they found a place near the five-piece orchestra that the Breckinridges had hired for the evening. "I had to think of something to get you away without causing a scene."

"I think it would cause more of a scene if you danced with me. I'm not exactly built for graceful movement at the moment."

She could laugh at herself. He hadn't expected that from her. He found it oddly pleasant. "I thought you weren't going to let this pregnancy impede you." Or so he had heard from a mutual friend.

She looked at him, wondering who had told him that. Obviously he had been talking to people about her, and it annoyed her.

"No, and neither has it made me simpleminded." Her tone low, her lips tightened as she spoke. "I'm not dancing with you, Travis. I'm not talking with you, I'm not doing anything with you. Is that understood?"

She didn't wait for confirmation. Determined, Marlene cut a space in the crowd and moved past the fifteen-foot Christmas tree with its antique decorations. Her goal was to reach the French doors that led out onto the terrace. They were slightly ajar, and she could do with a whisper of air. The press of bodies was making the room stifling. As was Travis.

A waiter stopped and lowered the tray he was carrying before Marlene as she reached the doors. Offering it to her, he waited for her to make a selection.

Marlene shook her head, a small, perfunctory smile on her lips. She would have enjoyed something a little stronger than mineral water right now, given the situation. But her condition was always uppermost in her mind. "No, thank you."

Marlene started as a glass seemed to materialize from nowhere at her right. Turning, she saw Sullivan holding out a filled fluted glass. Bubbles rose to the rim. "I'm not drinking champagne, either."

His eyes dipped to her abdomen, then back to her face. "I would hope not. This is ginger ale, disguised as something more potent." His mouth curved. "Rather like you."

She wanted to demand to know what the hell he was talking about, but that would only lead her down a road she didn't think she wanted to go. Accepting the glass, she took a tentative sip.

"Ginger ale," he affirmed again. "You're going to have to learn to be more trusting than that."

Sullivan looked away, surveying the room. He saw Cynthia looking in their direction, a satisfied smile on her crimson lips. He nodded at her, seeing no reason to burst her bubble at the moment. She would find out about her error soon enough.

Marlene took another sip, then drained the rest of the soda. There was no point in working herself up. For the moment she would endure him. The evening would be in the past soon enough.

Just like everything else.

Marlene looked at Sullivan's profile, all angles and planes. Funny how they seemed to come together to make him appear almost pretty. The impression was intensified by his long, dark lashes. Lashes most women would have killed for. It was only his mouth, firm and hard, that saved him from being labeled pretty.

He turned his eyes to hers.

Marlene felt something shimmy in her stomach, something apart from the baby's movement. It was tempting to look away, but she'd learned at the knee of a master that looking away only left you vulnerable for further attack.

"Why don't you stop trying to avoid the inevitable?" he asked quietly.

The feeling left. Marlene's eyes narrowed. "Meaning you?"

"Me, and our common problem."

She raised her head. A waiter came and collected her empty glass. "My only problem is you, and if you choose to think of yourself as common, well, you'd be the one to know about that."

"I don't want to spar with you, Marlene."

He had a very funny way of showing it. "Then go away."

The orchestra was beginning another piece behind them. Sullivan placed his glass on a nearby table. "I still haven't had that dance."

"And you won't," she replied mildly.

Instinctively, he knew how to get to her. "Are you afraid to dance with me?"

"Afraid of you? That'll be the day." She refused to be afraid. Marlene blew out a sigh. "All right. Remember, you asked for this."

He found himself smiling. She was feisty, all right. "I'll remember."

The slow piece the orchestra was playing was vaguely familiar. Very gently, he took her into his arms and began to dance.

She was lighter on her feet than he'd thought.

Her hand resting against his chest and covered by his, she looked up at Sullivan. The beat of the music and his heart swayed into her body.

She felt awkward and hated the feeling. "I'm too big to dance."

"You're doing fine."

His tone sounded patronizing, or maybe that was just her interpretation. "I don't need your affirmation."

"Fine, have it your way." Holding her other hand in his, he bent his head so that his cheek rested against her hair.

Marlene felt herself drifting. She could almost get to like this.

Her eyes flew open as her thought registered. She didn't want him this close to her. He was taking advantage of the situation.

"Look—" Marlene started to draw away.

"Shh," he murmured against her hair. "You don't want to cause a scene."

She didn't like the way her pulse had begun to accelerate, or the warm flush that was creeping over her entire body. She especially didn't like the way he was holding her, amusing himself at her expense.

Sullivan pressed his hand against the small of her back. He wondered what she looked like when she wasn't pregnant. And what she felt like.

It was all idle speculation, and he allowed himself to indulge in it. After all, nothing would ever come of it.

She felt ungainly. It was only a matter of time before she stumbled and stepped on his foot. But if that was the way he wanted it, that was his problem. She would continue dancing.

"All right. Your funeral."

He laughed, looking down into her eyes. "No, that's when you dance on my grave." He laced his fingers through hers. It formed a solid union, he mused. "This we do together."

There was something about the way he said the last word that sounded as if he were uttering a prophesy. She shook off the foolish thought.

His eyes slowly appraised her face. She was easily one of the most beautiful women at the party, without benefit of a plastic surgeon's scalpel or makeup that was strategically applied.

If he thought that he was softening her up, he was in for a disappointment. "This is the *only* thing we'll be doing together," Marlene countered.

Her answer amused him. She was sharp, but then he'd already learned that. He appreciated her mind. Nothing annoyed him more than gullible fools. "Tell me, are all pregnant women so cynical?"

The only other pregnant woman she knew was Nicole. Because of the length of her workday, her experience tended toward the denizens in the corporate world, mostly male. "I wouldn't know."

He had a feeling she was telling the truth rather than just brushing him off. "All right, I'll settle for knowing what makes you so cynical."

Her eyes gave nothing away. She probably played poker well, he thought. It would make for an interesting game someday.

"I thought by now you would have found out all about me." If she could resort to a private investigator, she had no doubt that Travis probably employed one to dig up what he could about her.

"Not enough," he confessed. He smiled briefly. "I like going straight to the source whenever possible."

It was time to place some space between them. She felt as if her air were being siphoned off. As well as her privacy. "The 'source' would like to stop dancing now."

Sullivan nodded as he immediately ceased. "That's good."

"Why?" She slowly drew her fingers from his.

Sullivan nodded toward the orchestra. "Because the music stopped."

She had been so wrapped up in the conversation that she hadn't noticed. Embarrassed, Marlene flushed and turned from him. As she began walking away, Sullivan joined her, taking her arm and guiding her past a waiter with a full tray of hors d'oeuvres.

Marlene tried to draw her arm away unobtrusively. She succeeded only marginally. "I can walk without you."

"I'm sure you can. However, this allows me to keep track of you. You're slipperier than you look." His hold tightened slightly.

Her eyes on his, she uncoupled herself from him. "If you'll excuse me, I'd like to get back to the rest of the party."

"We haven't talked yet," he reminded her.

But Marlene was already disappearing on him. "On the contrary, we've talked enough."

Sullivan caught up to her easily, managing to shoulder aside the man Marlene wanted to speak to, the head of Breckinridge's board of directors.

When she felt Sullivan's hand on her arm, she stiffened and turned around. "I don't need you to watch."

He intended to keep her within his sight until he got the opportunity to talk to her. "Who knows? I might learn something."

She raised her chin. He was laughing at her, but she knew how to deal with that. Her father had taught her well. "Maybe you might at that."

She took everything as a challenge, he thought, even when it wasn't meant as one. He gestured with his free hand.

"Lead the way. I'm all ears." He paused, thinking of another way he might be able to soften her. "Oh, by the way, I could arrange an introduction to Matthew Geodano for you if you're interested."

That, he noted, caught her attention.

The elusive designer was legendary. And Marlene knew his account ran well into the seven-figure range. But the introduction would place her in Sullivan's debt. The price tag was too large for her to pay.

"Thanks, but I'm afraid I'll have to pass on that."

He shrugged casually. "It's up to you."

Stubborn, Sullivan thought, to the very end. No doubt about it, he had his work cut out for him.

Chapter Five

With a satisfied sigh, Marlene silently congratulated herself. It had been a rather productive ninety minutes, even if she did say so herself. She'd managed to touch base with a number of clients and break ground with several would-be clients. She'd even convinced Carl Hays that her company could run a better TV campaign for his new line of perfume than his current advertising company did. Winning the Hays account would certainly send their stock up a notch or two. Not as much as getting the Geodano account, but at least she was still her own person.

Merry Christmas, she toasted mentally.

Throughout the evening, she'd been very aware that Sullivan was always somewhere close by, observing her. She had to admit that it was unnerving. In a way, it almost reminded her of her father. Except that Sullivan wasn't wearing her father's perpetual frown. And there was certainly no fear involved, no eagerness to please on her part. Only a growing sense of annoyance.

She tried to block his presence out, but it didn't work for long. Sullivan Travis wasn't the kind of man you could easily ignore. Especially not when he was within touching range.

Not that he did.

It just felt as if he had. Or would, even though his hands remained at his sides. She supposed what bothered her most was that having him so close created a latent anticipation that seemed to dance all through her. An anticipation of what, she wasn't certain. Pending doom, probably. It had her on her guard, which blew her attempt to ignore him.

Sullivan had trouble taking his eyes off Marlene. She was fairly glowing with triumph. The look on her face was probably identical to the one worn by Joan of Arc when she'd returned home after leading the French to victory in battle.

If Joan had been pregnant, Sullivan amended.

He would have actually admired Marlene's smooth tactics, he mused, if they weren't in direct competition with his own for the infant she carried. But they were in competition. And, since fate had seen fit to deal him this hand, it was time to make use of the opportunity. Taking two plates from the stack at the buffet table, Sullivan crossed to Marlene and handed her one.

Marlene looked down at the fine china with its delicate design. She recognized it as part of the huge set her father had given Breckinridge two Christmases ago when the account had been renewed.

"What's this?"

"A plate. It looks better with food on it." He turned on his heel and led her to the table.

She followed unwillingly. "I didn't ask for this."

"No." Sullivan glanced at her over his shoulder as he helped himself to a small serving of caviar. "But I thought that after sweeping half the room clean with your charm, you might have worked up an appetite."

His back was to her, and she couldn't tell from his tone if he was smiling or not. She moved next to him and pretended to survey the table. "Was that a compliment or a judgment?"

Examining it, he supposed that it was a little of both. "Interpret it any way you wish, as long as it keeps us on civil terms."

Marlene regarded the plate and decided that perhaps eating a little something wouldn't be such a bad idea. "I am always civil," she informed him. "Unless I'm threatened or challenged."

"I'm just here to have a good time."

His innocent tone didn't fool her. She knew better than to relax.

Marlene looked down the huge buffet table with its perfectly formed ice sculpture in the center. The sculpture, a jovial looking Santa Claus, complete with a pack of toys flung on his back, was only now beginning to melt. The food, artistically arranged around the sculpture, didn't move her. But then, she was never very hungry when she worked, and tonight had been work. It seemed to be the only way she ever socialized lately.

Marlene rotated her neck, feeling suddenly tired. Or was she just tense?

Sullivan perused the different servings and decided that having money didn't necessarily mean you had taste. He glanced at Marlene's plate. She obviously shared his assessment. There was very little on her plate, as well.

He inclined his head toward her, lowering his voice. "You really know how to work a room."

Marlene stopped contemplating a platter with a color-coordinated assortment of seafood to look at him. The comment sounded like something someone would have said to a saloon girl in the old West. Or to one of the women who frequented dark doorways and offered passersby heaven for half an hour and a price.

She frowned at him, absently settling on the avocado dip. "I wasn't 'working the room,' I was just touching base with some clients."

"Same thing." Following her lead, Sullivan took a symmetrically shaped celery stick and sampled the dip. It had looked like avocado, but its taste surprised him. The flavor was entirely different, entirely unknown, but very pleasing.

He wondered if it would be the same if he sampled her mouth.

Sullivan cleared his throat, clearing the thought away as well. "You know, you're an entirely different person when you talk business."

Marlene raised her eyes to his, her pulse beating a little quicker than she would have liked. She tried to remember that she didn't like being analyzed.

"I don't think—"

He took another taste of the dip. It was definitely growing on him. "Confident. Knowledgeable." His eyes skimmed her face. She looked a little flushed again. "Vivacious," he added.

Marlene worked hard at seeming uninterested in his assessment. "Conversely, under regular circumstances that would make me wavering, stupid and dull."

She meant the comment cryptically, but the words brought similar labels to mind. Judgments uttered by her father. That had always been the way he'd seen her—lacking in everything that was important.

"I doubt if you ever really wavered." Sullivan reached for the napkins and handed one to her. "You're definitely not stupid, and I'd be willing to bet you are never dull."

She shrugged off his words, intended, she knew, just to get on her good side. She'd been around enough smooth salesmen to know the signs. And there was a very large bonus at stake here. But yet, he didn't strike her as the slippery type. There was something in his eyes that didn't quite jibe with the specifications.

"That is one bet, Travis, you will never have a chance to collect."

Sullivan smiled. "The first rule of business my father taught me is never judge a book by its cover, and never be certain that you know your adversary. He might surprise you."

It was a nice, antiseptic word to describe the situation they found themselves in. "Is that what we are? Adversaries?"

He looked at her meaningfully over the selection of seafood. "That is entirely up to you."

Meaning, if she gave in, they wouldn't be. *Fat chance.* She let her fork slide to the plate. She would only concede so much, and no more.

"I am this baby's mother. You are, according to your claim, his or her uncle. That makes us bound, indirectly, by blood. Relatives of a sort, if you will." Her eyes narrowed. "Do you consider your relatives adversaries, Travis?"

He looked annoyed, then laughed. "Some." He nodded at her. "You're good."

His smile was infectious. Her guard went up another notch. "I've had to be."

Their hands touched as they both reached for one of the imported bread sticks. He withdrew his to allow her first choice. As she picked one, he resumed his assessment of her. "You're not the vain type."

He was flattering her again, and she knew she shouldn't be reacting to it. They were just vacant words. But somehow, in his mouth, they had a different sound. A genuine sound. But that, she reasoned, was probably part of his plan—to get her at her ease. To make her trust him. When she did, he would spring a trap for her baby.

There was no way that was going to happen. Marlene lowered her eyes as she poked at a huge, flattened shrimp coated in a glaze that caught the light from the chandelier. She decided to pass on it.

"In my own life, I deal in facts. The fact is," she asserted as she raised her eyes to his, "you're not going to get my baby, so stop spinning your web."

"Why don't we table this topic for a while?" he suggested mildly.

More like forever, she thought, but said nothing. She didn't want to get into an argument in a public place, least of all here.

Sullivan looked around the room. Marlene had been on her feet the entire time she'd been at the party. He saw an unoccupied chair against the wall. "Shouldn't you be sitting down or something?"

He was definitely the type who liked taking over, she thought. And she was the type who didn't like being taken over. She'd already paid her dues in that department. That automatically placed them on opposite sides of the fence.

Marlene raised her chin. "If I wanted to be sitting, I'd be sitting."

Someone brushed against his shoulder, and Sullivan moved closer to Marlene. He looked down into her eyes and saw the stubbornness shining there. "No," he said slowly, "I don't think so."

She squared her shoulders beneath the deep velvet padding of her jacket. "Meaning?"

He didn't think he really had to explain it to her. She knew. "Meaning that you're stubborn enough to stay on your feet even when every fiber of your body is begging you not to—just to prove a point."

Marlene shifted. Travis understood her a little too well for her comfort. She didn't like that. "And that point being?"

He shrugged good-naturedly, sinking his fork into the seafood array on his plate. "*That* I haven't figured out yet, beyond the fact that you're determined not to allow pregnancy to slow you down."

She didn't want him taking his analysis any further. "That would be enough."

"Maybe," he conceded, inclining his head. He took a bite before continuing. "But I think there's probably more."

She pushed around the few things that were on her plate, attempting to work up some sort of an appetite. She decided that she'd been gracious long enough. "I refuse to be psychoanalyzed over a plate of shrimp, Travis."

He would wager there were a great many things that she refused to put up with. Despite the initial circumstances that had brought them together, he found himself growing intrigued.

Sullivan pressed on amicably as if she hadn't attempted to cut him dead. "They're your ankles. You want them to swell up just because you have a point to prove to someone, that's your business."

Her ankles? What was he talking about? "My ankles are fine." Holding the plate in one hand, she lifted the hem of her velvet skirt with the other to show him.

He glanced down. She was wearing matching velvet pumps and silk stockings. Even from that small glimpse, her ankles looked sexy.

"Yes, maybe they are at that." Then, as if he'd won his point, he indicated the wall closest to them. "There's a chair over there."

She had no idea what made her stubbornly dig in. Maybe it was because she'd had to give in on so many points, small and large, before her father had died. Maybe he just rubbed her the wrong way. Or maybe she didn't like reacting to him when she knew that he was after only one thing: custody of the baby. Whatever the reason, Travis had set her off.

"Your powers of observation really are keen, aren't they?"

He let the sarcasm wash over him. He'd been subjected to a great deal worse. "There's no shame in sitting while you eat."

She turned her back to the chair and continued to pick at her plate, rearranging the items and eating nothing. "There's no need, either."

He shrugged as if it were all one and the same to him. "Well, if you won't, I will." Leaving her, Sullivan strode over to the chair.

Marlene counted to ten, then sighed and followed him. Sullivan caught Cynthia Breckinridge's scent before he saw her. Seventy-five dollars an ounce and used unsparingly. He raised his eyes in the woman's direction.

Cynthia placed a well-manicured hand on his shoulder. "Has she deserted you, Sullivan?" Disappointment throbbed in her voice.

He saw Marlene approaching. He felt a small note of triumph.

"No, I'm just reserving a chair for her." For Cynthia's benefit, he nodded toward Marlene who was behind her. "I would imagine that it's a little hard for Marlene to move quickly these days."

Marlene stopped short just to Sullivan's right. Alan Breckinridge's department store was one of the major accounts held by her company. She had landed it herself. It had been her first account when she had joined her father's agency. She was on very good terms with both Alan and Cynthia. Cynthia's friendship with Travis made her feel outnumbered.

Between them, she and Cynthia framed Travis like two uneven bookends. Somehow, she was going to make him pay for that last remark, she thought. Dearly.

"Thank you for being so thoughtful," she said to him tightly.

He moved away from the chair, and Marlene was forced to sit down or look like a fool. Something, she was certain, Travis would have readily enjoyed.

"Don't mention it." He turned toward Cynthia. "All in all, I think she wears the blush of motherhood rather well, wouldn't you say?"

Satisfied, Cynthia began withdrawing. But before she did, she hooked an arm through Sullivan's and moved him closer to Marlene.

"Yes, far better than I had thought. Now make nice, you two. Remember, this is the season for brotherly love. Nothing wrong with slipping in a little sisterly love, as well." She winked broadly, then released her hold on Sullivan's arm. "Well, if you'll excuse me. I have to go and mingle. So many stick-in-the-muds here. A hostess's work is never done." She sighed dramatically.

Marlene looked up at Sullivan as Cynthia disappeared into the crowd. "The blush of motherhood?"

The corners of his mouth curved. "Best I could do on short notice."

"You could have spared yourself the trouble."

He let his glance slide over her. "I live for trouble."

"Okay, I'll bite. Elaborate."

He laughed shortly, then decided that there was no harm in telling her. Maybe carrying Derek's child gave her the right to know a little something about his brother.

"Derek was what you might call a rebel, a prodigal son who never came home to sample the fattened calf." His mouth curved slightly. "My father doted on Derek even as he railed that he behaved like a heathen."

The description reminded her of Robby and the relationship her older brother had had with their father. Robby had been too young to really rebel, but even the slightest hint of willfulness had James Bailey turning red. Robby had known how to irritate him from a very young age. There was no doubt in her mind that he would have gone down his own path if he'd lived.

If anything, the peek into Derek's life Sullivan gave her made her feel close to the man whose seed she had taken. "I know how that is."

Sullivan looked at her sharply. He thought she was patronizing him and realized, as he looked into her eyes, that she wasn't. She really did understand. For the first time he found himself wondering about her and thinking of her as a person in her own right, rather than just an extension of the problem.

He relaxed a little. "It was always up to me to clean up Derek's messes." He shrugged. "There were women to buy off, incidents to keep quiet. Things like that." The family name had always been so important to his father. It was as if the name had a life of its own, apart from the rest of them, and it, above all, had to be honored and protected.

She couldn't say she cared for his analogy. "Is that what this is? Another mess to clean up?"

If he tried to smooth it over with words, she would see through them. He'd already learned that she wasn't the type whose head was turned with flattery.

"In a way."

His reply caught her off guard. Maybe she'd underestimated him. "I guess I should give you points for being honest."

His eyes held hers. "Only if you want to."

Her father had always favored a narrow approach to business, one that she found never worked for her. To him people were opponents. She preferred being friends with them. Maybe, if she could turn Sullivan into a friend, there would be no need to fear anything worse happening down the line. She didn't have to be told how powerful the Travis family was.

It was worth a try.

She looked down at his plate. He hadn't eaten any more than she had. The food was attractive to the eye but predominantly bland to the palate.

Marlene made up her mind. "I know this prime rib restaurant where the cuts are larger than most of the egos here."

"That would have to be very large." He laughed dryly. This was working out well, he thought. The more he knew about her, the easier it would be to find the right approach to use with her. "Sounds good to me. Is there anyone left you need to overwhelm with your charm?"

Marlene glanced around the large ballroom and did a quick mental roll call: McCarthy, Edwards, Winnow, Breckinridge, Andrews, Smith and Sakiota. She'd chatted with the heads of seven different companies, strengthening ties on old accounts and laying groundwork for possible new ones. Her father had always claimed that he conducted as much business at these functions as he did behind his desk. But she had talked about as much as she was going to tonight.

She winced slightly as she felt the baby kick. Marlene's velvet skirt rippled as if it had been caught in an unexpected breeze.

"No, I'm done."

He looked down in fascination as another ripple moved across her stomach. He couldn't imagine what it felt like to know that there was another human being inside of you. He nodded absently to her comment, still watching for further movement. "Just how fancy is this restaurant?"

She shrugged. "Fair to middling. It's a steak house, actually."

His brow rose. She was dressed for a posh party, not for an evening meal. "Aren't you afraid you're overdressed for a steak house?"

There had been a time when she'd lived in fear of other people's opinions. But although she was still very conscious of her professional appearance and reputation, she'd learned to be more relaxed when it came to her personal life.

Marlene smiled as she shook her head. "I am very rarely afraid these days. Besides, maybe everyone else is just underdressed."

He had to admit he rather liked her moxie. "Okay, let's find the Breckinridges and say our goodbyes."

She led the way toward the tall, white-haired man talking to a small gathering of men who obviously worked for him. Heads were bobbing like apples in a tub of water at an old-fashioned Halloween party.

"Leaving already?" Breckinridge asked, obviously surprised.

"Marlene's rather tired. I offered to see her home," Sullivan said quickly. He felt Marlene's eyes shift toward him in anger.

Breckinridge pointedly looked at Marlene's stomach. "Can't have anything going wrong at this stage of the game. You take care of yourself, young lady," he ordered affectionately.

She returned his light, quick kiss, brushing her lips to his cheek. "Will do."

She waited until they were out of earshot. "Why did you lie to him?"

The answer seemed pretty obvious to Sullivan. "What was I going to tell the man, that we were leaving his party to get something to eat?"

She wasn't taking exception to that part. "You could have used another excuse besides me."

"Next time." He shouldered a path for them toward Cynthia, who was closer to the front door.

Marlene was beginning to think that it would be wiser if there *wasn't* a next time.

"Leaving together?" Cynthia's small, bright eyes darted from one face to the other like a humming bird undecided which flower to light upon first.

"It certainly looks that way, doesn't it?" Marlene murmured, forcing a smile to her lips. She knew exactly what was going on in Cynthia's mind.

Sullivan decided to cut the woman short. "We really have to be leaving, Cynthia. I—"

She patted his hand. "No excuses, I quite understand and I couldn't be happier. You look out for her, Sullivan. She puts on a good show, but she needs a man in her life. Don't you, dear?"

Marlene clenched her jaw so hard forcing a smile for Cynthia's benefit, she thought it would crack. "Maybe later," she murmured.

Coming to her rescue, Sullivan ushered Marlene out of the house. "So what makes Cynthia think you need a man in your life, other than the fact that you're pregnant?"

She didn't want to have this conversation. "My guess is an old-fashioned upbringing. I'd like to drop the subject if you don't mind."

He smiled to himself. He enjoyed teasing her, he discovered. "Fine with me."

"Good." She fairly bit off the word.

The valet approached them, waiting for instructions. Sullivan turned to Marlene. "The '95 white 735 BMW." She gave the man her key.

"Black '94 Mercedes," Sullivan added, handing the man his key, as well. Pocketing both, the valet hurried away.

The wind had picked up. Marlene hunched her shoulders slightly beneath her velvet jacket. Inside the house, she'd felt unbearably warm. Now she felt cold.

He was tempted to place his arm around her, but that would be taking this association to a plateau he had no intention of scaling. The situation was already more complicated than he wanted it. He slipped his hands into his pockets and watched the valet pick his way through the sea of metal that had arrived. Headlights suddenly turned on in the distance. The valet had found his car first.

He watched as the valet attempted to maneuver his way out of the tangle of cars. They were apparently the first to be leaving, and a great many cars had arrived after them.

Doubts about going out with Marlene began to surface. Perhaps this wasn't such a good tactical move after all. "Maybe I'd better take a rain check on that restaurant," he told her. "I've got an early meeting in the morning."

Beside him, Marlene had begun to shiver. Hang propriety, he thought, slipping his arm around her and drawing her to him for warmth.

She was surprised by his action, but because she did feel cold, she rationalized that there was no harm in letting him leave his arm there. Marlene hoped the valet would hurry.

"Will the meeting go on without you?" she asked. Bringing Sullivan's car up the driveway, the valet jumped out and went to retrieve the other car.

"Yes, but—"

"Then you can be late," she stated.

He sighed, nodding. It was foolish to have this uneasy feeling. After all, this could only work to his benefit. "You'll have to lead the way."

"No problem."

She led the way all right, he thought, pulling up into the parking lot behind her. At sixty or faster. Did the woman have a death wish? She probably had the word *fast* tattooed on her heart.

Sullivan got out of his car and crossed over to her. Marlene was already standing at the restaurant's entrance. He thought of all the people she had touched base with tonight, all in a short period of time. "Do you do anything slowly?"

She shook her head in reply. There was always too much to do. She could never sit back and relax or take her time. When she had attended college, she had apprenticed at the agency, making do on five hours of sleep a night. When she graduated, she'd gone to work full-time. Full-time to her father meant working as many hours as a project needed, then going on to the next one.

"Doing things slowly usually doesn't cut it." It was something her father had continually hammered into her.

Sullivan had no idea what possessed him. He caught her arm at the door and very slowly ran the back of his hand along her cheek. He saw her eyes widen in surprise. And latent pleasure.

"Oh lady, you have no idea."

She felt the earth sway beneath her. But the building directly in front of her remained stationary, so it couldn't have been an earthquake. The quake she experienced had nothing whatsoever to do with shifting plates beneath the earth's crust. And everything to do with the man in front of her.

She took a long, deep, cleansing breath the way she'd been instructed by her Lamaze tutor. Unable to make regular sessions and with no partner, she had hired a teacher to come by the house one late Saturday afternoon. Cleansing breaths might help in childbirth, but they were useless against Sullivan Travis.

"Maybe," she heard herself answering. "C'mon, let's go inside." Not waiting for him to open the door, Marlene led the way in.

The restaurant was plain and dark, the booths small and intimate, and the food even better than Marlene had promised.

Sullivan's life was so structured that he ate on the run and had little appetite when an island of time presented itself. Tonight, he allowed himself to unwind and savor the meal. And the company.

He enjoyed watching her eat. She did it with such contented pleasure. It occurred to him that she might make love the same way. Startled, Sullivan raised his hand for the check. It was time to go, he told himself.

Marlene was going to insist on paying for the meal, since she had brought him here, then thought better of it. Instead she sat back and looked at him. "Was it good?"

He smiled and nodded. "Yes."

She grinned at him, feeling very pleased with herself. "Told you so."

Yes, he thought, she had.

Sullivan walked with her to the parking lot and stopped beside her car. "So now what?"

She knew that there was a great deal more to his question than the simple way the words made it sound. But for now, she went with the simple. "So now you go to your house, and I go to mine."

"And the baby?"

Her eyes narrowed as wariness entered them. "The baby has no choice. It comes with me."

"You know what I mean. We haven't discussed the situation yet."

That was what had made the dinner enjoyable. Marlene took a step back. Any further retreat was hampered by the car. "There's nothing to discuss. You and your father can have visitation rights if you want. I suppose it's only fair."

He knew that his father would never settle for that. "What would be fair is to raise him—"

"Or her," she interjected.

She was just trying to irritate him by interrupting. "Or her," he conceded, "as a Travis."

"Why?"

"There are advantages."

His answer was infuriatingly vague. She could see his point if she were an idiot, but she wasn't and he knew it. "I doubt if they outweigh having a mother around."

Marlene thought of her own life, a life without a mother, or a father for that matter. He had never been around while they were growing up, and even when James Bailey had been there, he really wasn't. Not for his children. Not emotionally.

Sullivan sighed, feeling stymied. "How do I make you see reason?"

That was exactly the way she felt about him. Why couldn't he see her side?

"In this case, reason is in the eye of the beholder." She pressed her lips together. "It was a fairly decent evening, Sullivan. Don't spoil it by threatening me."

Was that what she thought? That he was his father's henchman and he was threatening her? "I'm not threatening you. My God, I've never threatened anyone in my life."

Maybe he didn't hear himself. It certainly sounded like a threat from where she stood.

"Then don't start now." She paused for emphasis. "Or you may lose a great deal more than you can gain."

He had no doubt that she fully intended to carry out her promise. The better part of negotiations was knowing when to retreat. For now, he changed the subject. "I enjoyed tonight, Marlene."

That took her by surprise. What was he up to? She hesitated for a minute, attempting to analyze him. "Why did you say that?"

"Because it's true. I did."

Rather than say anything, she looked away and began digging through her purse for her car key.

Sullivan peered at her face, trying to see her expression. "Hasn't anyone ever told you that they enjoyed your company?"

She found the key and began to insert it into the lock. He took it from her. Marlene looked at him, her annoyance growing. "I don't go out very much."

He held on to the key for a moment. "Why?"

She blew out a breath. She shouldn't even be answering this. "Because I'm busy. I've always been busy."

There was busy and then there was hiding. "Always? All through high school? All through college?"

He sounded as if he didn't believe her. It wasn't his place to ask her anything. "That is none of your business, Travis."

"Maybe." He was getting in deeper, he thought. He inserted the key into the lock for her, then turned it.

And then he did something very impetuous. Or something very stupid, depending on the perspective. He knew he didn't have any. His had temporarily left. The woman before him had made it disappear.

The crisp winter air seemed to solidify all around him as he slipped his hands into Marlene's hair and lowered his mouth to hers.

Chapter Six

At the last possible moment, Marlene wedged her hand between them. Her heart was pounding. "You're not going to do what I think you're going to do, are you?"

His mouth was inches from hers, his breath on her lips as he answered. "What is it that you think I'm going to do?"

"Kiss me." Her eyes narrowed slightly. Maybe, just this once, she was in deeper than she could handle. "Because if you are—"

"What?"

"It might be a mistake."

"You're probably right." In fact, he knew she was. "But it's a mistake I want to make. God only knows why."

She certainly couldn't claim that he had undone her with sugary, seductive words. But there was something else at play here, something nameless and demanding. She wanted to kiss him. To be kissed by him. "That's hardly flattering."

"I'm not trying to flatter you. I'm not even sure I know what I am doing." Very slowly, Sullivan lowered his mouth to Marlene's. He moved his lips over hers, sampling, tasting. Enjoying.

Despite her very obvious condition and the iciness she periodically used like a rapier, he'd been right in his assessment. Beneath it all, she was a very sensual woman.

He'd expected her to shove him away after a beat. He would have understood that. What he wasn't prepared for was the wonder. There was a wonder in her kiss that took him completely by surprise. As did the degree of passion that shimmered just behind it.

Passion that aroused his own, sending it to the next plateau.

Common sense dictated that he end it, but common sense had taken a holiday. He played his lips softly along hers, a pianist coaxing a sweet, sensual melody from the keys, tapping an ability within himself he didn't even suspect he had.

He was sorely tempted to deepen the kiss and see her reaction. To see his own reaction. But that would be going too far too fast. Sullivan struggled to hold back.

Kissing Marlene was like chasing after a ball that was rolling downhill. The increasing momentum was astonishing.

And damn exciting.

Struggling for control, Sullivan filled his hands with her hair again, framing her face, drawing her even closer to him. He tried to remind himself that he had no business doing this, that it would only complicate everything. He tried, but he didn't get very far. She stirred something within him that had to be explored.

He heard an almost imperceptible moan, felt it traveling along her throat until it settled within his mouth.

Sullivan was accustomed to women of breeding who, when they kissed him, were busy thinking about his genes, his name, his background. He had come to expect that and knew how to handle it. But here was something else entirely. What he sampled, what he tasted on her lips, brought him back to the wonder he'd felt himself, eons ago, when he had kissed his first woman.

Then, as now, he found his breath completely stolen away.

My God, was she out of her mind? She shouldn't be doing this, kissing a man she hardly knew. A man who had made it clear that he wanted to take her baby away. She needed to clear her head.

The words drummed through her mind over and over again, but she couldn't seem to draw away from Sullivan. Away from his lips. It was as if she were sealed to them.

Sealed to the moment.

Her emotions ran wild. Like a newly uncaged animal, her feelings dashed in one direction, stopped abruptly, then dashed off in another. She wanted to attribute her reaction to mood swings, but knew that was a feeble attempt at rationalizing away her response.

The wind sent waves of cold swirling around her body. She didn't feel it. Instead she felt hot, much hotter than she could ever remember feeling.

Her fingers wound into his hair as she lost herself in the heat of his mouth.

In the heat of her feelings. For one isolated, shimmering moment, she felt as if she could touch the sky. She felt...

Desirable.

And certifiably crazy.

Self-control was something he prided himself on. He never overindulged. Never. But he felt as if he were doing just that. Losing himself in something he had no place experiencing. She was carrying his brother's child! In biblical times, he would have been stoned. Maybe he still should be.

Sliding his hands down to her shoulders, Sullivan drew back and looked into her eyes. "Wow," was all he managed to say. He realized, only after a beat, that he had used one of Derek's favorite exclamations. For a moment the word hung in the air between them as if it had depth and breadth.

She would have wanted to hug the moment, the word, to her as a compliment. But that was probably exactly what Sullivan wanted her to do, to be overwhelmed by him until she agreed to anything that he suggested.

No way, Jose.

She tossed her head, her eyes defiant. A small pin fell from her hair, followed by a curl. Bravado was the only way to handle this. She had to speak sharply, and hope to hell that he didn't notice that she was trembling.

"You look surprised. Didn't you think pregnant women could kiss?"

He didn't know what he thought. He had thought he knew, but now...he would have had to pause before correctly reciting his name and social security number.

Sullivan ran his hands along her arms. The velvet sleeves felt sensual against his palms.

Her eyes pinned him in place. "You shouldn't have done that."

She was probably right. It instantly complicated the situation. But talking about the pros and cons wasn't going to change the fact that it had happened.

"Moot point."

What wasn't moot was that he wanted to do it again. He toyed with the temptation, then for his sake as much as hers he stepped back. But one nagging thought wouldn't fade. A woman who could kiss like that, who had that much pent-up sexuality within her, didn't seem like the type who would allow herself to be artificially inseminated.

His eyes skimmed over the outline of her body. "Why?"

She knew exactly what he was asking. Maybe because it had been on her mind as well, all these months, a secret regret not to have created this life within her by the standard methods.

"My business, remember?"

He toyed with the curl that had come loose and saw her eyes widen even as she moved her head back. Funny how such an innocent thing could stir him. He generally didn't fantasize about women he couldn't have. He wasn't the type to pin his hopes to anything.

"As I see it," he said, leaning back against his car, "you've got a great deal to offer." He saw her annoyance mounting at his presumption. It amused him. "I suppose you were in between gentlemen callers."

It sounded like a line from a Tennessee Williams play. Did he lump her into the category of repressed, dried-up women?

"You might say that," she answered coldly.

He brushed his fingers against her cheek. The diamonds at her ear winked flirtatiously at him. "Might? And what could I say for certain?"

Marlene edged away from him. Her back came flush against the door. She stood her ground. "That you have a hell of a lot of nerve."

Sullivan maintained a mild tone, his voice soothing. "It's important in my line of work." Though he'd agreed that it wasn't any of his business, something urged him on. He had to know. "Why isn't there anyone in your life, Marlene?"

She suddenly felt very weary again. She pulled her jacket up around her throat to ward off the wind. Why hadn't she noticed how cold it was before?

Slender shoulders lifted and fell beneath velvet in answer to his question. "Things don't always work out the way you want them to. I haven't had time to build relationships."

So she had alluded. He still found that difficult to believe. He was alone, but that was by choice. He'd never met anyone who could really matter for more than a few nights. But that was his story. Hers, he had a feeling, was a different one. One, he found, that was beginning to intrigue him.

"Ever?"

She sighed, looking past his head into the darkness. "There was a guy when I first began college. I thought things might turn out for us."

Her voice trailed off as she remembered Ted. Her words fell carelessly. "There was some groping, some enduring, and I found it wasn't all it was cracked up to be." She shrugged. "It wasn't worth the effort."

He had a feeling there was more, but he didn't probe. As she'd said, it was none of his business. He had to remember that.

The feel of her lips hummed on his own. "You just met the wrong man," he muttered. He wanted to hold her, but he made no move toward her.

And was Travis going to try to convince her that he was the right one? She thought not. "Well, I won't say that this hasn't been interesting, but I do have an early morning."

He could respect her dedication and sense of responsibility. He could identify with those qualities. It was everything else he was having difficulty identifying with. He'd gotten too close with the kiss. Much too close and too intrigued. A little curiosity was a good thing. Too much clouded the other issues.

"We haven't resolved anything," Sullivan suddenly remembered.

"That all depends on how you look at it. As far as I'm concerned, it's all resolved." Her eyes narrowed as she placed her hand over her abdomen. "Possession, Travis, is nine-tenths of the law, and in case you haven't noticed, I have possession."

Sullivan inclined his head in acknowledgment. "I've noticed."

He stepped back and allowed her room to open her car door. Marlene slid in behind the steering wheel. He thought of how uncomfortable that had to be for her as he closed the door.

Sullivan pressed his lips together. There was no way anything would get settled tonight. But there was always tomorrow. "You still have my card?"

"Taped over my heart." Before he could say anything else, she revved up the motor and pulled away.

That had been a mistake, she thought. A gross, impulsive mistake. She should have gone with her first instinct and immediately pushed him away, not let the kiss flower.

Without thinking, she ran her tongue over her lips. His taste was still there, tart and tantalizing. Her heart fluttered, skipping a beat. Restless, Marlene dragged her hand through her hair. The remaining pins came loose, scattering like metal leaves. She had absolutely no idea what had come over her, why she had allowed him to kiss her.

Why she had wanted it.

No, she amended, taking a sharp turn. That wasn't true. She knew exactly why she had allowed it. Because she had wondered what it would be like to kiss him.

Marlene blew out a long breath. That still didn't excuse what had happened.

She was still upbraiding herself when she returned home. The feel of his mouth haunted her all the way into the house. It would probably haunt her, she thought darkly, all night.

Marlene frowned, slowly making her way up the stairs. It felt as if she were dragging a ten-pound sack with her.

Or rather a twenty-five-pound sack, she corrected herself, remembering the numbers from the last weigh-in. God, those weigh-ins were depressing. But then, she had known what she was in for when she had signed on for this.

Or believed she had known. She thought of Sullivan, a cryptic smile flittering over her lips.

The door at the top of the stairs cracked open just as Marlene reached the landing. Sally, her compact, bony frame swathed in a turquoise terry cloth robe, peered out into the hallway. She glanced at her wristwatch as if she hadn't been marking time since Marlene had walked out the door.

"You're back late." There was surprise in her voice, if not on her face. "Good party?"

Marlene attempted to get her feelings under control. Her nerves continued humming. She shrugged. "It was all right."

She thought of ending the conversation at that, then changed her mind. "I ran into Sullivan Travis."

Sally's face puckered into a deep frown. "With the car, I hope."

Marlene laughed. Maybe that would have been the better way to go. "No, at the party."

Sally stifled a yawn, but duty came first. "Need anything?"

Yes, answers. To so many questions. But nothing you can help me with, Sally. Marlene shook her head. "No, I'm fine."

Sally seemed grateful to hear that. Shuffling back, she withdrew into her room.

"See you in the morning." She shoved her hands into her robe, then stopped as her fingers came in contact with paper. "Oh, I almost forgot. This must have fallen behind the table in the foyer when I brought the mail in. It's got yesterday's postmark, so I must have dropped it today." She produced an official looking envelope.

Junk mail, Marlene thought as she accepted it. The return address sprang up at her. The letter was from the Travis Corporation. With a feeling of dread, she tore it open and quickly scanned the single sheet of paper.

"Anything?" Sally asked.

"The slimy bastard," Marlene declared, crumpling the letter in her hand. She envisioned it being Sullivan's neck. "The lousy, seductive, slimy bastard."

"Seductive? What do you mean seductive?" Sally demanded.

But Marlene didn't hear her. "To think I actually thought we could be friends."

"Friends don't describe each other as being seductive." Sally tugged on her arm, trying to get her attention. "What are you talking about?"

Marlene suddenly realized that Sally was still there and talking to her. The woman's questions played themselves back belatedly in her mind.

There was no way she was going to go into detail. "I'm talking about a mistake."

Sally tried to read between the lines. "Yours?"

"His. He just made a fatal one." Marlene brandished the letter in front of her. "His lawyer just officially put me on notice that I have an obligation to turn custody of my baby over to the Travises. That he hopes I'll be 'sensible' so that this can be resolved calmly." How could he have kissed her, knowing that this was on its way? "I saw him all evening, he never once gave me a clue that he had put his lawyer on the job—"

"Did you give him the chance?"

Sally's question had her pulling up short. No, she hadn't allowed Travis to discuss it. But that was no excuse. "That doesn't matter. He should have told me before—"

"Before what?"

The words came out before she thought them through. "Before he kissed me."

Sally's mouth dropped open. Recovering, she shook her head. "Hope you've had all your shots."

Too late for that, a small voice whispered.

Marlene's reply to Sally, the voice and Sullivan was to slam her bedroom door.

She couldn't sleep.

What was left of the night stretched out before her like a vast, darkened desert. She spent it in fitful naps, grabbing snatches of sleep and feeling the worse for it.

By morning she knew she looked like hell. She certainly felt like it.

And it was his fault, she thought angrily as she hurried into her clothes, getting ready for work. All his damn fault. She would see him in hell before she would see him with her child. And she was going to make him pay for last night. Pay for it dearly. As soon as it was humanly possible.

Dressed, Marlene hurried down the stairs. Outside, one of the worst storms of the decade was taking shape. Rain was coming down, striking the tiled roof in angry, rhythmic staccato beats. She envisioned it as fists, beating on Sullivan's body. It helped calm her down. A little.

Sally met her in the hallway and silently pointed toward the kitchen. Marlene ignored her. She was running late as it was. Something else she could blame that bastard for.

"It's raining. Stay home," Sally urged gruffly.

"It's the rainy season, Sally," Marlene reminded her. "It's supposed to be raining."

"You should still stay home."

Marlene checked her briefcase for her address book. "I can't kill Sullivan Travis if I'm home."

Sally nodded, smiling. "You have a point. Then you're not going to the office?"

She had three meetings today. There was still a lot to do before she went on maternity leave. "First business, then pleasure," Marlene told her.

Slipping on a raincoat, Marlene entered the garage through the rear of the family room. She threw her things over to the passenger seat and got in behind the wheel, her resolution clear. She was going to call Travis as soon as she got a free moment today and give him hell.

There were no free moments. Like a colorful paper chain forged by a determined child, one moment linked into another and another, leaving no spaces. And absolutely no time.

Normally, Marlene would have enjoyed the hectic pace. She was at her best under pressure, where free minutes were as scarce as oxygen in space. But not today. Today she just wanted to tell Travis what she thought of him. And she couldn't.

One of the clients she had spoken to the night before called just before her early morning meeting. Enthused by an idea she had suggested, he was requesting an immediate get-together. He wanted to work her idea into his advertising campaign in time for Christmas. It gave her a salvo of triumph, which she had two and a half minutes to savor, before she had to hurry to the meeting.

Which ran over.

By the time Marlene was finally sitting behind her desk, with no more meetings scheduled for the day and no telephone ringing, demanding her attention, the world had turned completely dark outside her window. In the distance she saw the palm trees in the parking lot swaying and bending at an alarming angle. The storm that had been promised was settling in.

She'd given her employees the opportunity to leave early and most of them had. Flash flood warnings were out for Malibu and the canyon roads. It promised to be a grim evening before the storm moved on.

She was about to get her things together when the telephone buzzed. She picked up the receiver.

"Wanda? I thought you'd left."

"Just going," her secretary told her, "and you should, too. But there's a Mr. Geodano on line one. Said Sullivan Travis told him to call you regarding a new advertising campaign he'd been considering."

Talk about dirty pool. He was playing both sides against the middle. Strong-arming her on one side, playing up to her on the other. Well, it wasn't going to work, even though the Geodano account was a lucrative one.

"Tell him I've already left for the day, Wanda. Then get yourself to high ground."

"I'm already on my way."

* * *

The wind was howling mournfully as Marlene got into her car. Common sense dictated that she go straight home before the roads became impassable, but first she had one stop to make.

Travis's office was on her way home. Not exactly in the direct path, but it only required a minor detour. It seemed a small price to pay for the satisfaction of telling him to go to hell in person.

The weasel. And to think for a moment she had actually been carried away last night when he'd kissed her. Obviously the letter of intent had reached her before he'd had a chance to undermine her even further.

She felt a hard twinge in her stomach. It wasn't the first time today. There had been strange, tingling sensations running over the lower portion of her body on tiny, spiked heels.

Another three weeks of this, she thought with a tired sigh. God, there were times she doubted that she was going to make it.

Marlene rubbed her hand along her neck. Another twinge, harder this time, rippled through her body. She bit back a moan, succeeding only partially.

The baby shifted again, moving over organs that felt as if they would never be the same. For the last week or so, Marlene had felt as if she were ready to push him or her out. Especially today. But her due date was still weeks away. Christmas Eve.

An eternity away.

The rain continued to lash at her windshield. She felt isolated. Tonight that bothered her. To keep herself company, she switched on the radio. A broadcaster came on. More reports of roads that were out.

The voice on the radio faded into the background. There was a rushing noise in her ears, blocking it out. She shook her head, trying to clear it. Maybe she had better just go home and...

No, she wanted to have this out. She knew she would get no rest tonight if she let it go another day. She wanted to tell Travis exactly what she thought of him—and that she intended to get a restraining order to keep him away from her.

Another kick had her wincing. She curved her hand over the swell beneath her tailored suit and looked down.

"You're going to be an active one, aren't you?" she murmured. In reply, she felt another kick. Her body seemed to contract in response. "Try to go easy on me," she whispered. "I'm new at all this."

Very new, she thought ruefully. She hadn't even played with baby dolls as a child. There had been no desire to play house with her brother or sister, no crying need to have dolls to dress up and pretend to nurture. There had never even been a hint in her childhood that she would wake up one morning with this incredible pull within her. A pull to hold a child of her own in her arms. An overwhelming desire to have a tiny being in her life to love and nurture.

It had taken form a little more than a year ago, beginning as a small, nagging thought. It had followed her like a persistent tiny pebble in the bottom of her shoe.

The pebble had grown into a boulder when her father died.

The windshield wipers struggled to give her a small measure of visibility. She squinted, turning up the defroster on her dashboard. After she told Travis where he could put his threat, she was going to go home and reward herself with a nice, warm cup of tea.

God, but she felt chilled.

Only a little farther to Travis's office. She wondered what the penalty was for justifiable homicide in this state and if her pregnancy would make any difference to the jurors.

Once inside the building, Marlene found her way easily enough. Sullivan's office was located on the seventh floor. When she got off the elevator, the area looked as deserted as her own office building had when she'd left. She sincerely hoped Travis hadn't gone home. If he had, she would track him down. She wanted to have it out with him while her anger was ripe and her strength lasted. There was no denying that she was feeling very odd.

There was no secretary sitting before his office door. The computer on the desk was covered, indicating that she had left for the night.

Good, no witnesses.

Marlene barged in.

Sullivan looked up, startled by the sound of his door banging against the wall. He thought it was an earthquake, ushered in by the rain. He took one look at Marlene's face and decided that it might as well have been.

She looked exactly like what he'd envisioned one of the Furies looked like—if the Furies had been beautiful and pregnant enough to burst.

He wondered how she'd gotten past his secretary and then remembered that the woman had left early for the day. Somewhere around four or five. Working, he'd lost track of time. One of Travis Corporation's developments had been badly affected by the storm. Manning the telephone, he'd attempted to do what he could in the way of damage control.

Throughout it all, Marlene had lingered on his mind like vapor hovering above a boiling kettle.

The vapor looked as if it were ten degrees past the boiling point. Trying to focus, Sullivan attempted to think of a reason for her sudden, obviously angry presence in his office.

He pushed back his chair and rose. "Did I forget something?"

Damn, she wished those funny pains would stop. She felt like an egg being cracked open on the side of a pan. "Obviously." Marlene took the envelope out of her purse and held it out to him.

He looked at it, but made no move to take it from her. "What's that?" And then, belatedly, he remembered the letter he had asked his lawyer to draft. But he had instructed the man to show it to him first, not mail it. Damn.

She dropped the envelope on his desk. Marlene braced her legs against the carved side for support. "The letter your lawyer sent me. He forgot to include the thirty pieces of silver."

A hell of a lot of damage control was in order here and fast. He walked around the desk until he was beside her. "You weren't supposed to get this now."

She raised her chin, though she didn't feel very feisty at the moment. She felt as if she were liquefying right where she stood. And being near him had nothing to do with it.

"When?" she demanded. "Just when was I supposed to get this? When is a good time to tell me that you intend to rip this child out of my arms no matter what?"

"Marlene," he began, then stopped. Given the situation, he would have expected her to be turning red. But she was white, a very deathly shade of white. "You're turning pale."

Her mouth was dry as dust, yet she felt damp all over. Just the rain, she told herself. But she felt woozy and her pulse was accelerating.

"It's very hot in here."

"No, as a matter of fact, it isn't. It's rather cold." The thermostat was set low, the way he liked it. "And if you were hot, you'd be flushed, not pale."

Sullivan placed the back of his hand against her forehead, checking for a fever. It slid against the sheen of perspiration.

Marlene jerked her head back. It made her dizzier. "I didn't come here for a medical opinion, Travis. I came for your heart—on a platter."

"Well, you're getting my opinion, such as it is." He reached for her hand. Marlene pulled it away. "You're perspiring and your hand is clammy. I'm going to take you home."

She didn't want him to take her anywhere. Marlene took a step back. "I can—oh!"

Sullivan grabbed her arm as her knees suddenly buckled beneath her, succumbing to the intensity of the pain that seized her.

"What is it?" he demanded.

It took her a moment to find her voice. "I don't know." She was bewildered. And scared. "I feel as if there's some sort of revolution going on inside. I—" Her eyes flew open. "Oh, my God."

He braced her against his body and moved her to a chair into which he gently lowered her. It wasn't difficult. Her legs had virtually collapsed.

And then he saw what had caused her to gasp. There was a damp pool on the carpet where she had been standing.

Unease slid over him like a heavy blanket, smothering him. "I think your water broke."

Oh, God, not here, not now. "There's that razor sharp mind again." She was almost panting.

He became stern. "Shelve the sarcasm for a minute. You need to go to the hospital."

She shut her eyes as another wave of pain assaulted her, then danced away. "Good thinking. You must have been first in your class at Harvard."

"How did you know I went to Harvard? Never mind. Save your strength." Slowly, he lifted her to her feet. "I'm taking you to the hospital." Behind him, the wind was attempting to rattle the windows.

She wound her hand around his. The retort on her lips melted in the face of her need. Later they would hash things out. Right now, it was all she could do to keep from collapsing.

"I would appreciate that," she whispered.

Chapter Seven

Sullivan wrapped his fingers around hers tightly as Marlene struggled up to her feet, but there was no need for him to make the extra effort. Marlene's hand was hermetically sealed to his.

She was stronger than she looked.

A fresh pain shot through her body. Marlene swallowed a surprised gasp and squeezed his hand even harder.

She was entirely too unsteady on her feet. He thought of calling for an ambulance. "Can you walk?"

Marlene hated admitting how weak she felt, even at a time like this. Carrying on no matter what had been inbred in her. It was her father's belief that the weak were walked on. They were taken advantage of, then ignored and tossed away.

But even so, there was no denying the truth. She was definitely not prepared for this kind of pain. Marlene had expected that labor was going to be bad, but not like this.

Anticipation and experience were definitely not in the same league. They weren't even close.

"I don't know." The words came out in a pain-filled whisper. She straightened up, but her knees began to buckle almost instantly. Annoyed, she pressed her lips together. "I think—"

Sullivan didn't wait to hear what she thought. He had eyes. "You're obviously in no condition to walk anywhere, even to the elevator." He knew everyone was gone by now. There was no one to call for assistance. Bracing himself to ignore a barrage of protests, Sullivan lifted her into his arms.

The protest that instantly materialized melted on her lips a moment later. She might be stubborn, but she wasn't stupid. There was no way she could walk, not right now. Marlene laced her arm around the back of Sullivan's neck. Though she hated the situation, she was grateful to him. He didn't have to do this.

"I weigh a ton." Her objection had very little intensity behind it.

She didn't weigh nearly as much as she seemed to think she did. "Not quite, and I've been working out," he said flippantly, "so don't worry about it."

The wave of pain receded, momentarily allowing her to think clearly. Marlene pushed back the hair that perspiration had plastered to her forehead. She didn't want to be carried around like some helpless sack of flour.

"But—"

He didn't want to hear it. The last thing he needed was to have her deliver the child on the floor right there. He prided himself on being ready for anything, but that was one thing he definitely wasn't prepared for.

"You're in pain, remember? Moan, don't whine."

Marlene drew in her breath sharply. "I never whine," she ground out between her teeth.

"Glad to hear that." He made his way into the hall. Usually the hub of bustling activity, the long corridor with its florescent lighting looked forlornly deserted.

Marlene let out the breath she was holding. The pain had ebbed away further. Maybe she was just panicking for no reason. Maybe she still had time.

Clinging to that hope, her breathing began to level off. Embarrassment nudged aside the remnants of panic. Marlene felt foolish. Not to mention self-conscious, even though no one else was around. No matter what Sullivan said, she knew she had to be heavy.

"I think I can walk now." She slipped her hand from around his neck.

Sullivan ignored her as he made his way to the elevator. He wasn't about to set her down and watch her sink to the floor.

"And just when I thought we were beginning to share a moment." He murmured the comment without cracking a smile. "Okay, we'll test your resilience." He nodded toward the wall. "Press the down button."

She reached out and pushed the circular button. The light that appeared behind the white casing glimmered feebly. Not unlike her, she thought.

"Travis, this is carrying chivalry a little too far."

Maybe, but he had started it, and he always finished what he started.

"Indulge me." She felt as if she were slipping. He shifted her weight slightly. "Besides, you're the one who crumpled at my feet. Or was that just my fatal charm bringing you to your knees?"

"Don't push it," she murmured.

She could feel a distant edginess sending out long feelers for her. Her breathing began to grow labored again. The pain was returning. Fresh perspiration dotted her brow as a foreshadowing of things to come.

The elevator finally arrived, and he carried her inside. Sullivan could feel her impatience mounting. "All right, we'll test your sea legs in here."

The door closed behind them as Sullivan gently set her down. The sudden change in orientation made her feel dizzy. Panic spilled through her, and she clutched at his arm. Perspiration poured down her brow.

She looked as pale as the snow-capped mountain peaks in the dead of winter. Sullivan was growing seriously concerned. "Maybe I'd better pick you up again."

"No, I'm fine." The words were uttered breathlessly. Swallowing, attempting to coat a throat that was suddenly parched, she gritted her teeth together. Damn, but this really hurt. She pressed her hand to her abdomen, as if that could hold off the encroaching pain. "But I really hope that there's no traffic between here and the hospital."

He braced himself against her, holding her steady, and she made no attempt to push him away. He doubted that she even realized what he was doing.

"I'll get us there," he promised. Even if he had to drive on the sidewalks.

She drew in a breath, hoping it would somehow subdue the erratic flutter of her heart. It didn't. Her head was pounding like a timpani in a classical orchestra.

"Didn't anyone ever teach you not to make promises you might not be able to keep?" She was beginning to feel oddly light-headed, and struggled to focus.

"If worse comes to worst, I can call 911 from my ca—" He didn't get a chance to finish as she gripped his hand again. Hard.

Marlene sucked in her breath as another wave swept over her, subjugating her in its power. The next moment, the lights flickered spasmodically overhead, as if undecided whether or not to remain on. They settled for on as the elevator creaked and groaned, then jerked to a sudden stop.

Was she imagining it? No, the elevator had stopped. Panic surged through her. This couldn't be happening. "Travis?"

He wound his other hand over hers and the hand she held captive. "Just a little delay," he assured her. His calm voice belied what he was feeling. The storm had been battering at them all day. What if it had affected the power, knocking it out?

Damn, not now, he thought. *Please, not now.*

Holding her to him with one hand, Sullivan pressed each button on the wall in turn with the other. But like a car sealed off in rush hour gridlock, the elevator refused to budge in either direction.

Marlene's eyes were wide with pain and what looked like mounting panic.

"We're stuck?" It was a question that ended in a cry of anguish.

"Only temporarily. Stay calm." Forcefully easing his hand away, he stripped off his suit jacket and laid it on the floor. "Why don't you sit down?"

She had to get hold of herself, she thought desperately, trying to rein in her fear. She wasn't going to make matters any better by getting hysterical. They were in a malfunctioning elevator in a building in the middle of Newport Beach, not lost somewhere in the Himalayas. It would be all right.

All right, hell. She was about to give birth stuck in an elevator with a sarcastic, would-be baby snatcher. How much worse could things be?

Marlene bit down on her lower lip. *Get a grip.* Stabilizing her fear, she shook her head in reply to his suggestion. "Because if I sit down, I may never get up again."

"Don't worry." He ran his hand along her arm. "You'll get up. I'll be right here to help you."

She wanted to say something sarcastic about relying on his help, but didn't have the strength. She didn't like having to depend on him, even for something so simple as helping her regain her feet.

But she had no choice. She *had* to rely on him. "All right."

Sullivan took her hand and gently helped her lower herself to the floor.

"We'll be out of here in a few minutes," he promised, hoping to God that he was right. Didn't these things have backup generators or something?

He pressed the emergency button and an alarm began to whine. The noise fueled the panic that was mounting within her, even as she tried to shut it off. It was like a car alarm that defied deactivation.

Here it comes again. Marlene dug her nails into the palms of her hand. She looked up at Sullivan. He seemed so much taller from this vantage point. Her mind was winking in and out and she struggled to focus it, just as her coach had instructed.

"How long does it usually take for someone to come?" She hoped she didn't sound as frightened as she felt.

It's too long already. "Not long."

She wasn't stupid. He wasn't fooling her. "But that's in the daytime, isn't it?" And it was way into the evening now.

There would be a security guard on duty at the desk. Unless he was off making rounds or somewhere grabbing a quick nap. Sullivan didn't want to think about that. "This is hooked up to a main office where they maintain surveillance."

So where were they? She swallowed again. There was a lump growing in her throat to match the size of the one in her belly. His answer was diluted as a roar of pain engulfed her. She couldn't catch her breath.

"Oh God, Travis, I feel like I'm being broken in half."

He didn't know very much about childbirth, but that couldn't be a good sign. A terrible premonition overtook him.

"Just when are you due?"

No, she refused to believe that she was going into labor. She didn't know what was happening to her body, but it couldn't be settling into the birth mode. She just wouldn't allow it. She didn't care if her water had broken. She wasn't ready. Dear God, she wasn't ready. What did she know about having a baby? There were so many books she still had to read before she felt qualified to be responsible for a child.

Marlene bit her lip. "Not for another three weeks. It's supposed to be a Christmas baby."

Women and babies never did what they were supposed to. And the latter was as unpredictable as the weather. "Christmas may be coming early this year."

She shook her head, her damp hair clinging to her neck and forehead. "I can't be giving birth *here*. In a stuck elevator. With *you*," she added after a beat.

He could empathize with her. In her position, he wouldn't have wanted to give birth here, either. "Don't worry." He closed his hand over hers. "These things are supposed to take hours."

That wasn't comforting, not when she felt like a wishbone two people were wrestling over.

"I'm supposed to feel like this for hours?" Her voice hitched as another pain speared through her. It felt as sharp and hot as if a knife were cutting her open.

Damn, why wasn't anyone answering that alarm? He was certain that it was loud enough to be heard from the street.

"You'll feel better once your doctor gives you something." If they ever got out of here, he thought dismally.

She looked around the dimmed silver container that held them prisoner. It felt smaller somehow, as if they had slipped into a metal canister. "How is she supposed to get into a stuck elevator?"

"I don't know." Exasperated, Sullivan hit all ten buttons on the wall with the flat of his hand. Nothing happened. The elevator didn't budge.

Exhaling a short, exasperated breath, he leaned on the emergency button. The piercing ringing only continued, underlining his frustration.

Behind him, Sullivan heard Marlene stifling a moan. He felt chagrined. Hitting the elevator wasn't going to accomplish anything. He squatted down beside her again, taking her hand.

Comforting women in labor wasn't in his repertoire. He tried his best, though. "It's going to be all right."

No, it wasn't. She could feel it. "Easy for you to say. You're not having a baby."

He laid a hand over the swell of her abdomen, willing the child within to wait. "And neither are you. Not yet."

Her eyes narrowed as fresh pain wrenched her. She didn't know how much more of this she could take. "Are you a betting man?"

"Not usually." Gently, he brushed back the damp hair from her forehead. She looked as if she'd been in a sauna. He wondered if he should be loosening her clothing. "Maybe you'd be more comfortable lying down."

He debated stripping off his shirt and creating a makeshift pallet for her. It wasn't much, but it was the best he could do under the circumstances.

"I'd be more comfortable behind my desk, working," she panted. Another contraction was starting. Tears gathered in her eyes. "Oh God, this was a stupid idea."

Because he felt she needed someone to agree with her, he did. "Yes, it was."

She tried to focus on his face. In the limited light, it was becoming hazy. "You don't know what I'm referring to."

She had him there. "I haven't the foggiest," he admitted.

He wasn't making any sense. Men never made any sense. "Then why are you agreeing with me?" It wasn't easy, attempting to get the words out without slurring or crying.

He stroked her arm, trying to soothe her. "I thought it would make you feel better. This is hardly the time to get into a debate over anything."

She barely heard him. Marlene began to rock, trying to hold the pain at bay. It didn't help. It just continued coming, like an army of unrelenting soldiers.

"I shouldn't have done this," she whispered to herself. "I shouldn't have gotten pregnant."

On that point he agreed with her, not with the method she'd employed at any rate. But he didn't think she wanted to hear that. What she needed was something positive. "All mothers feel that way just before they give birth."

Blinking, she looked at him. It was so very hot in here, Marlene thought. She felt as if she were melting. "How would you know?"

He smiled at her. He was making this up as he went along. "Hearsay."

She looked past his head at the red button on the opposite wall. The one that had set off the alarm. "No one's answering." Her eyes shifted to his face. "Why aren't they answering, Travis?"

"I don't know." Impotence drummed through him. Sullivan wished he had something more hopeful to tell her. He hated not being able to do anything. "But they will. Soon."

If there was just some way that she could call for help.

"Call," Marlene suddenly repeated aloud. The word thundered in her brain as her eyes darted excitedly to his face.

He looked around, but there was no telephone lodged within the shiny walls. Hell of a time for him to notice poor design. "They didn't put a telephone in," he told her, irritated.

He didn't understand, she thought frantically, her head throbbing in rhythm to the pain in her body. She pointed to the black object on the floor in the corner.

"No, my..." Marlene licked her lips as her breath was stolen away. "Purse...my purse...get my purse."

Sullivan couldn't begin to understand why she would want her purse at a time like this, but he didn't bother asking. She wanted it and that was reason enough. He could do little for her as it was.

Stretching, he reached for the shoulder strap and pulled the purse toward him. He thought of offering to go through it for her, retrieving whatever it was that she wanted, but he had a feeling she wouldn't want him to do that.

He handed the purse to her and was surprised when she shook her head, refusing it.

She couldn't concentrate, couldn't straighten her fingers. She'd been clenching them so hard for so long, they felt as if they were permanently curled. "Phone...my cellular phone...in there."

Of course. She was head of her company. It stood to reason that she would have a portable telephone with her. He should have thought of that himself. Feeling like an idiot, Sullivan took the phone out.

But when he opened the flip phone and pulled the antenna up, static met his ear. The signal was weak. He doubted if he could get through, but there were no other options available to them.

He pressed 911 and prayed. There was a buzzing noise that sounded like ringing on the other end.

"Hurry, Sullivan, hurry." Her breath was coming in short pants as she pushed her back to the wall.

The buzzing stopped. Something else took its place. It might have been someone answering, but he couldn't swear to it.

"This is Sullivan Travis. I'm calling from 725 Westcliff Drive. I'm trapped in an elevator with a pregnant woman who's about to give birth at any minute. Send an ambulance immediately—and someone to get us out of here."

An ear-piercing squawk came out of the phone. He held it away until the noise subsided, then repeated the message, hoping that someone on the other end heard, or could piece enough of the message together.

"Did you get through?" she whispered, her eyes shut as she rocked her body. *Please, please, let him have gotten through.*

"Yes, I got through."

Hoping that at the very least they could trace the faint signal, Sullivan didn't end the call. Instead, he placed the opened telephone on the elevator floor.

She looked as if she were fading. He placed his hand over hers. "Are you still with me?"

She nodded as she rocked, her eyes remaining closed. "I wish I weren't." And then her eyes flew open as a new shock wave traveled through her, stronger than the last. "I think . . . the baby's . . . coming."

His voice was firm when he spoke, a lot firmer than his knees were at the moment. "Marlene, didn't the doctor tell you that first babies usually take a long time to be born?"

She couldn't remember what the doctor had told her. All she knew was what her body was telling her. "This one didn't read the handbook." She grasped his forearm, pulling him to her. "I know what I feel. It's coming, Sullivan, the baby's coming."

He could feel the scratch marks forming beneath his sleeve as Marlene dug her nails into his forearm. Her eyes were huge, luminous with fear of the unknown. That made two of them. The only thing he knew about women giving birth he had acquired while watching television. It wasn't a hell of a whole lot.

But what he did know was that he had to find a way to keep her calm.

Gripping her wrists, he forced her to look at him. There was no denying that he sincerely wished they were both somewhere else right now, but they weren't and they had to deal with this brand new life that was struggling to be born.

"Okay, Marlene, you signed on for this and now it's show time." His voice exuded confidence. "I think we can do this."

What "we"? How was he involved in this? It was her body being shredded apart, her body being speared with swords.

But if she had been alone in this elevator, she didn't know if she could stand it. She kept the sharp retort to herself. "Have you done this before?"

He had to be honest with her. She would know soon enough if he lied. "No."

She gulped in air. If only she could put a cushion of air between herself and the baby. Between herself and the pain. "That makes two of us."

"Here, lean against the back of the elevator." He moved her as best he could into a sitting position so that her back was flush against the tarnished silver-colored wall. "You need to brace yourself, and I can't be in two places at once."

She looked at him uncertainly. A sliver of embarrassment reared its head through the sea of pain. "Where are you going to be?"

They both knew the answer to that one. He phrased it as best he could. "Catching the football after you make the forward pass."

She shivered, growing cold, then hot again. Over and over the sensations traded places. And always, there was the ring of pain. It didn't recede any more. It was just there. Growing harder, then softer, then harder again.

"I can't do this, Travis."

He felt for her. "It's a hell of a system someone thought up. The next time around when the universe is formed, maybe babies could be delivered by mail." He saw what might have been a weak smile on her lips. "But right now, I don't think you have much of a choice. The police may or may not have heard us and even if they did, they might not get to us in time. And I haven't got the slightest idea where the security guard is." He squeezed her hand. It was clammy and damp, just like the rest of her. "You seem determined to have this baby the way you do everything else. Fast."

But that was just it. She wasn't determined to have the baby. Not yet. She had things to do. She wasn't ready for this. She wasn't.

"I don't want to have this baby. Not here."

Sullivan searched his mind for reassuring things to say to her, things a woman in her condition would want to hear. Words materialized from deep within his soul.

"It doesn't matter where the baby's born, Marlene. What matters is how you take care of it, how you love it once it is here."

He would have made sense if she could think. She would even have given him points for sensitivity. But the pain was slicing through her like the blades of a whirling blender, shredding any coherent thought she was attempting to hang on to.

She bit down on her lower lip until she felt a trickle of blood seeping into her mouth.

Without ceremony, his eyes on hers, Sullivan lifted her dress up to her hips. Then he stopped. He sank back on his heels, looking at her incredulously.

"You're wearing panty hose?" And heels. Nine months pregnant, and she looked like the perfect businesswoman. The woman was either incredible—or crazy. Or both.

"My legs were cold," she said hoarsely.

He hesitated. He'd undressed more than his share of women. But this time, it was awkward. He didn't know how to make it easy on her.

"I have to—"

She nodded, swallowing, rocking, doing everything she could to refrain from screaming.

"I know." She waved a clenched, impotent hand. "Just do it."

Sullivan kept up a steady stream of conversation, trying to keep her mind off the pain as much as possible. "So, do you want a boy?"

"No." She moaned.

She sounded rather adamant about it, he thought. "A girl, huh?"

"No."

"Those are the only two choices you get, honey." The endearment had come out of nowhere, surprising him. He glanced up at her face to see if she had heard, but she didn't seem to have noticed.

"No, I don't care what it is, as long as it's healthy. And out." She'd dug her fingernails into her palms so deeply, she was bleeding. "I just want this to be over with."

Amen to that. Sullivan looked down and saw the crown of the baby's head peering out. She was ready, all right. He only hoped he was.

"It will be soon. I promise." He braced himself. "Okay, Marlene, I'd say we were about five minutes away from a debut." He had no idea if he was right, only that she needed to be reassured that this onslaught of pain was going to end.

She tried to lean forward and look, but the effort was too much for her. Her shoulders slid against the back of the elevator. Marlene raised her eyes to his. "Can I push?"

Even if he said no, she didn't think she could refrain. The urge was the strongest one she'd ever experienced.

It seemed only logical to him. "Yes." He only hoped he was saying the right thing. There were thousands of things that could go wrong between now and five minutes from now. "You can push on the count of three. Ready? One, two, three."

Marlene screwed her eyes tight and clenched her hands as she concentrated on doing just that one thing. Sweat seemed to cover her from head to foot, flowing out of every pore in her body.

But nothing else did.

Sullivan felt his own stomach muscles contracting in empathy.

"Okay, once more. On the count of three." He looked at Marlene. "You can do this. I know you can. C'mon. One, two, three."

Holding her breath, Marlene squeezed hard again, pushing, feeling light-headed. Feeling as if she were going to burst.

But she didn't.

He wondered if anything was going wrong and fervently hoped not. Where the hell were the police when you needed them? Why hadn't they arrived yet? "Take a break, Marlene."

She looked at him accusingly. "I *am* breaking."

He had no doubts she felt that way. "Soon, Marlene, soon. Just a few seconds more."

The scream of the emergency alarm was grating away at his nerves. What must it be doing to hers?

"You can do this, Marlene," he repeated, trying to make her believe that. "You know you can."

Her eyes darted to his face. "Are...you...making...fun...of...me?"

"Not at a time like this. I wouldn't dare." He could see the head. It was right there. Why couldn't she make the baby come out? In preparation, unconsciously mimicking her, he took a deep breath. "C'mon, Marlene, just one more time. The baby's almost here. One, two—"

"Threeeee," she screamed, pushing for all she was worth. Her face turned a deep shade of red.

The air stopped in Sullivan's lungs as he looked down in wonder. A tiny head, covered with damp, dark hair slid into his waiting hands.

"Okay, I've got it! Just a little more. Push out the shoulders. You're almost done."

"It?" Her voice quavered. She'd never felt so tired in all her life. "What...do you...mean...'it'?"

"You pushed out the head, Marlene. I need to see the other end before I can give you a gender."

With the baby partially in his hands, blood seeping through his fingers, Sullivan looked up at Marlene. She was flushed, exhausted—and he would have sworn on a stack of Bibles that he'd never seen anyone look so radiantly beautiful in his life.

"C'mon, push, Marlene. Push."

"I am, I am," she cried. Her head felt like exploding, and what light there was in the small elevator was growing dimmer. Marlene thought she was going to pass out at any moment.

The alarm sounded as if it were getting louder, pealing like church bells on a holiday as she pushed her child into the world.

"And we have a winner," Sullivan announced. He held the baby in his hands, turning it so that Marlene could see. He'd never held anything so precious in his life. "You have a son, Marlene. It's a boy."

Chapter Eight

The wail of the ambulance's siren cut through the heavy rain plundering the streets of Newport Beach like the sound of a foghorn on an ocean liner. Sullivan was only vaguely aware of the grating noise.

He looked down at Marlene as the ambulance raced down the semiflooded streets to Harris Memorial Hospital. Cars sent up sprays of water as they pulled over to the right.

He was still stunned at the chain of events that had brought him to this moment. To this woman. It sounded like something out of a movie he wouldn't have bothered watching. It certainly hadn't been one of the more run-of-the-mill days of his life, he mused, as he rubbed his thumb unconsciously over the hand that still clutched his so tightly.

Before today, Sullivan would have readily said that he didn't believe in miracles of any kind. That kind of belief had died in his childhood. And yet, a miracle was what he'd been part of. There was nothing else he could have called it. He had been there to look down into the face of another human being as he drew his first breath.

Tonight, as he coached Marlene through the pain, as he held her baby in his arms, as he held her when the rescue team and paramedics finally arrived, something had occurred within him. A different sort of feeling had been born in the wake of the infant's arrival. A satisfied happiness that he had never experienced before.

"Are we almost there?" Marlene looked up at him, indigo eyes as huge as twin pools of water in the Carolina Keys.

"Almost," he assured her. He didn't look up toward the front of the vehicle to verify his reply.

It felt as if they should have arrived already. They'd been traveling long enough. But looking out the windshield would have given him no further clue as to where they actually were. The street signs could have been nonexistent for all the visibility he had.

All Sullivan could really see, if he craned his neck, were the twin beams of light coming from the ambulance's headlights, slicing through the sheets of water.

Marlene nodded, taking his word as gospel.

When the paramedics had hurried her cot into the ambulance, she'd held on to Sullivan's hand tightly, refusing to let go. Her eyes had silently asked him to come with her. It was quite a switch from the go-to-hell attitude he'd seen her display earlier.

But then, tonight was special. Tonight was the night her son had been born.

Her body felt battered, as if she had been turned inside out. There was a sleeping baby nestled in her arms, wrapped in Sullivan's jacket. The paramedics had cut her cord, rushed her onto the cot and then into the ambulance. It was as if she had been cast headfirst into a dream.

But it wasn't a dream, and despite her pain and the exhaustion pressing down on her body, there was an incredible euphoria echoing through her.

Marlene looked up at Sullivan's chiseled profile turned slightly away from her as he stared out of the window. It was a hard thing for her to admit, given the circumstances between them, but she knew she couldn't have made it without him.

"Travis," she whispered. She cleared her throat, wishing it didn't feel so dry. "Travis."

He realized that she was saying something. But her words were being absorbed by the scream of the siren. Sullivan bent over her. "What?"

He didn't understand. Marlene felt groggy and hazy, but she wanted him to know. It seemed only right.

"No. Travis." She looked down at California's newest resident. He was so small, so helpless. She thought her heart would burst from the love she felt. "That's what his middle name is going to be." Marlene wrapped her tongue around the sound. "Travis."

"Not bad." For the moment, he pushed aside what he knew his father's reaction to that would be. He would want Travis to be his last name, not the one sandwiched in the middle.

Sullivan just barely skimmed his palm over the sleeping infant, afraid of waking him. He raised his eyes to Marlene's face. "What's his first name going to be?"

The smile faded from her lips, replaced by a solemn expression that had its roots in the long ago.

"Robert." Marlene shifted her aching body on the cot, unconsciously bracing herself as the ambulance finally came to a stop. Her throat was no longer dry. Tears filled it. "Robby." She whispered the name fondly. "That was my brother's name."

Was. Which meant the man was dead. He didn't have to be told how attached she'd felt toward her brother. He could hear it in her voice. Sullivan wondered how he had died.

The ambulance doors dramatically flew open. Suddenly, there were faces all around them, talking, issuing orders, meshing and drowning each other out as they pulled the cot from the ambulance.

Surprised, Marlene dropped Sullivan's hand. She turned her head to see that he was beginning to recede into the background. Instantly, she grabbed for him. The movement had been involuntary, like breathing. Need had taken over.

He'd meant to let everyone else take over. Instead, his fingers clutched in hers, Sullivan found himself trotting along beside the cot as it was rushed through the automatic emergency room doors.

A tall, rangy man in green livery joined the ensemble. Several others fell back to give him access to Marlene. He assessed the scene quickly.

"Doesn't seem like there's that much left for us to do," he said kindly, smiling at Marlene and her son. He tugged on the ends of the stethoscope that he wore carelessly thrown over the back of his neck. His eyes, so small behind the rimless glasses, shifted to Sullivan. "You the father?"

Sullivan shook his head. "No, I'm just the uncle." He looked at Marlene. She smiled weakly in response. What had happened in the elevator had forever bonded them, whether they liked it or not, far more than the blood that flowed through the infant's veins.

The doctor shrugged, taking the response in stride. "Are you able to give the admitting desk some information on her?"

Sullivan nodded. He had no idea what sort of insurance she had, though he assumed she could pay her way. If she couldn't, he would cover the bill. That was his nephew she held in her arms. Derek's son. The words throbbed in his temples.

"I can get them started." He eased his hand from Marlene's and saw the question in her eyes. "I'll be back," he promised.

Two orderlies continued down the hall with the cot, pushing it toward the elevator. Sullivan heard a tiny cry from the baby. He smiled to himself as he was led off by the receptionist to the admitting desk.

The session with the admission's clerk went far smoother than he had anticipated. Within fifteen minutes Sullivan was free to find a pay phone and call his father. Osborne answered.

"How is he tonight, Osborne?"

Sullivan shifted, uncomfortable within his confinement. Five old-fashioned booths were lined up in a row, each with a door for added privacy. But they weren't much for space. He felt cramped.

"He's complaining that everything hurts. It's to be expected with the rain."

Even when he was being friendly, Osborne sounded formal, Sullivan thought. "Put him on. I've got something that might make him feel a lot better."

"Very good, sir." There was a pause as Osborne handed the telephone to the senior Travis.

"'Bout time you got back to me. What are you doing out on a night like this?" his father demanded as soon as he took the receiver.

Sullivan was accustomed to the rough greeting. Social amenities were for associates and business dealings, not him. He knew that beneath the tone, his father was worried about his safety. Now more than ever since Derek was gone.

"Delivering your grandson."

There was no response on the other end. Then, in a subdued voice that was choked equally with disbelief and emotion, Oliver asked, "What did you say?"

"Your grandson arrived early." Sullivan couldn't help wondering if their scene in his office had brought her labor on early. He supposed he would never know. "In a stuck elevator in our building. She went into labor and I had to deliver the baby." He still had trouble believing that it had all happened. Sullivan scrubbed a hand over his face and managed to hit his elbow against the folding door. "Now I know why I didn't become a doctor the way mother wanted. I was never so terrified in my life—"

Oliver cut Sullivan's narrative short. "But he's all right, isn't he? The boy, he's all right?"

His father sounded anxious. "He's fine, Dad. The paramedics arrived and got us out of the elevator. I'm calling from the hospital." Shifting again, he opened the door to let some air in. The booth was getting stuffy. "Marlene's fine, too."

"Who?"

In typical fashion, his father disregarded what he felt didn't concern him. "Your grandson's mother. Marlene Bailey."

"Oh." That information was tossed away as soon as it registered. She wasn't important in the scheme of things. Only the baby was. A boy. He had a grandson. Damn, but there were times life could still be sweet. "Make sure he has the best."

Sullivan laughed. "They don't have private rooms for infants, Dad. He'll be in the nursery with all the other newborns."

His father snorted. "Well, pay for it."

Sullivan knew that it was pointless to argue. "Sure, Dad."

Oliver felt younger than he had in years. Heaven had handed him another chance. "Stop by later, Sullivan. I'll wait up. We'll have some cognac and toast the new generation."

He was tired and wanted to beg off, but decided that perhaps his father needed this little ritual. They didn't share much these days. Since the stroke, his father rarely got out. If he needed company, he summoned it to him.

"Sure, soon as I can. I've got to go, Dad. There are other people waiting to use the phone," he lied. Sullivan broke the connection.

By all accounts, it had been a long night. Sullivan knew he should be leaving. He'd done everything he'd been called on to do. And more.

But as he picked up the telephone receiver again to call for a taxi, Sullivan changed his mind. He decided to hang around just a little while longer. Just until Marlene was settled into her room. Maybe he would even stop by to see his nephew after he was cleaned up, processed, bundled in a sleeper and placed into a glass bassinet.

The storm was beginning to subside somewhat as he passed the window by the fifth floor waiting area. Automatic doors slid open, admitting him to the section of the floor reserved for the nursery.

He stopped before the nursery window. There was a sea of tiny bodies before him. It seemed like an incredible amount of humanity to be crammed in such a small space. Sullivan surveyed the long rows filled with newborn infants, their identities neatly entered on pink or blue cards and mounted at the foot of their tiny cubicles.

Sullivan leaned his shoulder against the wall next to the window, watching as nurses milled about, tending to the occupants. As he watched, a large-bosomed, maternal-looking nurse lifted a squawking baby and held him against her, rocking and cooing something that the glass wouldn't allow to be heard.

A nurse who looked as if she were barely out of high school brought in Marlene's son and gently placed him into his bassinet.

Sullivan studied the infant now that he was all washed and dried off. He cleaned up well, Sullivan mused. With his startling shock of black hair, Robert Travis Bailey looked more like him, Sullivan mused, than his blond mother.

His mouth curved, but the smile was a sad one. *See what you could have had, Derek? If you'd only stuck around, you idiot, you could have been standing here instead of me.*

Sullivan sincerely doubted that he would ever have children of his own. The world was too rocky and uncertain a place to willingly thrust a child into it. But if he were to have one, he would imagine that the baby would look exactly like the one he'd held in his arms.

The one who now lay sleeping, butt end up, in the bassinet.

He stood and looked at him for a long time.

Sullivan straightened. It was really getting late. He would just look in on Marlene and then leave. He still had his father to see, and he needed to get some sleep before he dropped where he stood.

The corridor was quiet as he made his way down to room 526, where the woman at the admission's desk told him Marlene had been assigned. It was positioned directly opposite the nurse's station. Always a good thing, he mused. Maybe she would get faster service.

He cracked the door open as silently as he could, afraid of waking Marlene if she was asleep. She was. Her eyes were closed. Very carefully, he began to back out.

"Come in." Her voice sounded groggy as it floated to him.

Sullivan slipped back into the room, letting the door close behind him. "I thought you were asleep."

She smiled at him, or thought she did. It was hard to tell what was real and what was simply in her mind right now. The doctor had given her something for pain, and she was floating in and out.

"Almost. After all the excitement, I'll probably sleep for a week." She took a breath, pushing back the exhaustion for just a little longer. "But I was hoping you'd come by."

She would have lifted her hand to his if she'd had the strength. "I wanted to thank you for helping."

He shrugged. She looked as if she were only eighteen, lying there with her hair pulled back from her face. She'd probably been a sweet kid, he mused. Someone he might have wanted to get to know, before life had become so complicated.

"It seemed only fair, seeing as how I probably made you go into early labor. Besides, I didn't do that much. It was more of a spectator event for me. You did all the work."

It had felt that way at the time, but now she knew differently. "Maybe, but you helped calm me down."

The smile deepened on his lips and filtered into his eyes. "You were calm?"

He was teasing her. It felt nice, she thought, as sleep hovered an inch away. Teasing was nice. "Considering what was happening, I was very calm."

He brushed back the single strand of hair that had fallen on her forehead. His fingertips gently skimmed her skin.

"Then I'd hate to see you excited." *Or maybe I would,* he added silently. "I'd better let you get some sleep." He began to retreat.

It was an effort to push the words from her mouth. "I came to give you hell, you know."

Sullivan stopped and slowly turned around. Whatever they'd given her had made her forget that she had done just that.

She could barely see him. Her eyes kept insisting on shutting. "But under the circumstances, I think maybe I'll give you another chance."

He bent over her. Her voice was fading away like a vapor. Maybe, being half asleep, truer answers would emerge. "Why?"

She forced her eyes open. He was so close, she thought. So very close. And he smelled so good. She realized that her mind was drifting. "I don't know. I guess I feel sorry for small puppies and fools."

"I take it I don't fit into the small puppies category."

Because it seemed right, Sullivan kissed her on the forehead. "Get some sleep."

But she already was.

The very first thing Marlene saw when she opened her eyes late the next afternoon were the yellow roses. The next thing she saw was Sullivan, looking vaguely uncomfortable, as if flowers weren't something that he was accustomed to holding.

She didn't even remember dozing off after the nurse had taken the baby back to the nursery, but she must have. Breast feeding had been a disaster, and Marlene had felt hopelessly incompetent. She didn't think, after her father's death, that she would ever experience the sensation to such a degree again, but she had. Depression had claimed her as much as sleep.

A faint noise had roused her, like a door opening and closing. A noise and the warm, sensual fragrance of roses had seeped into her senses.

Marlene dug her fists into the mattress, raising herself into a sitting position. She looked questioningly from the bouquet to Sullivan. Last night seemed like a dream now. "Roses?"

Sullivan curved his fingers around the white vase. There was a festive bright yellow bow just above them. He wasn't in the habit of bringing roses to anyone.

But bringing her flowers had somehow seemed appropriate. Now, he wasn't so sure. He felt vaguely guilty because bringing her flowers inadvertently was in keeping with his father's plans. "Win her over any way you can," he had said over the snifter of cognac. Ordered, really, though the words had been softly spoken. But Sullivan wasn't doing it to win her over, that would be later. He was here, bearing flowers, because he wanted to be.

"I thought that since this was my first delivery, the occasion dictated something special."

He looked around the room. Obviously, others had thought the same thing. There were baskets and vases of flowers sitting on every available surface in the room. Word had spread quickly.

"Maybe not so special," he amended casually. "Seems everyone else beat me to the punch. It looks like you've single-handedly sent the florist trade up fifteen points on the stock exchange." There was absolutely no place to set the vase down. Feeling a little foolish, he nodded at the vase. "Maybe I'll just take these over to the nurses' station. They'll find someone who might—"

Marlene shook her head. "No, not my flowers."

She flushed, knowing how possessive that must have sounded to him. Or how spoiled. But she wanted these flowers. Much more than she wanted the others.

"There." She pointed toward a spot on the small bookcase against the wall that was closest to her. "You can put them over there."

It was already occupied by a basket filled with a profusion of birds of paradise and some flower Sullivan couldn't even begin to recognize. He'd never seen anything so gaudy looking in his life.

"That spot's taken."

"Those flowers are from the head of Montgomery Shoes. They've never had much taste." Wanda had gotten the word out this morning, right after Marlene had called her and Sally from the hospital. Flowers had begun arriving an hour later.

Marlene indicated the space near the sink. "You can move them to the floor. I want to be able to see the roses when I open my eyes." She realized how that must have sounded to him and hurried to add, "Yellow's my favorite color."

He knew that. The detective he had hired had been very thorough. He knew almost everything about her. And yet, somehow, as he looked at her, it didn't seem like enough. It didn't seem as if he knew anything at all about her.

Picking up the grotesque arrangement from the shelf, Sullivan laid the basket on the floor and then placed the vase he'd brought in its spot.

He turned to look at Marlene. She had a great deal more color in her face than she'd had last night. But there was something in her eyes he couldn't quite decipher.

He leaned a hip against the foot of the bed and crossed his arms before him, studying her. There was obviously something on her mind. His father's mandate rang in his ears. Perhaps he could get her to talk to him again.

"So, how are you feeling this morning?"

She always gave a stock answer to that question, believing that people really didn't want to know when they asked. Feeling that way, she had no idea how the truth rose to her lips.

"Incompetent."

That was an odd answer. He'd expected her to say "fine" or "tired" or something that fell in between. His mouth quirked as he reminded himself that the lady was all business.

"Why? The hospital doesn't want you to handle their ad campaign?"

She shook her head, already regretting the slip of tongue. "It's personal."

Yes, he could see that it was. Something was wrong. His voice softened as he sat down on the edge of her bed. "I think that last night you and I became as personal as a man and woman can ever get. Now, what's the matter, Marlene? Maybe I can help."

The offer temporarily melted the dissatisfied feeling she was harboring. She laughed at the image it evoked. "I doubt it. Unless you've ever nursed a baby."

"Oh." Sullivan paused. He was way out of his element here. "I think you'd better talk to your doctor."

She laughed again as she nodded. "Good idea."

Years seemed to melt away from her when she laughed. She looked eighteen again, just as she had last night. For a moment, he was tempted to lay his hand over hers, but then refrained. He'd already overstepped the boundaries he had set for himself. Getting emotionally involved was never part of the deal.

"About the only thing I can tell you is that everything new takes time. If something isn't working out," he said nebulously, "give it a chance. It just might."

He was right, of course. That still didn't erase the inadequate feeling she had, but he was right. Maybe she was just being too anxious.

Marlene ran a hand over her hair, wishing she'd had a few minutes to fix herself up before Sullivan had arrived. It wasn't him so much, she told herself, as her just wanting to appear at her professional best. Appearances were very important to her. People always judged what was on the outside first before they bothered to take stock of what was within.

If they bothered doing that at all.

She would have killed for some lipstick. Nicole had promised to bring her overnight bag and a few dozen necessities of life when she came to see her today. But as of yet, she hadn't arrived.

"Thanks, I'll keep that in mind," she murmured.

There was a quick rap on the door a second before it opened. Sullivan turned a moment before the petite, dark-haired woman entered. She looked even more pregnant than Marlene had last night. Maybe they traveled in pairs, he mused. Sullivan stepped aside. Carefully, he edged toward the window.

Marlene had a good view of the harbor from her room, he thought. The choppy sea beyond was empty. They were between storms, but the darkened sky dictated that all the boats be moored at the dock for the day.

Marlene brightened as she saw her sister. "Sullivan, this is my sister, Nicole Logan. Nic, this is Sullivan Travis."

Nicole's eyes opened wide as she shook his hand. So this was Sullivan. Marlene had given her all the details of the harrowing experience. "Thanks for taking care of my big sister."

He nodded. "There wasn't much else I could do under the circumstances."

Well, at least he wasn't conceited, Nicole thought, then turned her attention to Marlene. "My God, for a woman who's been through hell, you look terrific."

She took Marlene's hand in hers as she searched her face for telltale signs, something that could unlock the mystery of what still lay ahead for her. Something no textbook or video could really prepare her for.

"So, how was it?" The question, despite her efforts, came out breathlessly as Nicole braced herself for the answer.

How was it? Excruciating, terrifying, like falling into a well without a bottom. Like being a giant wishbone caught in a celestial tug-of-war. Marlene's mind sorted through the pain, the panic and the fear as she looked at her sister's tense face. She debated what to say. At the very least, odds were that Nicole wasn't going to be having her experience in an elevator that was stuck between floors.

"Special," she finally answered.

Her eyes shifted toward Sullivan, silently asking him not to say anything that would contradict her. She glanced at her sister's face. What was the point of launching into a horror story and dwelling on the negative? The upshot of it all was that she had a healthy baby boy, and that was all that really mattered in the end. All that would ever matter in the years that were to come.

Nicole let go of a shaky breath, unsatisfied. She was more of a realist, more down-to-earth than Marlene. "What about the pain?"

The memory of the pain still lingered in her body, as it would, Marlene knew, for a while. It was like a throbbing calling card. But somehow, it didn't seem quite right to admit that. And maybe it wouldn't be so bad for Nicole.

"It passes."

He was out of place here. He'd come to look in on her and bring her flowers, and he had done that. The two women would probably feel more comfortable if he left.

Sullivan nodded toward the door. "It's getting a little crowded in here." He began to edge his way out of the room. "I'll be seeing you—"

Marlene nodded in reply. Her emotions still felt as if they were being tossed about in the center of a huge blanket that was being raised and lowered in the wind. She didn't know quite how she felt about his coming to see her. Or his leaving.

Reflexive manners covered that department for her. "Thanks for stopping by."

He nodded as he passed Nicole.

"So when are they letting you go home?" Nicole asked, settling in for a long visit.

"Day after tomorrow." She said it mournfully. Lying around made her feel restless and unproductive.

"Day after tomorrow?" Nicole groaned. "I'm going to be busy all day." There was no way she could beg off. The gallery was having its big showing. She bit her lip, thinking. "Can you wait until evening?"

Sullivan stopped in the doorway. The forecast was for more rain on Thursday. Evening travel would be hazardous. He let the door slip from his fingers and turned around.

"You won't have to wait," he told Marlene. She stared at him in surprise. "I'll bring you home." He crossed back to her bed. "I can be here within an hour after the doctor signs you out." Taking a card out of his jacket pocket, he handed it to Marlene. "Here's my beeper number."

She was already more in his debt than she'd wanted or intended to be.

"Don't you have meetings to go to? Some widows and orphans to dispossess?" she quipped dryly.

"We don't deal in widows or orphans." The Travis Corporation bought and developed former farmland. As of yet, they weren't in the business of knocking down old buildings to make way for shopping malls. "We only dislodge squirrels and relocate them," he informed her mildly. "As for my meetings, let me worry about them." He pointed to the card as he walked out again. "Call me."

Not a chance, she thought, watching the door close. Her gratitude to him hadn't made her stupid, just slightly vulnerable. Which was why she was going to see as little of him as possible.

Chapter Nine

The rain lashed against the car's windshield like so many needles attempting to pierce the glass. The wipers, set on high, struggled to maintain a modicum of visibility.

The world directly in front of the car shimmered like a surrealistic painting done in shades of gray. They moved past distorted streets, buildings and trees as Sullivan picked his way slowly up toward Spyglass Hill and Marlene's house.

When Marlene hadn't called by ten that morning, he had called her at the hospital and discovered that she had decided to take a taxi home. She wanted neither her sister nor her housekeeper driving in the inclement weather.

"All things considered," he'd guessed, "you'd have no objection to my being out in it."

She had no thoughts about that one way or another. "No."

He hadn't let her continue. "Fine, then I'm leaving now. I can be there within fifteen minutes, barring any flash floods," he added wryly.

"Don't leave yet," she had protested. "The doctor hasn't been here to sign me out." She sighed, as if debating whether or not to continue resisting. "I'll call you."

He had his doubts, but there wasn't much he could say. "Okay. Do that."

He'd waited until one, then called to check on her. Her doctor had been detained, first by the rain, then by a delivery that was far more complicated than Marlene's had been. A nurse had promised her that Dr. Pollack would be by before two. He'd left the office immediately after the call. He didn't want Marlene leaving without him. He didn't waste time examining why.

It was almost three by the time she and the baby were released. A temporary break in the storm lasted long enough for them to get into the car and pull away from the hospital. Then it restarted with a vengeance. Visibility went from fair to almost nonexistent.

Sullivan couldn't make anything out in his rearview mirror. There was nothing discernible beyond three feet of the car in either direction.

There were no sounds other than the ones caused by the rain as it beat against the car. Beyond that, there was silence.

He usually liked silence. Comfortable with his own company, silence gave him an opportunity to reflect. Right now it was driving him crazy. The rhythmic thud of the wipers as they hit the bottom of the windshield mimicked the throb that was beginning to take over his temples.

His radio had temporarily become a victim of the storm, deprived of clear transmission. It crackled and snapped. Finally he gave up trying to find a station and shut it off. The baby, secured in an infant seat he'd had the forethought to purchase the day before, was sleeping calmly through it all.

For a talkative woman, Marlene was maddeningly quiet, he thought, glancing at her. She sat staring straight ahead, pensively watching the rain come down.

Just up ahead, a glittering ruby took on the dimensions of a red light. Sullivan eased his foot off the gas pedal and onto the brake. He took the opportunity to turn toward her.

"Are you all right?"

His question penetrated the haze that engulfed her mind. Marlene looked at him, surprised by his question. Surprised by a great many things, such as the thoughtfulness that had prompted him to bring the infant seat for the baby.

Her baby, she thought, with a wave of protective possessiveness. Not his. That's where all this was leading, she reminded herself. He was just being kind because he wanted to get her to lower her guard.

"Yes, why do you ask?"

He shrugged. The ruby light disappeared, to be replaced by an emerald one. He moved his foot onto the accelerator and pressed down.

"You're awfully quiet. I was just wondering what you were thinking." He'd conducted board meetings with brilliant aplomb. Why did he feel so tongue-tied now around this slip of a woman and her child? A child he helped bring into the world.

Squinting, Sullivan looked around. The roads were relatively empty. Thank God for small favors. In bad weather there was usually some fool going too fast, causing chain reaction accidents. The cargo he had was too precious to risk.

Marlene licked her lips. Her voice sounded strangely hollow to her ears when she answered. Almost as hollow as she felt.

"I don't know what to say."

"About anything?" Sullivan shook his head. "I find that very difficult to believe."

She let out a long sigh as she rotated her shoulders a fraction beneath the leather coat. She felt numb from the neck down.

Marlene looked over her shoulder at the baby in the infant seat. The baby who was going to turn to her to satisfy all his needs, turn to her for guidance. Turn to her for everything.

A shiver of panic cut through her. What did she know about being a mother? The closest she had come to dealing with babies had been designing a diaper ad which had been carried by all the major womens' magazines.

She sighed deeply without being aware of it.

He interpreted her silence correctly. It wasn't difficult. "Scared?"

Her eyes darted to meet his, a denial ready on her lips. But the words faded in the face of her surprise. She hadn't thought that she was that transparent. It bothered her.

"How did you know?"

It had been pure speculation on his part. "My guess is that very few things leave you speechless. Motherhood might be one of them." He took a right turn. Water sprayed from beneath his tires as he hit a puddle deep enough to pass for a small creek. "And besides, you've got that look about you."

She hated being so easy to analyze, especially by him. Not for a moment did she forget what he represented. Well, maybe for a moment, she amended, remembering when he'd kissed her. But not any longer than that.

Marlene raised her chin, as if she were raising a drawbridge, leaving behind only a moat and no access. "What look?"

She was taking offense again. The woman blew hot and cold, he thought, wondering what buttons he'd touched off this time. There was no shame in being afraid of the unknown.

"The look that says, 'Oh my God, what have I gone and done.' "

"I do not have that look. I know exactly what I have 'gone and done.'" He certainly wasn't going to use her edginess against her to win custody. She would manage. Somehow.

He said nothing. Instead, he reached over and flipped down the sunshade on her side. There was a mirror in the center of the flap. With his free hand, Sullivan angled it toward her.

She huffed and flipped the flap upward again. "The light's bad."

Sullivan looked out at the road. The rain was coming down even harder now. Despite the sweep of the windshield wiper blades, there was less than half a beat between visibility and complete obscurity.

"Can't argue with that." And he didn't feel like arguing over anything else. Not today. He needed to remain alert. Road conditions were so hazardous, he was surprised that they hadn't encountered any accidents yet.

"Damn, when California liquid sunshine decides to fall, it goes all out. Not like back East."

Back East. Had he lived there? She realized that there were gaps in the information the detective had gotten for her about the man at her side. Gaps that needed to be filled if she was to be prepared for any contingencies.

She turned toward Sullivan and tried not to let the curiosity she felt creep into her voice. "Did you live on the east coast?"

She'd forgotten, he thought. "I went to Harvard for my M.B.A." He steered through another puddle, then eased around a corner. "But I'm a Californian, born and bred."

When she made no response, Sullivan continued talking. He thought perhaps the sound of his voice might soothe her. It helped him at any rate. He didn't much care for the tense silence hovering between them.

"I like the weather here better. Most of the time," he amended.

Something unidentifiable darted across their path into the street. Probably someone's cat, he thought. Pumping the brake to keep from skidding, Sullivan slowed the car down to a crawl.

He struggled to curb the impatience drumming through him. He was anxious to get Marlene and the baby home and off the streets.

"I've never lived anywhere else." It was something she realized that she regretted, not traveling to different places. She had lived her entire life in Newport Beach.

She sounded almost wistful. "Not even when you went away to college?" he asked.

"I didn't go away." But she should have, she thought. She really should have. It would have been better all around if she had.

But looking back, that had never been an option to her. She had wanted so badly to please her father. That meant devoting all her energy, all her time, to what he demanded of her. What a waste all that misspent emotion had been, she thought.

"My father wanted me close by. And then I joined the business, working at the office on the days I didn't attend classes." She shrugged away the rest of her explanation. "Things meshed."

That wasn't the way he saw it. And he had a suspicion that she didn't, either. Not deep down. "Sounds more like your whole life became enmeshed in something your father dictated."

It was different for him, he mused. He'd known right from the start that Derek, despite his blemishes, would always be his father's favorite. He had done what he did because he'd felt as if he belonged in the family business. He had wanted to be there. Like his father, he had a flare for land development, for finding empty, wasted spaces and making them flower with prosperity, with families building their dreams.

He had done it for himself—and because he loved his father. In his own way, he knew that Oliver Travis loved him as well. But after years of relying on him, Oliver had just naturally taken him for granted. Sullivan was like an arm or a leg, there to be used, only missed if it was gone.

She felt defensive anger rising within her. He was being arrogant again. "Don't judge me, Travis."

Sullivan reminded himself that it was none of his business how she had lived her life, or would continue to live it. Their only link was the baby—well, only until he found the right approach to make her to give up custody. Setting things right, that had to remain his only concern.

It was a hell of a lot easier said than done.

"Back to Travis, is it?" he asked wryly. Just as well. It helped reinforce the barriers. "And for your information, I wasn't judging. I was making an observation." Even though it was obvious that he should back off, he didn't. "It wouldn't have sounded like a judgment unless you thought that way, too." He spared her a glance as they stopped again. "And regretted it."

The traffic light changed immediately to green, and Sullivan wove his way through the residential streets, hoping no dog or cat would come running out again.

"I don't regret anything." She said the words emphatically, then hesitated. "Except for one thing...." Her voice trailed off.

Sullivan hated to be left hanging. He had a feeling she already knew that about him. "And that would be?" he probed.

Her voice was small, distant, as if she were a young girl again, experiencing the pain for the first time. "That my brother died."

He wanted to ask her about that. He had a feeling it might be the key to a great many things about her. But her house was just up ahead. Questions would have to be tabled for now.

Relief washed over Sullivan as he took the winding path to the front entrance of the Doric-columned two-story house. They'd made it without any mishaps.

Sullivan parked the car as close to the house as possible. The housekeeper was standing in the doorway, as if she'd been waiting there indefinitely. She had a dull brown sweater thrown over her shoulders, an anxious expression etched deeply into the lines on her face. At her side was a huge black umbrella. She had it open before he even turned off the ignition.

Sally came hurrying down the steps to meet them, brandishing the umbrella overhead.

"Such a day to come home," she muttered.

She raised the umbrella, stepping out of the way as Sullivan opened the door for Marlene. The older woman was quick to reposition herself so that she could cover Marlene as she reached for the baby. As for Sullivan, she seemed to think he could fend for himself against the rain.

"We won't forget this day for a long time, I'll wager," Sally confided loudly to Marlene, raising her voice above the din that nature had created.

Sullivan ducked as Sally nearly poked his eye with one of the umbrella's ribs. He helped Marlene to her feet as Sally hovered with the umbrella.

The baby, still asleep, frowned and puckered his face reflexively as a stray raindrop hit him. Marlene's heart quickened. This was her son. *Her* son. She glanced at Sullivan. And nothing in the world was going to change that.

Looking in her eyes, he read her message loud and clear. But messages could be erased—or changed.

"Hurry inside." Sally had a protective hand draped around Marlene's back as she hustled her into the house. "I've got hot tea waiting for you." She glanced over her shoulder at Sullivan, taking care to keep Marlene and Robby covered. "I suppose you can come in, too. Can't have you catching pneumonia after doing your only good deed." A small smile quirked her mouth. "Although that might be your only chance of making it to heaven—dying at this moment."

He should be getting home. He debated leaving, then remembered that Marlene's things were still in his trunk. Hunching his shoulders against the rain, he went to the rear of the car and inserted his key into the trunk.

"I'll get the suitcase and the flowers first," he called after Sally.

Marlene had insisted on bringing a few of the arrangements home with her. He noted that his roses were among them. The rest she'd asked to be distributed to women on the floor who hadn't received any flowers. She had sensitivity, he mused, something he would have found charming had the situation between them been different.

But it wasn't, he reminded himself. He couldn't lose sight of that.

With Marlene and the baby safely inside, Sally turned on the front steps and frowned at him. "They can keep," she shouted. "And there's nothing in the suitcase that she doesn't have five of in the house. Move your carcass before you wash away!"

There was no arguing with the woman, and he had to admit that he got a kick out of the way she issued orders. She made him think of a wrinkled, old Napoleon.

Sullivan gave Sally a three-finger salute. "Yes, ma'am."

Raising the collar of his raincoat, Sullivan hurried toward her. Reaching the shelter of the overhang, he shrugged his raincoat back into place and dragged a hand through his wet hair. Droplets scattered like the beads of a broken necklace.

Sally nodded her approval. "That's better." Turning on her squat heel, she walked into the house.

Marlene stood in the foyer holding her son. She looked around as if she'd never seen these surroundings before. Perhaps she hadn't, she thought. Not in this light. It actually felt good to come home. She rarely experienced that feeling.

She'd *never* experienced that feeling before, she thought after a beat. But then, she'd never been a mother before. It made a world of difference.

Marlene looked down into the face of her sleeping son, and so many feelings hopscotched over one another within her. She'd wanted this child more than she had wanted life itself. But now, the feeling was not without a smaller, darker mate.

She was terrified of what lay ahead.

All the feelings of inadequacy that her father had stoked so diligently, like a fire whose embers he refused to let die, rose, flaming high, inside of her now. It had begun when Robby wouldn't take her milk at the afternoon feeding. Or the evening one. And then again this morning. All three times, she'd resorted to the small, four-ounce bottle the nurse had provided as a substitute. And each time, she'd felt as if she'd somehow failed her son.

She was determined not to. If she succeeded at nothing else, she was going to succeed at this.

Sally closed the door behind them. "Lord, will you listen to that rain?" She sneezed as she took a quick survey of Marlene's face. "Do you want to lie down? You look a little pale."

Sullivan shrugged slightly beneath his damp raincoat. The house appeared far too pristine to have someone standing in the foyer, dripping on the marble floor.

"She refuses to accept that observation," he told Sally. He had said the same thing to Marlene when he had arrived at the hospital.

Sally was instantly protective of Marlene. "Maybe she doesn't like criticism from a so-called uncle." She said the last word as if it were synonymous with the plague.

The old woman made him think of a lioness protecting her cubs. He supposed he couldn't blame her.

"The connection," Sullivan told her mildly, "is on record."

Small, dark eyes squinted as wispy eyebrows gathered over her nose, "Not any I'd be interested in playing."

Marlene placed a hand on Sally's arm. Robby was waking up and beginning to fuss. The trip home had been more exhausting than she'd anticipated. She just wasn't up to listening to any harsh words being exchanged between Sally and Sullivan. Sally's tongue could be as sharp as any saber.

The environment was getting a little too hostile for him. He'd done what he had set out to do. This wasn't the time to try to change Marlene's mind about relinquishing custody. He would give her a few days to recuperate. He felt he owed her that much.

"I think I had better be going."

Marlene glanced toward the narrow windows that framed the front door. If the rainfall kept up like this, the only way to get around would be by boat. Not to mention that the roads would become impassable because of mud slides. "You're not planning to leave now, in this, are you?"

He wanted to point out that he had just arrived in "this" less than five minutes ago. But before he could, the lights went out. A moment later, they flickered back to life.

"Terrific," Marlene moaned. She didn't need this tonight. Not on her first night home with the baby. She had enough to handle without having to do it in the dark.

Marlene looked around the foyer as the lights winked again. This had the definite feel of déjà vu about it. She looked at Sullivan. "Why do the lights always flicker when you're around?"

His grin rose of its own accord. "I was just thinking the same thing about you."

Sally looked from one to the other. "Is this some sort of secret code?"

The baby's fussing increased. He wasn't crying, but he was about to. Marlene patted his back awkwardly and swayed slightly, hoping to soothe him. Sullivan couldn't help thinking how natural she looked.

"The lights flickered in the elevator just before it got stuck." She thought she had told Sally that part. "Robby was almost born in the dark."

The next moment, the lights went out again. This time, they remained off. The darkened sky cast shadowed light into the house through the stained glass on either side of the door, creating an eerie, surrealistic atmosphere.

Marlene moved a step closer to Sullivan as she looked around uncertainly. "Sullivan?"

Back on a first name basis, he thought, amused. "Right here."

He was laughing at her, she thought. Even if she couldn't quite see his face, she could hear it in his voice. She should send him on his way, storm or no storm. But she didn't want him out in this because of her. What if he had an accident? Besides, she didn't like the idea of being left standing in the dark with a brand-new baby. She already felt in the dark as it was.

"I know, I can see you," she answered tartly. "But for how long?"

He strained to make out the numbers on his watch. It was 3:40. There would be light for perhaps another hour and a half. Then it would be pitch black. If power to the house wasn't restored, Marlene was going to be spending her first night home with her son—his nephew—in the dark.

"There's less than two hours of daylight left at most."

Sally interrupted him. "There's a circuit breaker on the side of the house." She reached for the dripping umbrella she had deposited in the stand beside the door. "Here, I can show you the way."

Sullivan turned to look out the front window. From his vantage point, he could just make out the house farther down the hill. It was dark as well. And it shouldn't have been.

He shook his head, releasing the gathered curtain. "I don't think a circuit breaker is going to do the trick this time. I think you have a full-fledged power outage on your hands."

The house felt cold already. Without electricity, there would be no heat, Marlene thought. The baby was going to need extra blankets to stay warm. And right now, she realized as she sniffed the ripe air, he needed something else.

Sally was way ahead of her. "I think someone needs changing," Sally announced. Putting the umbrella back in the stand, she took the baby from Marlene. There was a hint of a smile on her lips as she carried her new charge off to the nursery. "Come on, young sir, let's you and I become acquainted. My name is Sally. You, in time, can call me ma'am. I don't think that's going to be for a while yet, but it never hurts to be forewarned of things."

Amen to that, Sullivan thought, glancing in Marlene's direction.

In the fading light Marlene looked like a waif, definitely not like a woman who had given birth forty-eight hours before.

"Shouldn't you be lying down?"

"Not yet." She looked out the window. "I really don't think you should go home in this."

He was inclined to agree with her, but he had no options readily open to him. "Well, I can't stay here."

She supposed she had been inhospitable. For the moment, she stopped thinking of him as someone who threatened to take her child away and saw him only as the man who had delivered her child, who had held her and calmed her. Who had kissed her and definitely *un*calmed her.

"Why not? I don't bite." She forced a smile to her lips and found that it was far less difficult than she would have thought. "And one good turn deserves another. I can't have Robby's uncle drowning or getting stuck in a mud slide. There's plenty of room here. Besides, you can make yourself useful."

"How?"

"You can help me gather the flashlights together before it gets dark. I have a feeling this is going to get worse before it gets better."

That could also be used to describe their situation, Sullivan mused. "How can I refuse such a tempting offer?"

Because she felt a little unsteady on her feet, she hooked her arm through his. "You can't. C'mon."

It didn't take long. There were five flashlights in all, three of them camping lanterns.

"Do you go camping?" Sullivan deposited the armload of flashlights on the coffee table. She didn't remind him of the type who liked to sleep outdoors and slap away insects.

Marlene moved the largest lantern to the center of the table. They would need it to light the front door and the bottom of the stairs.

"No. We have these in case of earthquakes and other whimsical acts of nature. Like tonight," she said, turning around.

The lantern cast warm shadows on the walls. Their silhouettes overlapped and blended into one. Marlene shifted, pretending not to notice. She turned on the second one. The silhouette disappeared with the added light.

The wind picked up, howling as it continued to dash rain against the windows. Sullivan drew his eyes away from her and toward something that didn't tighten his stomach in a knot.

He walked over to the window. Not a single light anywhere in the area. "This doesn't look like it's about to let up for a while. The electric company is going to have its hands full."

Marlene ran her hands along her arms, trying to ward off the uneasy feeling. "I never liked the dark," she murmured. "Things always seem twice as bad then."

"I know what you mean." He'd lain awake at night and battled the same feeling more than once. "But it's just your mind working overtime."

She smiled in response to his words. Sullivan felt himself being drawn deeper into the fabric of her life.

The house was cold.

They were going to need a lot of blankets, he thought. The high, vaulted ceilings created a drafty atmosphere.

"Do you want some tea?" Marlene asked, remembering Sally's offer. She paused. He wasn't a man you offered tea to with a straight face. Only Sally could have pulled that off.

"The tea's cold by now," he reminded her.

She'd forgotten about that. Marlene sighed as she pushed a curtain aside to look out the window. She watched the rain come down relentlessly, as if someone had upended a huge pail of water. She pitied the men who had to work in this sort of weather—and prayed that they would hurry and restore power.

"Not much of a homecoming for the baby," she murmured to herself, unconsciously echoing Sally's words.

He stood behind her. For a fleeting moment, he felt the oddest yearning to stroke her hair. But his hand remained at his side. She wouldn't have wanted him to touch her.

And he wanted to touch her too much.

"I don't think your son was counting on hot tea. Besides, it's who you come home to that counts, Marlene, not what."

Marlene turned around to look at him. Sullivan couldn't begin to fathom the look in her eyes. It was far too complex.

"Yes," she said softly to herself, "I know."

Chapter Ten

Marlene let the curtain drop. It swayed slightly as it slid into place against the window. Beyond it, the world was still being held captive by the storm, though it appeared to have settled in for the night.

She turned around to look at Sullivan. Having brought in her suitcase and the flowers, he was sitting in her living room, as out of place as a steak in a vegetarian meal.

He looked pensive, she thought, like someone sitting on the edge of an arrow, waiting to be launched through the air. She couldn't for the life of her understand why. If anyone should feel that way, it should be her.

Upstairs, the baby was sleeping peacefully. Sally had retired early, silently for once, succumbing to the ravages of the cold that was encroaching over her.

For all intents and purposes, she and Sullivan might as well have been alone. It certainly felt that way.

Almost intimately so. Marlene tried not to dwell on how romantic the atmosphere was, with only the light from the lantern pooling around them. Sullivan wasn't a man to be romantic with. He was a man to be leery of.

And yet, there were these . . . conflicting *feelings* that refused to leave her, coloring everything. She felt happy, energetic, yet tired and extremely vulnerable. Vulnerable because he was staying and because she wanted him to. There was no way he could leave now, not with the storm raging the way it was.

She walked over to the sofa slowly. "This is a night that only Noah should venture out—and only if his life insurance was paid up."

He had been hoping it would let up, but that obviously wasn't going to happen. It had only gotten worse since he'd arrived. Sullivan was annoyed with himself for lingering. He should have left as soon as he brought her home. "They didn't have life insurance back then."

Given half a chance, he would probably argue with God. "I was just making conversation." Feeling restless herself, she began to move about the room. "The point is, I wouldn't want Robby's uncle getting into an accident because he did a good deed."

He turned his eyes to her. Even in the dim light, they looked as blue as the Pacific during an idyllic summer morning. She moved farther away.

Marlene cleared her throat and tried to sound friendly and unfazed. "As I said, we have plenty of room. My father always liked lots of space—I think he was trying to lose us in it."

There was no bitterness in her voice, he noted, only amused resignation.

"Not that he was ever here that much to misplace us. Except for his parties." Marlene bit her lip as she glanced up at Sullivan. "I'm talking too much." *And probably giving you ammunition to use.* Wary, she moved back toward the window, feeling safer there.

"I didn't notice."

Impatient, Sullivan crossed to the window. Reaching around her, he moved aside the curtain to look out as if he needed to be convinced one last time. He was. It was as if there were no world outside the cold glass pane.

Sullivan sighed. "I think we've had more rain in three days than we normally have in an entire year."

He'd heard on the radio this morning that this December was the wettest one on record. He could well believe it. There was only so long he could struggle against the inevitable.

"Maybe I will take you up on that offer."

She looked at him, her brows drawn together quizzically. Damn, what was that scent she was wearing and why did she have to be wearing it now? It felt as if it were seeping into all his pores, stirring his imagination in directions he didn't want it to go.

"About staying the night," he added.

He was standing so close she could feel the heat of his body. It felt good, comforting. She argued with herself that it was only because the house was cold, but tiny fragments of the other evening returned to her. When the lights had begun to dim in the elevator, she had felt herself bordering on hysteria. He had been tender and kind. No matter what else happened, Marlene knew there would always be that bond, that underlying sense of gratitude she felt existing between them.

She found herself wishing that nothing would ever strain it.

Dreamer. Of course it'll be strained. He wants what you want. Custody of Robby.

She knew she should step away from him, from this blossoming feeling. She stood perfectly still, holding her breath like a small child standing in the dark, thinking that the sound of her breathing would give her presence away. She realized that she could care about this man, really care, if only he wasn't who he was.

But there was no getting around that. She sobered. "I'll show you to the guest room."

Sullivan nodded, then thought of his father. He had promised to stop by tonight. He didn't like to leave things hanging.

"I need to make a phone call."

She wondered if there was someone in his life that he had to check in with, a fiancée, a girlfriend, some significant other who had staked a claim on him. That was something else she hadn't thought to ask Spencer. At the time, it hadn't seemed important.

And it shouldn't now. It's none of your business, Marlene.

She bit her lower lip to keep from asking. Instead, she indicated the telephone on the small table in the living room.

"It'll only be a minute," he told her, looking away. Why would someone gnawing on their lip make him want to do the same?

Maybe because her taste seemed to still linger in the recesses of his mind.

He wished he was leaving instead of staying.

Sullivan raised the receiver to his ear. There was no dial tone, nothing but dead air. He tapped the telephone twice, then returned the receiver to the cradle.

Marlene raised a brow as he turned around. "It's dead," he told her.

"Will she worry?"

Preoccupied, exasperated and trying to deny the feelings that were raising their small, demanding heads within him, he looked at her as if she had lapsed into a foreign tongue. "Who?"

Marlene shrugged nonchalantly. "Whoever you were trying to reach."

He shoved his hands into his pockets, feeling out of sorts. He didn't like being isolated this way. And he tried not to think about what the rain was doing to three ongoing developments in the county that were just in the beginning stages.

Most of all, he tried not to think about the woman before him.

"I was going to call my father, to tell him that I'd gotten you home and decided to stay."

An ironic smile twisted her lips. They had something in common beyond the baby. She would have done the same once. "A dutiful son."

His eyes slanted to hers, wondering if she was amusing herself at his expense. But the look on her face was guileless. "He likes being kept informed."

Marlene nodded, remembering. "I had one of those myself once." He looked at her curiously. "A father who wanted to be kept abreast of every move I made," she explained. "At least as far as the company was concerned."

He read between the lines. "Doesn't sound as if you liked him very much."

She began to protest, then paused, thinking. Though she hated to admit it, he was right. There seemed to be no reason to deny it.

"I loved him with all my heart. But, no, you're right. Looking back, I really didn't like him." She shrugged. It was all in the past now. Robby was her future, and she was never going to allow him to feel the way she had. "My father wasn't really a likable man, but I suppose he had his reasons."

Sullivan almost asked what they were, but that would just lead to more conversation—personal conversation—and he didn't want to get involved any further. He had to remember that. The less he knew about her personal life, the less entangled he would feel.

The less guilty he would be about separating her from her son.

Derek's son, he amended silently. And there was nothing to feel guilty about. It wasn't as if the child had been conceived during a night of lovemaking or even spontaneous heated passion. Robby was practically a test tube baby, for God's sake.

So why the hell did he feel as if he were the villain in some Dickens novel?

He didn't want to stand here any longer, mentally debating with himself. He was tired. "Maybe you'd better show me to my room."

Marlene picked up one of the lanterns and placed a small flashlight into her pocket. Shining the lantern on the stairs, she led the way to his room. He was withdrawing, she thought. That gave her the upper hand. She smiled to herself and relaxed.

"I'd like to meet him sometime." The words floated over her shoulder as she led the way up the winding staircase.

That comment had certainly come out of nowhere. "Who?" he asked cautiously.

She came to the landing and stepped to the side as she turned to look at him. "Your father. Robby's grandfather."

Sullivan never trusted a situation where the pieces fell together too easily. "Why?"

She raised the lantern up higher. She wanted to clearly see the expression on his face. Wariness highlighted his features. Was it so difficult for him to understand? She was looking to giving Robby as normal a life as possible.

"Because I think that Robby should have at least one grandparent in his life. I didn't." Turning again, she walked down the hall to the guest room. "My father's father was dead by the time I was born, and my grandmother lived in England. I didn't even know she existed until she died. She mentioned us, Nicole and me, in her will."

"What about your mother's parents?"

"I have no idea." Her voice turned formal. "My mother left when I was very young. I have no idea about her family. I think they like it that way." She stopped at his room and opened the door. He could just about make out a bed from where he was standing. "A child should have a sense of family. A strong sense." She looked at him pointedly.

She wasn't just making idle conversation. "What are you trying to tell me?" he prodded.

They weren't on the same wavelength, but they would be, she promised herself. It was the only solution for Robby. Sullivan had to withdraw his claim for custody.

"Things that I don't want to discuss out loud." Her eyes held his. "When things are said, they can't be unsaid." She gestured behind her. "Here's your room." She took the flashlight out of her pocket and handed it to him. "Good night."

"Good night," he murmured, but he doubted that it would be.

He slept badly, tossing and turning, plagued by formless dreams that eluded him as soon as they passed through his mind. Eventually, a low, whining noise began to bore a hole through the dark fabric of his fitful sleep. It grew in volume until it penetrated his subconscious.

Sullivan sat up in bed, listening.

It wasn't a dream, or the wind howling. The soft wailing was coming from the room next to his.

The baby.

Sullivan listened again. Robby sounded as if he were in pain.

Rising, he felt around for the trousers he had slung over the footboard the night before. Finding them, he tugged his pants on, then searched for his shirt. It was crumpled to one side of the bed. Unless he tripped over them, he wasn't about to hunt for his shoes. The floor wasn't cold anyway.

The significance of that hit him a moment later. There was light pooling under his door from the hallway. More light than could be cast by the lantern that Marlene had left on the hall table.

He opened the door and saw that a lamp had been turned on. Apparently the power had been restored sometime during the night. But from the sound of it, the rain still hadn't let up.

Squinting, his eyes adjusting to the light, Sullivan looked down at his watch. It was a little after three. He dragged his hand through his hair as he struggled to focus his mind. He wasn't at his best at three in the morning.

The wailing continued.

Sullivan didn't bother buttoning his shirt. He planned to be back in bed shortly. The two sides flapped about his torso as he went out into the hall and to Marlene's room to investigate. He paused outside her door, listening.

He could hear Marlene, softly attempting to soothe the baby. It seemed to be to no avail.

She could handle this. Eventually. Sullivan turned to walk back into his room, but he stopped just shy of the threshold. Something wouldn't let him retreat. With a sigh, he returned to stand before Marlene's door.

He knocked softly, but there was no answer. Very slowly, he turned the knob. The door was unlocked. Placing his fingertips against it, he pushed the door open a crack at a time until it was completely ajar. Until he saw her.

Marlene was standing at the window, her head bent. The room was dark except for one small lamp, its base shaped in the form of a duckling. The dim light from it outlined her body softly, blurring the edges, casting her silhouette on the wall and leaving very little to his imagination.

Leaving everything to his imagination.

Where it would have to remain, he upbraided himself suddenly. In his imagination. There was no way he was going to cross the line and become more involved with her than he already was. It would only be disastrous to the situation they were embroiled in. He needed to hold on to his objectivity, and he couldn't if his emotions were entangled.

And yet he lingered, watching her. Wanting her.

He could see the reflection of her face in the window. She hadn't heard him come in. He could still leave. Sullivan debated slipping out. Intellectually, it only seemed right. If it was him, he wouldn't want anyone invading his space.

So why was he still standing there like some moonstruck adolescent?

She turned then. If she was surprised to see him standing in the room, she didn't show it. "Did the baby wake you?"

He nodded. "For someone so small, he's got a good set of lungs." He walked toward her. "What's wrong with him?"

"Well, I've just changed his diaper, and he doesn't feel warm, so my next guess is that he's hungry." She looked down at the tiny being in her arms. It was still hard to believe he was finally here, finally hers. "God, he's so little."

Sullivan looked down at his nephew. "They usually are when they start out."

He was teasing her, but she didn't mind. It felt rather nice...she was vaguely aware of having felt this way before, but couldn't quite remember when.

"I know, but I never had one of my own before. Somehow, I thought he'd be bigger." She smiled at her son. "But you'll be a linebacker before I know it, and then this'll just be a golden memory. Won't it, Robby?"

The baby continued to cry as he tried to shove his fist into his mouth. The resulting sound reminded Sullivan of a mewling kitten.

Marlene lifted her head. Sullivan saw how tired she looked. But even exhausted, she was beautiful. Untouched beauty. It was a little like finding a new type of flower no one else had discovered yet, he mused, forcing himself not to touch her face, not to cup her cheek.

It wasn't easy. The sexual pull he felt toward her was strong.

Her eyes traveled over him. Sullivan's shirt was hanging open. He was a great deal more muscular than she would have thought. The room grew a little warmer.

She wasn't supposed to think about things like that, she reminded herself. Not about him.

Uncomfortable, Sullivan looked around her bedroom. It was pristine, giving the appearance that no one had actually slept here. Nothing looked out of place. Even the covers of her bed were neatly folded back. He thought of his own bed and the rumpled mess he always left in his wake. And then he thought of her in his bed and knew he was on dangerous ground.

"Where did you put the complimentary formula the nurse gave you?"

Marlene paused, thinking.

"I think it's still in the suitcase you brought in. In the foyer." She hadn't bothered to bring it upstairs. She had attempted to nurse the baby once, and he'd fallen asleep rather than work for his meal. Stubborn, she thought fondly. Like his Mom. "Here, hold him for a minute, will you?"

Before he knew it, there was a baby in his arms and Marlene was heading for the hallway.

"Hey, wait a minute." Sullivan managed to catch her by the wrist, slowing her down. "Why don't you let me get it, and you hold the baby?"

She shook her head, easing her wrist from his grasp. "That's all right, I can manage. See if you can keep him amused."

Marlene hurried from the room. He followed in her wake, then watched from the landing as she went down the staircase.

"I wasn't going to steal anything," he called after her.

Only my son, she thought as she padded on bare feet into the foyer. "Yes, I know."

With a shake of his head, Sullivan walked into the nursery. Muted light tiptoed about the room from the duckling lamp. The walls were professionally decorated with scenes from various nursery rhymes. He would guess that the cost of the furnishings in the room alone could probably have outfitted an entire house.

His father certainly couldn't use the argument that they could provide better for the boy than she could, he thought. What it was all boiling down to was wishes, hers versus his father's.

He looked down at the baby she had placed into his arms. He felt awkward, as if he were going to drop this bundle at any moment. And yet, there was something very comforting about holding this tiny squirming bit of humanity.

"Hi," he murmured.

The baby continued squirming and bleating pitifully. Sullivan felt inept. "Look, I don't know anything about taking care of a baby." He could identify with the way Marlene had said she felt earlier. "Where's your mother, Robby?"

Apparently attracted to the sound of a deeper voice, the infant ceased crying and stared up at him with Marlene's eyes. Sullivan felt something move within him, creating a bond with this small person.

He stroked the boy's head. This wasn't so bad after all.

"You don't look very terrifying, but I guess you cast a longer shadow." He looked at the length of the infant tucked against him. Robby had measured eighteen and a half inches at birth. Sullivan smiled. "I guess you'd have to, half-pint."

Robby's eyes were indigo. Sullivan absently wondered if they would change. He vaguely recalled reading somewhere that most babies had blue eyes when they were born, only to change to another color within a year.

He hoped Robby's eyes would stay the color they were.

"You're going to be able to do incredible things with those eyes of yours in about fifteen years," Sullivan promised the boy.

"Are you corrupting my son?" Marlene asked, laughing as she entered.

"My nephew," he corrected.

There was something a little too possessive about the way he said that, she thought. She wasn't out of the woods yet by any means. Just because he was being nice to her didn't mean he was going to be reasonable about Robby's custody.

"Here, you've suffered long enough. Let me have him." She took the baby into her arms.

"I was just getting the knack of it." His hand brushed against the bottle as he surrendered Robby to her. "Hey, isn't that supposed to be warmed or something?"

Damn, she'd been so intent on returning, she'd forgotten to heat the bottle. Talk about feeling incompetent. She looked from the bottle to Sullivan. "Warm it up for me? It should be a little warmer than room temperature."

He was surprised by the request. "Are you sure that won't interfere with your independence?"

"Maybe, but I'm too tired to go downstairs again." She raised an inquiring eyebrow. "Would you?"

"Sure, no problem. Where's the kitchen?"

"Just past the family room."

He nodded, leaving.

Marlene sat down in the rocking chair. It was made out of ash and had a honey gold finish that she had applied herself while dreaming of moments just like this. Of sitting and rocking with her child. She'd had an idyllic vision of motherhood that wasn't mired in feedings and diapers.

Yeah, right. It made her smile now to think how foolish she'd been. The only part that had gone according to plan was the love she felt. That she had vastly underestimated, she thought, her heart swelling as she looked down at her son.

For once it felt nice to be wrong.

Sullivan flipped a switch as he entered the kitchen, fluorescent light flooding the room. The kitchen was as immaculate as her bedroom, he thought. The house needed a little clutter to make it seem like a home.

He figured the baby would take care of that soon enough. Sullivan stopped, realizing what he had just projected. If he was successful, the baby wouldn't be here to create the chaos he'd just envisioned.

So this was what it meant to be stuck between a rock and a hard place, he thought darkly. He couldn't say that he much cared for it.

Pushing the thought to the side, Sullivan looked around for the microwave oven. It was built into the wall, set apart from the stove. There were three independent rows of buttons along the side. It looked a great deal more complicated than the little microwave he kept in his office.

Placing the bottle inside, he pressed what he hoped was the right combination of buttons and waited for the bell to go off.

Or the bottle to explode, he mused, whichever happened first.

The bell went off before the bottle cracked. He considered that a victory. Taking the bottle out, Sullivan tested the liquid on the inside of his wrist. It still felt a little cool, but better that than too hot, he thought. In any case, he didn't want to fool around with the controls again. There was no sense in pressing his luck.

Bottle in hand, Sullivan hurried up the stairs. The door to the nursery was still standing open the way he had left it. The night-light sent out its scattered beams along the floor, hugging corners like a low-lying fog. The light mingled with the shadows.

Marlene was sitting in the rocking chair, the baby pressed against her breast. She was cooing to him, rocking gently back and forth. Her face was soft, radiant. Moved, Sullivan stood there watching her for a moment. If he was a painter, he would have entitled the scene, *Portrait of a Young Mother.*

When she looked up in his direction, Sullivan coughed, feeling like an intruder caught trespassing. "Milk's ready." He held up the bottle for proof.

She extended her hand. "I'm not sure we still need it," she said softly. "I think he decided that he'd rather go back to sleep."

Sullivan gave her the bottle anyway. Marlene gently rubbed the nipple along the baby's lips, coaxing him to begin sucking. After a moment he responded. Drops of formula gathered about the rosebud mouth, trickling down his chin.

Sullivan wasn't aware of holding his breath until he felt the tightening sensation in his chest. It was like watching a tiny miracle unfold. He passed his cupped hand lightly along the downy head. As he did, his fingertips accidentally brushed against Marlene's breast.

A strong emotion dove through her, rivaling the maternal instincts that were solidifying. She looked up at Sullivan, her eyes wide with wonder.

He felt it, too, she thought. She could see it in his eyes. He'd felt that sudden jolt, that incredible charge that flashed through her like a thousand Fourth of July sparklers.

He knew he should withdraw. This was a very private moment between mother and child—and father, if Derek had been alive to see this.

But he was here, and he couldn't help himself.

Just as he couldn't help what he did next. Drawn by a force he had no control over, Sullivan lowered his mouth to Marlene's.

Ever so slightly, as if he were afraid of shattering the moment, he brushed his lips over hers.

The salvo of sweetness that shot through Marlene almost left her gasping. It occurred to her that she had never felt so happy, so complete as she did this very moment.

And that she probably never would again.

The sobering thought receded into the background as she reached up and slid her hand along Sullivan's neck, drawing him just a fraction of an inch closer to her.

Seize the moment, her father had always counseled. There were times, she mused, when her father was right.

Chapter Eleven

Instant passion, just add lips. That was the label that should have been affixed to her, Sullivan thought, his mind spinning. The woman packed a lethal punch that immediately sent him reeling.

And wanting.

For only a moment longer, he allowed himself to taste the incredible combination of sweetness and sex that she exuded. Anything more and he might not recover fully.

As if he were capable of doing that now.

Sullivan swallowed as he took a step back. Reluctantly, he drew his hand away from her hair. This attraction was certainly something he hadn't bargained on.

"Maybe I'd better go."

Holding Robby to her, she reached for Sullivan's hand. "No."

Marlene realized that she had said the word too quickly and too emphatically. In the wake of his kiss, she realized a great many other things about herself as well. Such as, despite the baby, there was a part of her that still felt incomplete. That still needed something—or someone.

She cleared her throat. "I mean, it's still the middle of the night." She looked toward the window. Through the opaque curtains she could see the sheets of rain sliding down the panes. She didn't want him leaving in this. She didn't want him leaving, period. But that was a foolishness she would have to work out for herself. "It's still raining. Wait until morning."

She'd misunderstood. An amused, affectionate smile curved his mouth at the image of the dramatic exit she'd envisioned. Maybe both of them were a little on edge. "No, I meant maybe I should go back to my room."

"Oh." She flushed, embarrassed, and lowered her eyes. "Maybe you should," she agreed quietly.

Marlene looked down at Robby. The baby had dozed off. The bottle's nipple was pressed to his cheek. A tiny drop of formula oozed out. She placed the small bottle on the nightstand and rose. Very gently, she laid Robby in his crib, then slipped a blanket over him. Marlene held her breath, hoping he wouldn't wake up.

She leaned against the crib railing, her back to Sullivan, the gauzy nightgown she wore softly folding around the curves of her body.

His mouth felt like cotton.

Distance was in order here, and maybe a long, cold shower, even at this hour.

He would see about both later. Right now, he just wanted to be next to her. To breathe in her scent and let his mind go lax. Standing beside her before the baby's crib seemed a safe enough place.

Curiosity nudged at him again, more urgently than before. He had tasted the passion. It just didn't make sense. "Why did you want to have this baby—or any baby at this time in your life? Going to that Institute seems so... so—"

"Impersonal?" she supplied.

Whatever he had to say, she'd heard it all before, from Sally, from Nicole, from well-meaning associates who had advised her to wait, that love would enter her life and then things could proceed naturally. But she hadn't wanted to take the chance and wait. What if love never came?

She slanted a look at Sullivan's profile. And what if—?

Marlene quickly buried the thought.

Impersonal. There was no better way to describe it, he supposed. "Yes."

She shrugged. "Maybe, but I had this sudden, overpowering need, and there was no one around to fill it. I wanted someone to love." She looked down at Robby. He looked so peaceful, so innocent. She memorized the moment. "Someone to take care of." *Someone who'll love me without making judgments.*

Right now, she was too tired for rendering explanations. "I just didn't think it was going to be this difficult."

She was standing barefoot, with her hair loose around her shoulders, part dream, part reality. Her vulnerability reached out to him, drawing him in. He struggled to resist. Sullivan didn't want to get entangled any more than he already was. He didn't want to care about her. He didn't need complications in his life. He liked his life just the way it was, smooth and simple. And she represented just the opposite.

"Relationships usually are," he said casually. "They require a great deal of work." He saw the interest enter her eyes. "Or so I've been told." He nodded toward the crib. "Even fledgling ones."

His eyes skimmed over her lips and he knew that if he remained, he was going to kiss her again. It was as much of a certainty as the sun rising in the morning. And that spelled trouble with a capital *T.* The only way to avoid the whole problem was to leave now.

"Well, like I said, maybe I'd better go." He crossed the nursery threshold, then paused in the doorway. "See you in the morning."

She nodded, lingering by the crib. He turned toward his room.

"Sullivan." He stopped, waiting. "Thanks. For everything."

He turned to look at her and grinned. "Don't mention it."

She pressed her lips together, tasting him. Her heart still hadn't gone back to normal. "Maybe I shouldn't have," she murmured softly to herself. "Maybe I really shouldn't have."

Marlene shifted slightly. The awkward, out-of-place feeling wouldn't abate. Robby whimpered in her arms, as if sensing her discomfort. The noise was absorbed by the floor-to-ceiling books that comprised three of the four walls within Oliver Travis's library.

She had no one to blame for this but herself. She had asked for this meeting. Robby was almost two weeks old, and she'd thought it was time to have things out with Sullivan's father. Having stopped by several times to look in on the baby and spend the evening with her, Sullivan had made her feel that perhaps things could be worked out. He'd made her relax her guard.

Undoubtedly that had been his intent all along, she thought grudgingly.

Bearding the lion in his den, that had been her idea. She'd hoped to forestall any major problems by offering a tentative hand in friendship. Right now Marlene felt as if the hand had been examined and then severed off at the wrist.

She had thought, after years of her father, that she was immune to this sort of intense scrutiny. But her father could have learned a thing or two from the man who sat in the wheelchair. He'd been a handsome man once, she judged, perhaps almost as good-looking as Sullivan. But something had robbed him of that, leaving in its place a man who was hunched and whose mouth had a bitter set to it.

She wished she had never come.

Oliver Travis's blue eyes looked her over very slowly, as if she were a piece of land to be evaluated for its ultimate worth on the market. His expression was partially hidden behind a steel gray beard. Given the season, he could have passed for Santa Claus, except that his eyes were judgmental. And Santa Claus's mouth would never have been turned down.

Very slowly, Oliver took measure of the young woman his son had ushered in. Making his decision, he looked at the baby in her arms.

His grandchild. His grandson. A world of promise within a small body.

He felt the same stirrings he'd experienced when he had looked upon Derek for the first time. That had been a lifetime ago. But he was older now, and wiser he hoped. At least he knew that plans, like as not, didn't always come to fruition no matter how grand or well formed they were. He'd given Derek the world, and Derek had thumbed his nose at him and thrown it all away.

All but this tiny infant. There was still a chance. And he meant to take it, no matter what the obstacles. The world owed him that. And Derek owed him that chance, whether he was gone or not.

Pressing buttons on the armrest, Oliver propelled his wheelchair forward until he was directly before her. He had given her the barest of greetings when Sullivan introduced her.

"Let me see him."

It sounded like a royal command. Everything about Oliver Travis reminded Marlene of her father. Unsmiling, demanding, with eyes that were cold and never saw beneath the surface. Glancing at Sullivan for reassurance and then damning herself for it, Marlene pressed her lips together and carefully handed Robby to his grandfather.

She saw what appeared to be a smile on the old man's lips. He had made a connection. Marlene held her breath and prayed she hadn't made a mistake coming here. The law, if it came down to that, was usually on the mother's side. But Travis was an important, powerful man, not to be underestimated. There were ways that he could take Robby from her and she knew it.

"Sullivan tells me his name is Robert," Oliver addressed his words to Marlene without looking up.

"Yes." Marlene strove not to feel fidgety. She felt Sullivan move closer to her, but didn't know whether to feel comforted or outnumbered.

Oliver shook his head, dismissing her choice. "It's too common."

Marlene squared her shoulders. "It was my brother's name."

That made no difference to him one way or another. This was his grandson they were discussing. The boy needed a name to be proud of. A name that was distinguished. "It can be changed."

"But it won't be." Oliver looked up at her sharply, but she didn't back down. Her eyes on his, Marlene took her child back. "Nothing about Robby is going to be changed except his diapers."

Sullivan could see this was not going well. When Marlene had again suggested meeting his father, Sullivan had agreed. He had hoped that perhaps things could be amicably resolved between them so that everyone was satisfied. He should have known better. The strange thing was that his sympathies had shifted from his infirmed father to this wisp of a woman in the last few days. Somehow, heritage wasn't nearly as important as he had once thought. There were far more important things to consider.

He could see that he was going to have to mediate. "Dad—"

Oliver waved him into silence. "I am prepared to offer you—"

Indignation hardened Marlene's features. She was not about to be intimidated, Sullivan thought.

"It better not be money, Mr. Travis, because I came here ready to try to like you for Robby's sake. A boy needs grandparents, and you're the only one that he has now. But if you insult me by asking to buy his affection—or him—I'm afraid that this visit is over."

The tufted eyebrows formed an angry ridge across Oliver's forehead as his eyes shot lightning. "You impudent little nothing!" He gave the impression of rising within his chair without moving a muscle. "Do you mean to stand there and dictate to me—?"

Her tone and bearing matched his. Anything less and she would have lost. "No, but I won't stand here and be dictated to, either."

"I am his biological grandfather—"

"And I'm his biological mother," she countered. "We know who we are. And I know how we'll *both* figure into Robby's life—unless you force me to cut you out. I don't want that to happen, and I don't think you do, either, but the law is on my side, so why don't we—"

His breath rattled in his lungs as his anger grew. "The law has a great many gray areas, young woman, and I have a squadron of lawyers on retainer. I can take you to court. I could have *you* cut out of *his* life."

Sullivan saw Marlene turn pale. He'd let this go on long enough.

"Dad, you don't mean that," Sullivan said firmly. He exchanged looks with Osborne, who was standing discreetly off to the side. Maybe it was time for Marlene to leave.

"The hell I don't. And you'd better stay back if you don't want to find yourself on the unemployment line, Osborne," Oliver warned without bothering to look in the man's direction. Osborne froze where he was.

The man was a tyrant, pure and simple. There was no reasoning with him, and no way that she was going to allow him to get his hands on her son, no matter what she had to do. Marlene held Robby closer to her.

"I'm sorry I came. I'd hoped that you might be different from what I imagined, that I was being unfair to you. If anything, I was being overly generous. I can see now why Derek ran off." She was beginning to feel a great deal of empathy for her son's late father.

She was angry and had a right to be, but Sullivan didn't want to see her leaving this way. "Marlene—" He took her arm.

She couldn't pull free without jerking the baby. Her eyes cut Sullivan dead. "Let go of my arm, Sullivan. Let go, or I swear I'll make you both regret the day you came into my life." She had no idea how she would carry out her threat, only that she wanted to get away. Now.

Startled by the look in her eyes, Sullivan dropped his hand. "Stay," he asked. "Maybe we can—"

"It's too late," she told him. "Way too late. I never want to see either one of you ever again." She turned away and walked out of the room.

"Young woman, come back here. You come back in here, do you hear me?" Oliver bellowed after her.

I hear you, Mr. Travis, she thought. *I hear you all too well.*

She hurried out of the house as fast as she could.

Marlene's fury hadn't abated a single degree by the time she arrived home. Exhausted, her emotions spent, she felt as if she had crossed the Mojave Desert on her knees. That was what she got for trying to be fair, she upbraided herself. For being taken in by a pair of crystal blue eyes.

Well, another lesson learned. And paid for, she added, feeling a sadness slipping through the anger she felt. Trying to calm down, Marlene busied herself with the baby. When Sally asked her how the meeting went, she said very little. For once, Sally knew when to back off.

After giving him his bath, Marlene brought Robby to his room. Toweling him dry, she glanced at the discarded sailor suit lying on his bureau. She'd dressed him in it for his first visit to his grandfather.

His first and his last, she thought, her mouth hardening.

"I'm sorry to have put you through that, honey." She slipped yellow terry cloth jammies on him. "I didn't know that your other grandfather was as heartless as my father was. But I should have." She thought of Sullivan, of the offer he had originally made to her, trying to buy her out of her son's life. "Yes, I definitely should have known."

Maybe she'd overreacted, but Oliver Travis hadn't sounded as if he were willing to listen to reason or compromise. He wanted her son. He wanted to take over his name, his life, everything. She wasn't about to let that happen.

"You're mine, sweetie, and no one is going to take you away from me, ever," she whispered to the baby. Robby responded by kicking his legs.

She knew it was time to put him down for the night, but she had an overwhelming need just to hold him. She picked Robby up and pressed him against her.

His head rubbed against her cheek. She felt infinitely soothed. "Uncle Sullivan's not going to be any help. Looks like you and me against the world, Robby." A sad smile curved her mouth. "It's not so bad, really. I've been there before."

Sullivan. She frowned as she thought of him. He should have done something, said something.

She struggled to be fair. What could he have said? She'd had a father like that herself—overbearing, unwilling to listen, or even to acknowledge the existence of anything beyond his opinion or scope of things.

Her frown melted slightly. No matter how angry she was, there was no denying that Sullivan did make her feel like a woman. Whenever he touched her, however casually or accidentally, it made her long to feel like a flesh-and-blood woman instead of the head of an advertising agency.

No use dwelling on it; it was over. Besides, it was best not to venture into uncharted territory. She was good as the head of the advertising agency, and she was gingerly making her way through the confusing jungle of motherhood. That was taxing enough. Any feelings she had for Sullivan made her feel naked, knee-deep in emotional quicksand and completely unaware of how to pull herself out.

The best way to avoid being sucked in by the quagmire was not to step out into the field and risk sinking in the first place.

No chance of that happening now, she thought. The next time she saw Sullivan would probably be across a courtroom. God, she hoped it wouldn't come to that.

She placed a blanket over the tiny form. Robby, his cheek pressed against the mattress, was bathed, fed and changed. And fast asleep. It gave her an overwhelming sense of satisfaction.

She tiptoed out of the room and went downstairs. This was her last evening on maternity leave. What a way to end it, she mused. With fireworks. She found herself wishing for one more week, one more day, but she'd already made up her mind to return to work tomorrow. It hadn't been an easy decision, or one she'd made lightly. She was going to miss Robby more than she'd thought possible. But there was no way around it.

Her firm needed her. There were accounts going begging because she was tied up at home, feeling her way around this brand-new continent she found herself in. The office had been in constant touch, almost from the beginning of her maternity leave. She'd conducted some business via telephone and fax, but she just couldn't continue to put things off any longer. Not with the Saunders account in the balance. Miles Saunders was demanding that she handle the campaign personally, which for him meant in person. It did wonders for her ego, but very little for her stress threshold.

Marlene struggled to put a positive spin on the situation. The best way to place everything into perspective was to get back to work. Work had always been the steadfast part of her life. It was her anchor. She needed work in order to forget about the whole ugly incident today. And to forget about Sullivan.

She entered the kitchen and paused. Sally was there, still tidying up after dinner. She looked at Sally closely for perhaps the first time in a long time. The woman was getting on in years. It was a jarring realization. Though she had always assumed that Sally would care for the baby, maybe other arrangements were going to have to be made.

"Sally?"

Sally turned from the stove, a sponge in her hand. "Yes?"

"Will you be all right here with Robby?"

"Of course I'll be all right with Robby. Why? Are you going out tonight?"

She knew Sally wasn't going to like this. She'd never liked her working at the ad agency and had made her disapproval clear the very first time Marlene had gone to the office. Sally had never understood how important working with her father had been to her.

"No," Marlene answered firmly. "I'm going back to work tomorrow."

Sally looked at her, stunned. "It's only been two weeks, girl."

"I know," Marlene nodded slowly. "And I can't stretch it out any longer."

The doorbell rang, but Sally remained where she was, staring up at the woman she had raised from a child as if she had never seen Marlene before. "You're kidding... aren't you?"

"No, I'm not."

She didn't like the look in Sally's eyes. It made her uncomfortable, as if she'd failed to live up to some secret standard. Damn, why was it that everyone held up a yardstick to measure her by? It was her life, not anyone else's. The doorbell rang again. It was like a bell signaling the end of a round.

"The doorbell, Sally. It's ringing."

"I know it's ringing. I'm not deaf." She spared her a dark look. "Not like some people who refuse to hear." She scowled and muttered under her breath as she went to answer the door.

Her scowl intensified when she saw who it was.

Sally grudgingly opened the door all the way. "Oh, great, more trouble." She looked over her shoulder. "It's for you, and he's bringing a gift. And I'd give serious thought to the story about the Trojan horse if I were you."

Marlene was in no mood for riddles. "Sally, what are you talking about? Oh." Marlene stopped dead in her tracks. The last person she'd expected to see at her door was Sullivan. She glanced at the large, hand-painted rocking horse beside him. Now what? "I didn't think you'd be here after what happened earlier."

Coming here hadn't been easy for Sullivan. Part of him was ready to say the hell with it. He'd done what was required of him, tracked down his brother's "contribution" and brought her and his father together. The rest should be up to his father and Marlene. He could wash his hands of it.

But that would be lying. He couldn't wash his hands of it. Not after he'd kissed her. Not after what he'd felt when he had held Robby in his arms. It couldn't just end this way.

He'd come to apologize and to mend fences. And maybe to hold her just one more time.

"It's because of what happened earlier that I'm here." He didn't want to have this conversation on her doorstep. "Can I come in?"

"The horse can." She stood at the door, barring the way. "I'm not too sure about you."

He glanced at the rocking horse. "We're a set."

"Too bad for the horse. All right, come on in." With a sigh, she led the way in.

Sullivan lifted the rocking horse and carried it into the house. The horse was a lot heavier than it looked. "It's Derek's."

Puzzled, Marlene stopped and turned around. "What is?"

Sullivan set the rocking horse down. He had spent the better part of two hours looking for it in the storage unit, and then another hour cleaning it up.

"The horse. Derek got it for Christmas one year. He was about six." Sullivan smoothed the flaxen mane down on the wooden neck. With a push of his hand he set it rocking gently. "He loved riding on it, pretending he was a cowboy. My father saved it, hoping to pass it on to his grandson one day." Sullivan lifted a shoulder, feeling somewhat awkward. Maybe he should have just stayed away from her. Being here, being close to her, did things to him. He didn't know quite how to handle it. "I thought that Robby might like it."

It was a beautiful toy and just the sort of thing she would have wanted for her son. A gift with a history to it. Still, she was cautious. "What's the catch? He can only ride it in your father's house?"

"I brought it here, didn't I?" Sullivan worked to curb his temper. He hated that wary look in her eyes. Hated it because it was directed at him. "No catch. I thought he should have it, that's all."

She ran her hand over the flaxen mane. There was no doubt in her mind that it was handmade. She felt herself softening. Calculated or not, Sullivan's gesture touched her.

"Thank you." Marlene looked up at him. "Did you get one, too?"

Sullivan shook his head. "No. I wasn't into horses." It was Derek who had always received the preferential treatment, Derek who had gotten everything he wanted as a child.

Something in his voice told her otherwise. *Yes, you were,* she thought, looking at his expression. *But you didn't get one.* A kinship rose within her. Marlene slipped her hand into his. "It was very nice of you to bring it. I'm sure Robby'll treasure it when he's old enough."

"So, are you letting him stay?" Sally demanded as she walked out of the kitchen.

"Yes, Sally," Marlene answered patiently. "I'm letting him stay."

"Never did know what was good for you, did you?" the woman muttered loud enough for them both to hear. "Well, I'm going to bed. Scream if you need me." She made her way up the stairs.

Marlene looked at Sullivan, chagrined. "Sorry about that."

It didn't take a Rhodes scholar to see that Sally was particularly disgruntled tonight. "She seems angry with you. Is it because I'm here?"

She thought of saying yes, but that would be lying and he deserved better. "No. She just doesn't approve of my returning to work tomorrow."

"Tomorrow?" That seemed so soon. She'd given birth—when? A week, no two weeks ago.

Marlene could read his mind. He disapproved, too. Why did she always have to defend everything she did? "That doesn't make me an unfit mother, just a responsible human being. Besides, Sally is very capable. She can look after him. She looked after me when I was growing up."

"Sally's not his mother," he pointed out. He'd sided with her earlier because he felt a child belonged with its mother. If that mother was going to turn her back on her responsibilities, maybe he would have to rethink his position. "*You* are." He struggled not to let his emotions get the better of him. "And you're abandoning him."

Her eyes grew wide at the accusation. He was angry, she thought. What right did he have to be angry with her? "I am not abandoning him." Marlene stopped abruptly. She was shouting. With a sigh, she lowered her voice. "I'm providing for him."

"If it's a matter of money—"

There was that infernal Travis checkbook. Did they think that they could just throw money at a problem and it would be solved?

"No, it's not a matter of money. It's a matter of pride. My pride. His pride in his mother. This is what I do, and despite the way I got into it, I am damn good at it. I want to hand him something when it comes time for that."

"He won't care." He remembered his own childhood. It was one filled with nannies and boarding schools. "All he'll care about is that you weren't there for him when he needed you."

She raised herself up, angry, hurt. Did he think she was some kind of self-centered monster? "I will always be there for him when he needs me. Now I'll thank you to take your accusations and your gift and leave."

"I'll go, but the gift stays. It's a piece of his heritage, too."

With that, Sullivan turned on his heel and walked to the door. He yanked it open with a jerk and strode out.

Damn, she shouldn't have said that. She was letting her emotions get the better of her. He'd come here with a peace offering, and she was all but burning it because, maybe, some part of her agreed with him. Maybe she *should* be staying home.

Guilt consumed her. "Sullivan," she called after him.

He didn't turn around.

Marlene hurried after him, afraid that if he left now, he would leave forever. Maybe she would regret this later, but she couldn't just let him go like this.

"Sullivan."

"What?" He ground the word out between clenched teeth.

She stopped behind him and laid a hand on his arm. "I'm sorry."

He didn't turn around. "Yeah, so am I."

They were talking about different things; she could feel it. She had no idea what he was sorry about. She only knew what she felt. She was ashamed that she had allowed her guilt and anger to get the better of her.

Marlene slipped her hand into his. "Come back inside."

His own anger cooled in the face of her apology. Still, there were feelings within him that were dangerously close to the surface. Feelings that he couldn't give in to. It would only muddy things up.

Following her, he crossed the threshold then loosened his hand from hers. "Maybe I'd better leave."

Her eyes held his. For the first time, she felt protective of him. That, and something more. Something that had been hovering on the outskirts of her mind for some time. "Now who's running?"

"I never run, Marlene," he told her quietly, feeling his control sliding away. He tried vainly to hold on to it. "Not from anything." Her eyes were playfully mocking him. "Sometimes, though, I just walk away."

She allowed a triumphant smile to grace her mouth. "Like now?"

God, stronger men than he had succumbed to a beautiful woman. He thought about the road to hell and the good intentions it was paved with. From where he stood, it was a clear slide down a chute, straight into the fire.

He took her into his arms. "I should."

Marlene didn't resist. She raised her chin. "Can that be taken up to a vote?"

She smelled good, he thought. The scent was a mixture of expensive perfume and baby powder. It was a heady combination.

He toyed with her hair. "I kind of like dictatorships myself."

Her smile was wide. "So do I. When I'm holding the reins."

He liked the way she fit against him, neatly, as if every curve of her body had a complimentary niche in his. "I noticed that."

"Did you, now?" She could feel the thread of excitement pulling through her. "What else did you notice?"

Everything. The way your breasts rise when you challenge something I've said. The way the sunlight falls into your hair, getting trapped there. Just like me. "That you've got the greatest mouth I've ever seen."

Was it just her, or was the room getting warmer? "Moving or closed?"

"Moving. And not uttering a sound."

Cupping her face in his hands, he brought his mouth down to hers. This time there was passion. Such passion that it rivaled the magnitude of the storm that first night he had brought her home.

His hands dove into her hair, and he dragged her against him. The feel of her body ignited his own. His mouth slanted over hers again and again. He had no idea that he could lose control so quickly. He'd never lost control before.

She'd caught him at a vulnerable moment and made him pay with her ripe mouth and her silken skin.

Lord, but he wanted her. Wanted what he couldn't—what he shouldn't—have.

Blood pounded in his veins, demanding release of the pent-up emotions. It took every fiber of his being to draw back.

"Hey." He blew out a long breath as he tried to focus on her face. "If we're not careful, I'm going to lose what little good sense I have. We can't do this. You can't do this. You just had a baby."

She felt as if she had been bodily tossed into a furnace, and there was only one source of relief. "I'm fine. I went to the doctor today before I met with your father. Except for not being able to produce any milk for the baby, she says I'm fine."

He swept her hair away from her face, framing it again. Her eyes bored into his soul. "You're sure?"

If she didn't do it quickly, she wouldn't be able to do it at all. And she wanted to. Desperately. "I have it in writing."

"I'll read it later." Sullivan picked her up into his arms and turned toward the winding staircase.

Chapter Twelve

The door to Marlene's room stood open. Very gently, Sullivan set her down on the floor, his eyes intent on hers. There was something there, an uncertainty that mirrored his own.

"Second thoughts?"

Marlene shook her head, but there were second thoughts. Thoughts that had to do with Oliver and Sullivan's true intentions. What if all this was just an elaborate ruse? What if it was happening to get her off her guard? To undermine her and somehow use this to prove that she was an unfit mother and get the baby away from her?

She knew men like that existed, knew that her own father had been one of those kinds of men. And yet, looking into Sullivan's eyes, she couldn't make herself believe that he was like that.

Maybe she was a fool, but this pull toward him was so overwhelming she couldn't find the strength to resist.

Damn, this was all wrong. He was allowing too many ends to tangle. And yet, he couldn't stop himself. He didn't have the will to stop himself.

She would have to do that for him if it was to happen.

Sullivan ran his hands along her arms, resting them lightly on her shoulders. His thumbs teased the tender skin along the slopes of her neck. Marlene reacted to his touch even as the tiniest part of her struggled to maintain control.

He saw that, too. Was she afraid of him? Or was there something else she was afraid of? He needed to know. Even as he tried to convince himself of the fact, he knew his reaction to her wasn't merely physical. It was more, so much more that it unnerved him.

It was time for honesty. "Marlene, right now I want you more than I want anything else on this earth, but this won't go any further if you're afraid."

Afraid? Did he think she was afraid of him? Marlene slowly moved her head from side to side. If she was afraid of anything, it was herself and the magnitude of the emotions building within her. She'd never felt anything like this before.

"I'm not." Her denial was firm. And then came the coda. "Exactly."

"Then what, 'exactly'?" He paused, waiting. But she said nothing. She didn't have to. He knew. His voice was low, caressing her, surrounding her. "There's only you and me involved, Marlene. Only you and me in this room. There isn't space for anyone else. No past lovers, no one passing judgments." His eyes were on hers. "No ghosts or specters. I'm not here as Derek's brother or Oliver's son. I'm just Sullivan. And I want you."

She let out a shaky breath. When he touched her like that, he scrambled her senses. She wanted him more than she wanted anyone else in her life.

But what if—?

Tomorrow. She would deal with all her uncertainties tomorrow. She always thought clearer in the morning. All she could think of at this moment in time was him.

His fingers feathered along her face, gentle, coaxing. The ache was building within him even as he struggled to rein it in. "If you want me to stop—"

"No," she said a little too quickly, a little too breathlessly. "I don't."

Marlene looked up into his eyes. Whatever had gone down between them, whatever was to come, at this moment it was exactly as he had said. Sullivan was here with her as himself, not as Robby's uncle, not as his father's emissary. Not as Derek's brother. Just as himself.

And she could deal with that.

Yes, she could more than deal with that. She raised her face to his, her lips curving in a small smile. "Kiss me, Sullivan. Kiss me before we both come to our senses and realize what we're doing."

His eyes washed over her, pulling her to him. "Sense? What's that?"

Dear Lord, but she felt as if she were self-igniting. It was as if all these years, she'd been waiting for him. Only him. She didn't want to talk any more. "Something I seem to have lost along the way."

There was a different world in his arms, a different world than one she'd ever known. And she wanted to be submerged in it.

Very slowly, Sullivan tilted her head back with the crook of his finger under her chin. Her eyes were bright with anticipation. He lightly brushed his lips against hers, stroking the soft column of her neck with his fingertips. He felt her pulse accelerating. He could feel his own heart slamming into his rib cage, eager to meet hers.

The kiss deepened, being drawn out by the need he sensed within her. The need that rose to meet and mingle with his own.

The arousal he felt was incredible.

Once again he was surprised at the fervor with which she responded. The need he tasted on her lips humbled him and broke so many barriers within his own soul. If any doubts of his own lingered, they dissolved. He sensed that all her dreams, all her needs, were locked up within that one kiss.

It took extreme control to bridle his own reaction to her. Not for the world would he risk making her back away now by frightening her, but it felt as if there were explosions going on within his veins. Explosions fueled by urgent demands that had to be kept in check until Marlene was ready. As for himself, he felt as if he'd been ready from the first moment he'd laid eyes on her.

As passionate as she was in his arms, he sensed that she wasn't quite ready yet. His mouth worked over hers again and again, his hands brushing along her body, caressing, gentling, reassuring.

Making her crave.

Making her crazy.

This was joy. This was anticipation and an eagerness she'd only sampled in moderation once or twice before. But each time it had turned into dust and ashes. The promise had never flourished.

This was different. Dear Lord, this was different. Somehow she knew that what lay ahead would not lead to disappointment.

There were desires rumbling through her, climbing on one another like acrobats in a circus, rushing to form a pyramid to the top.

She wanted everything he could give her. Quickly, before her common sense returned and stopped her. She knew that what was unfolding was happening too quickly, that these things took time. She hardly knew him. But somehow, none of that mattered. None of that got in the way.

Eager, her breath backing up in her lungs, Marlene tugged on his shirt, pulling it free of his waistband. Her hands splayed across his bared skin as she burrowed her hands beneath the shirt.

Despite wanting her to continue, Sullivan stilled her hands, holding them in place. She had no idea what she was doing to him. His self-control was being eradicated by the sweep of her fingertips along his skin.

"Hey." His breath skimmed along her throat. "Slow down." Sullivan could feel her pulse fluttering wildly beneath his lips, like the wings of a hummingbird. "We have all night to do this."

His lips curved against her skin. It tickled her even as it sent her blood rushing through her veins. "Or until the next feeding," he amended.

From somewhere, the information seemed to filter in. "That would be in four hours." Her words were thick, her head spinning.

"I can work with that." He raised his head and looked into her eyes. No, this wasn't just another woman making calculations as she entered his arms. There was infinitely much more at stake here. He had no idea if he should even be sitting at the gaming table, but he couldn't help himself. His expression sobered.

"We'll take this one step at a time, Marlene," he promised. "And if you want to stop—"

If she felt like this, like someone on the verge of diving off a cliff into the bracing waters beneath that called to her, how must he feel?

She stared at him in wonder. What sort of a man was he? "You'll stop?"

His hands worked over her shoulders, molding her, seducing her. Seducing himself. He knew he would keep his word, but it would be at a tremendous cost.

"I'll stop. It would probably kill me, but I'll stop."

It was what she wanted to hear, what her soul needed to hear. The uncertainty that had held her in its iron grip seemed to melt like a glacier that had moved into tropical waters.

It was gone.

And she surrendered herself to what was to be. What she wanted to be. Arms twined around his neck, Marlene raised her mouth to his.

With every pass of his hand, every hot, longing touch of his mouth, he created a world for her that robbed her of her breath, her thoughts, her mind. And gave her so much more in return. It gave her a world of sensations. And truths.

He made her discover things about herself she'd never known. She felt wanton, wild, eager. The woman in Sullivan's arms was light-years away from the young girl who had so desperately attempted to curry her father's favor and from the more than competent executive who handily increased her company's profits by giving up a piece of her life.

It was as though she'd been blind all these years and suddenly was being able to see. Bathed in colors, she had no idea what to savor first.

She savored it all. The taste of his mouth, the feel of his hands along her body as he stripped away her clothes, garment by garment, inch by inch until she was no longer wearing anything but happiness, and the sensation of his body, hot, hard, pressed against hers.

She reveled in all of it.

She was eager. Eager to touch him, eager to be shown more. Eager to feel her blood rush and her body hum with a strange music.

With hands that were amazingly steady, she opened the button that held his trousers closed. Sullivan sucked in his breath as she lowered the zipper, her fingers feathering along his torso like rampant kisses raining down on his body. Her fingers were warm, her touch hot. He could barely think.

It amazed him. He could hardly keep up with her. If he had meant to seduce her, as his father had covertly suggested, he found himself now seduced. There was no question that he was no longer in charge of what was transpiring. How could you be in charge of the wind?

Marlene felt like unharnessed energy, a volcano that had been dormant for years, only suddenly to be roused into activity.

She made him feel free. Freer than he'd ever felt in his life. There were no boundaries, no barriers, no limits for him.

Sullivan kicked away the last of his own clothing, his body melding against hers as they rolled along the length of the bed. He fisted his hands in her hair, kissing her mouth over and over again.

A wildness seized him, as if it had telegraphed itself through the medium of her body. It electrified him.

He was afraid of hurting her, of not being able to hold back, and yet he seemed to have no say in it. His body throbbed with demands that she had stoked. She had undone him, taken all the knots that held the package together and ripped them away.

Their limbs tangled as they rolled along her bed, the comforter scrambling beneath them like a large crumpled tissue.

This was too singularly wonderful to be real, like a glorious celebration of life. Like something very important and precious. She could have cried if all her energy hadn't been focused on him.

Marlene buried her fingers in his hair, her mouth eager on his, as she felt his hot body sear against hers.

She arched against him, her hips locking to his, her body begging for entry, for release.

He had wanted to prolong this, to make it last even longer, to show her how it could be. But he was only a man, only so strong, and his own needs slammed into him as her body pressed against him, silently imploring.

Rolling over so that he was looking down into her eyes, he crossed the last threshold and entered. She gasped once against his mouth and then, almost as if she were in a trance, began to move with him in the rhythm he created, a dance that took them both into the clouds.

When the last note faded, Marlene was so awed she felt like crying.

She did. Soft, small tears of happiness.

He felt the moisture against his cheek as it rested against hers. Pivoting up onto his elbows, he looked down at her face, his heart freezing.

She was crying.

Damn, this was exactly what he had wanted to avoid. He shouldn't have lost his head this way. He thought of her condition and was filled with self-disgust. What was he, a rutting pig? She'd just given birth, for God's sake.

"Hey," he whispered as he bracketed her face between his hands. "I didn't hurt you, did I?"

She sniffed once, then slowly moved her head from side to side. "No."

He didn't understand. Something was obviously wrong. "But you're crying."

She didn't think she had enough strength to move anything, but she managed to curve her mouth into a smile. "I always do when I'm happy."

Relieved, Sullivan flicked a finger along her cheek and captured a single tear. He examined the bit of moisture that could bring a man to his knees.

"Then this is a good thing?"

She took a breath, trying to steady her pulse. Her breasts brushed against his chest as they rose and fell. "It's a good thing."

Lovingly, he swept her hair away from her face and just looked at her. She'd taken him completely by surprise, and that rarely ever happened. Warmth spread through him like a huge smile. "I think so, too."

Still watching her, he lightly licked the tear from his fingertip. Then rolling off Marlene, he tucked her against him on the bed.

Because the room was chilly, he drew the comforter over both of them.

She smiled. "You know, it's true what they say."

He had no idea what she was talking about, only that the sound of her voice against his ear was soothing. The feel of her warm breath was anything but. How could he want her again so soon? And yet he did, with every fiber of his being. The woman was part witch, and he was more than willing to have her weave her spell on him.

He smiled down at her. "And what is it that they say?"

"That still waters run deep." She tilted her head back so that their eyes met. "Who would have ever thought to look at you that there was all this untapped passion just beneath the surface?"

Not him, that was for sure. "Obviously you can't judge a book by its cover."

Her grin widened. "Obviously."

He couldn't remember when he had felt this way. He'd had women, but she was woman with a capital *W.* He had no desire to leave, the way he normally did. No desire to leave her bed. Ever. "You were incredible."

Perhaps too incredible, he added silently. He needed time to clear his head. There were feelings within him that had been touched, feelings that he'd never quite experienced before. Feelings that pointed in a direction he'd never taken. Sullivan wasn't quite sure he was ready to follow that route just yet, if ever.

And yet, here she was, supple, wanting. His, at least for tonight. It was too much to walk away from.

He shifted, pressing a kiss to her shoulder. Her eyes grew smoky with fresh desire. He felt his own growing.

"So, what do we do now?" she asked in a breathy whisper. She knew what she wanted to do.

"We do it again."

Her lips spread into a smile that had its roots in her soul. "Again?"

He nodded, attempting to look solemn. He failed. "Again. Until we get it right."

She could feel the breath backing up in her lungs as his hand gently played over her nipple, teasing it until it was hard. Keeping her voice steady wasn't easy. "How long do you think that'll take?"

"All night, if we're lucky."

She wanted to be lucky. Very, very lucky.

It had been one hell of an incredible night. He'd never made love to a woman and fed a baby, then gone back to making love all in the same night. One for the books, he mused, watching Marlene sleep beside him as dawn nestled in between the slats of the soft blue blinds.

She was one for the books. In a volume all her own. The title would be a question mark.

He didn't want to get up and leave, which was precisely why he had to. This was going too fast for him, and he had to put brakes on the toboggan before he went over the precipice. He had to think.

Of something else besides Marlene.

He thought of slipping quietly out of bed, but he couldn't bear leaving her just yet. She'd been too alone most of her life. They both had.

Sullivan leaned over and pressed a kiss to her shoulder. She stirred. A moment later, her eyes opened, wide with wonder. And something more. He refused to classify it just yet. It was a lot better for both of them if he didn't.

Things were getting much too complicated as it was. And they were getting more so every moment he lingered.

"It's morning," he whispered.

"So it is." She stretched and her body rubbed against his.

Damn, but he wanted her again. He would have thought that after last night, he would be sated instead of inspired. "Maybe I'd better leave before Sally gets up."

Sally. The name brought back images of a walking frown. Sally would probably call out the National Guard if she saw Sullivan coming out of her bedroom.

"You have a point." Sullivan began to rise, but she pulled him back. "Of course, she sleeps like a rock when she takes cold medication." A smile danced along her lips. "And she took cold medication." *Bless her.*

Marlene dug her palms against the bed, raising herself to a sitting position against the headboard. She pulled the sheet up with her. It rested invitingly along her outline and she knew it. "Of course, if you want to leave this early—"

Want? The word was tangled up with visions of her in his arms. With needs that were bursting to resurface again. He struggled with the urge to pull away the sheet and nuzzle her. "I really should..."

Marlene felt cold. And bereft. There was no regret, the way she thought there would be. Not about last night, only about this morning...and that he was leaving. "Is this how it goes, the morning after?"

"Yes. Life has to go on." *No matter what it had in store.*

Sullivan reached for what was now a very rumpled shirt at the foot of the bed.

As he slipped one arm into the sleeve, he looked over his shoulder at her. Her hair was loose, splayed about her bare shoulders, begging for his hands to run through it. And then there was the rest of her, barely hidden beneath the sheet that had slipped off and was now hugging the swell of her breasts.

He felt his gut tighten.

"Oh, the hell with it." Pulling his arm free, Sullivan tossed aside the shirt and came back to bed.

He'd just drawn her into his arms when her alarm clock went off. He thought of shutting it down now, but opted for later. His hands were full at the moment.

"You make bells ring, Marlene."

Her eyes had drifted shut with the lazy, exciting pleasure that had overtaken her as his mouth found hers. They flew open now as his words and the sound belatedly registered. "The alarm!"

"That's what it is." Maybe he should shut it down. He reached behind him with one hand, blindly searching the night stand for it.

But for Marlene reality and responsibility clawed their way to the top. "No, I'll be late for work." She had forgotten all about that. He'd chased everything out of her head.

But she had already placed him on a path that he had no control over changing. He skimmed his lips along the side of her throat, making her tremble even as she tried to drive a wedge between them.

"Bosses are never late. Work starts when they get there." He grinned. "You taught me that, remember?"

She had said something along those lines the night of Cynthia Breckinridge's party. Trust him to use her own words against her. She felt giddy. Her breathing was ragged again. It was as if he took away all her air and substituted stardust. "You're making it very difficult to think."

"The feeling is mutual." He lowered his mouth, his tongue skimming her nipples now. Marlene could feel her stomach muscles tightening like a clenched fist. "I'm doing it to both of us."

She was losing the battle, and she didn't care. Marlene slid her shoulders back down onto the bed. "You don't want to think?"

He hovered over her, his body poised, his mind already possessing her. "Not right now."

But he thought later. He thought about her a great deal. About the way she'd felt in his arms. Like heaven. His own piece of heaven.

And he thought about the fact that for the first time since he could remember, he was in way over his head. He was going to have to swim toward shore. He knew he couldn't sort this out until his feet touched bottom.

The best thing to do right now was not think about her at all. Not as a woman. Only as the mother of his nephew. The nephew he was supposed to return to the fold. For his father's sake. And quite possibly, for Derek's.

He glanced at his reflection in the office window. And what of his sake? What was it that *he* wanted?

He wasn't so sure he knew. Until now, he had just wanted to be a success. To run the Travis Corporation to the best of his ability and build it up to be even more prosperous than it was.

He'd never thought of himself as having a wife. Never thought of really going through life except on his own. And there was no reason to think of it now, he insisted, as he turned his chair around to face his desk again. He had come to terms with his life, and he intended for it to remain just the way it was.

The word *lonely* whispered through his mind, but he managed to block it out.

Chapter Thirteen

Who would have ever thought it? Marlene smiled to herself like someone cherishing a precious secret. She was actually watching the clock. Some change. But then, it had been a month for changes. Important changes.

Marlene was aware of glancing at her watch at least a dozen times that day, perhaps more. And it was never to see how much time she had left until her next meeting, but because she was counting the minutes until she was free to go home.

Free to fly home to diapers, to just barely grasping fingers and to what she would swear—no matter what Sally said to the contrary about gas—was a drooly smile.

She'd been back to work for three days, and each day it was the same thing. It was no longer a matter of arriving early and staying late the way she had done for so many years under her father's scrutiny and his grueling, high expectations. Now the process was reversed. She arrived late and left early. It was a matter of priorities. Hers had changed drastically.

She was no longer leaving from something but leaving *to* something. She was leaving work to go to her son.

It made all the difference in the world.

Time, she thought, saving the last bit of work on her computer. It had been a long day, and she couldn't wait to place it out of mind.

Flipping the locks closed on her imported leather briefcase, the one her father's secretary had signed his name to for her graduation, Marlene rose.

She felt a smile welling up, spreading like golden honey all through her, leaving no room for anything else, no doubts, no negative feelings. No thoughts of work.

Wasn't life funny? she mused, pausing.

It was a strange thing to suddenly find yourself born at thirty, but she had been. It wasn't just a rebirth, it was more. In retrospect, she realized that she hadn't been really alive until now.

Her life was still hectic, still teeming with so much activity that it was bursting at the seams. Maybe even more so than before. But now she felt a satisfaction that had nothing to do with ads splashed across billboards or displayed within the bindings of a magazine. Nothing to do with awards or the ethereal rewards of knowing a job had been well done.

Now her satisfaction derived from something more. It came from a small, vulnerable human being. Her contentment was locked up in the feel of a small child's head nestled against her own as she burped him. Or simply when she held him.

Her father would have thought she'd lost her mind. Her father, she thought with more than a trace of sadness, never knew what he had missed. This was what it was all about, not accolades, not money, not connections. It was about who you loved—and who loved you back.

Marlene looked at the gold-framed photograph on her desk. It was a close-up of Robby at two weeks. Sally had propped Robby up so that he appeared to be sitting. He was wearing his sailor suit, and her heart melted just to look at him. The photograph had been taken the day before she returned to work.

The afternoon, she added silently, remembering, before she had stepped into an entirely different world. A world with Sullivan. Now, as always, she struggled to place that in perspective. She knew what they had was just temporary, even though he had called several times and sent more gifts over for Robby. Robby was what was permanent in her life.

She brushed her fingertips over the glass. The joy in having a child was absolutely unimaginable.

She'd been right to do this, to have a child at this juncture in her life, before it became too late. Marlene set her mouth grimly. And nothing Oliver Travis had in mind was going to change that.

Oliver made her think of Sullivan again. He looked nothing like his father. She sincerely hoped that he *was* nothing like his father. More than that, she hoped that the night they had shared had not been part of an intricate plan to win custody of Robby.

She pushed the thought from her mind. Sullivan couldn't be that deceptive. She would know if he was. Somehow, she assured herself, she would know.

Marlene closed her eyes for a moment, reliving that night. Warmth shimmered through her just as it had then. She hadn't realized she was capable of such feelings, that desire and passion existed within her to such depths.

You're never too old to learn, she thought with a bittersweet smile.

She ran her hand along the desk top. Yes, a great many things had changed. Only a few months ago, she'd sat here long after everyone else had left, finishing one more idea, structuring another. Preparing for a meeting. Working hard and believing that it was a life. And it had been. But it had been her father's life, not hers. Now she no longer felt as if she were only defined by the quality of her work. There was no longer that compulsion to relentlessly keep at something until she put a campaign to bed.

Now she had a son to put to bed. Nothing else would ever be more important than that.

Humming, she picked up her briefcase and crossed to the door.

Wanda looked up as Marlene walked out of her office. "Going home?"

Marlene nodded. She knew exactly what was going on in Wanda's mind. "There's nothing going on here that everyone else can't handle. Or that can't keep until the morning."

"Nothing at all," Wanda agreed. "Go home, Ms. Bailey, and enjoy that son of yours while he's still young." She glanced at a framed picture of her own family. "God knows they grow up fast enough."

"So they tell me." She smiled warmly at the woman. "Good night, Wanda."

As she turned to leave, Marlene barely missed colliding with Joe Stamos, an artist who had started with the company the same week she officially had. Over the years, she had found his judgment to be flawless. He had a happy aptitude for simplicity and taste. When her father had died and the reins had fallen into her hands, she promoted Joe to a junior partner. Her father had never had partners. He hadn't believed in them. But she did. In more ways, she realized, than one.

Joe's lips spread wide, giving her a slightly gap-toothed smile. "Hey, Marlene, Abernathy liked your ideas for that radio spot showcasing his dealership. It's a go. The spot starts airing next Monday."

"Was there ever any doubt?"

There was a time the news would have elated her. Now it just slid into perspective. Winning the high-profile account meant more clout for her company, which translated to more power in negotiating and more security for her and the people who worked for her.

More security for Robby—if he wanted the company some day. And if he didn't, well, that was okay, too. She wanted him to be happy just being himself. A lesson, she thought, she'd learned from her father—in reverse.

Joe noticed her briefcase. "You leaving?" He raised an eyebrow in surprise.

"Yes." She was in a hurry to get going. "Call me at home if there's an emergency. Otherwise, I'll see you in the morning."

Joe nodded, closing his mouth.

"You know, Marlene, motherhood certainly agrees with you."

Marlene turned around and saw her sister standing almost directly behind her. Nicole wore a light gray cape thrown over her shoulders in deference to the weather and a huge, satisfied smile on her lips. There was a very festive Christmas wreath slung over her forearm.

Homemade, Marlene guessed. The wreath had Nicole's touch written all over it. She had an unerring eye for color and blending. Her sister had definitely shifted gears and changed direction. She was light-years away from that wild child she'd seemed so bent on becoming only a few short years ago.

"I think so." Marlene eyed the wreath. "Taken to selling wreaths from door-to-door, have you?"

"Very funny. I brought you a gift for the holidays." Nicole handed her sister the wreath. "Looks like I arrived just in time. Five minutes later and I would have missed you." Her relief was sincere. Traveling anywhere these days was a challenge, and extra trips were as wanted as an extra ten pounds.

Marlene studied the wreath more closely. Nicole had dried and lacquered the tiny berries individually. She acted offhandedly about life in general, but Marlene knew that Nicole was a stickler for perfection.

"It's beautiful, Nic." Marlene leaned over and brushed her lips against Nicole's cheek. "Thanks." Marlene wore the wreath like an oversize bracelet as she picked up her briefcase again. "C'mon." She hooked her elbow through Nicole's. "I'll walk you back to the elevator. I'm on my way home."

"Home?" She'd thought that Marlene was on her way to an early dinner with a client. "You?" Nicole placed her hand to her chest and gasped dramatically. She would have stumbled backward if there had been twenty-five pounds less of her. "But it's not even dark yet."

"Wise guy. I know that. But I just don't want to spend all my time here anymore." Marlene led the way toward the elevator. "I've got more important things to do these days."

Nicole fell into step beside her. She looked enviously at her sister. Marlene had already gotten her figure back. God, she hoped it would be that easy for her. "Like changing diapers?"

"Yes." Even that didn't bother her, now that she had gotten the hang of it. The first few attempts had resulted in Robby wiggling out of his diaper, or said diaper sliding off as soon as it was damp.

Nicole pressed the down button. She gave Marlene a knowing look. "Anything else?"

She could never keep anything from Nicole. Somehow, she always seemed to know. A smile played on her lips. "I don't know what you mean."

Nicole laughed as the elevator doors opened. "Sure you do. In my experience, that sort of contented look comes along only when there's a man involved."

Marlene got on the elevator. Nicole followed, treading heavily. She was beginning to feel as if she were leaving dents in the floor with every step she took.

"Your experience is . . ." Marlene paused. What was the sense of pretending? She felt too happy to lie, and she wanted to share this feeling with someone. Who better than Nicole? "Absolutely right."

Satisfaction was stamped all over Nicole's small features. "Thought so." She'd never seen Marlene as happy as she was right now. Whoever Marlene was involved with, the man certainly had her approval, sight unseen. "Is it anyone I know?"

Marlene was about to say no, then remembered that they had met in her hospital room. "Only by sight."

That took in a lot of men. Then it came to her. The elevator stopped, but Nicole remained where she was, stunned. "You don't mean..." Her voice trailed off as her eyes grew larger.

Marlene lifted her shoulders and let them drop nonchalantly. Because Sullivan was uppermost in her mind, she assumed he was in Nicole's, too. "Maybe."

Nicole's mouth dropped open. "Sullivan?" she whispered in disbelief. The man was utterly drop-dead gorgeous.

Marlene's grin gave Nicole her answer before she said a word. "Yes."

Nicole couldn't bring herself to believe it. She followed Marlene from the elevator down the hall, hardly aware of her surroundings. "You and he . . . ?"

Marlene nodded. She pushed open the glass door and held it with her back while Nicole walked out. The early evening air was chilly. Marlene hunched her shoulders slightly. "He and I."

There was a huge ache traveling up the length of Nicole's spine. She pressed her hand to the small of her back to ease it as she studied her sister's face. Marlene really did look happy enough to burst. She thought of their last conversation regarding the senior Travis.

"Then everything's okay?"

Marlene turned to look at her. "In what way?"

"About his father?" Nicole looked at her hopefully. "He's backing off?"

Marlene raised her chin unconsciously. "That still remains to be seen."

But Marlene didn't sound as beleaguered as she'd once been. Things seemed to be under control. Nicole grasped the handrail as she went down the six steps to the parking lot. "Well, at least with Sullivan in your corner, you have an ace up your sleeve."

He was hardly that. She hadn't worked any of this out satisfactorily for herself yet. Seeing her sister's car, Marlene shook her head as she began walking in that direction. "Does being pregnant make you talk in clichés?"

Nicole laughed, not taking offense. "No, but being pregnant makes me very, very hungry."

Marlene looked at her, puzzled as to where that had come from.

She'd forgotten, Nicole thought. Typical. "Dr. Pollack's party tomorrow, remember?" Nicole could feel her appetite springing to life just at the thought of it. "Rumor has it that the restaurant where she's holding it has a cook who performs miracles in the kitchen daily."

Marlene stopped at the white T-bird she'd forced on Nicole as a birthday present the year before. "I'll be there," she promised.

Nicole unlocked the door and turned to look at Marlene before beginning the arduous task of getting in. "Significant others are invited, too. Why don't you bring Sullivan along?"

She didn't want to jeopardize anything by placing too much emphasis on it. "He's not a 'significant other,' yet."

Who did Marlene think she was fooling? "Isn't he? From that look on your face, I'd say that he seems pretty significant to you."

She shrugged, her shoulders moving beneath the red wool winter jacket. "Maybe, but I don't push."

"Yeah, right." Nicole laughed. "Who are you, and what have you done with my sister, the overachiever?"

"Very funny." She nodded toward the car. "Drive carefully, Nic."

"Will do."

Nicole attempted to hug Marlene, but it wasn't easy. Nothing was easy these days. Her bulk got in the way of everything, throwing her off. She backed away, relieved that she hadn't squashed the wreath.

Nicole looked down at her stomach. "I can't wait until I don't feel as if I'm carrying around the entire Raiders football team inside of me."

How well she knew the feeling. Marlene patted her sister's stomach. "Less than a month to go, Nic."

Nicole sighed loudly. "Not soon enough for me."

Bracing herself, Nicole angled in behind the steering wheel. She had the seat back as far as she could and still be able to reach the pedals. But the wheel still managed to rub against her abdomen. It felt as if she had always been pregnant. And would always be doomed to remain that way.

Marlene nodded knowingly. "I know that tune." She closed the door for Nicole, then stepped away from the car. Her own was parked near the building. "Hang in there, Nicole."

What choice did she have in the matter? "Yeah." This too shall pass, Nicole told herself, as she pulled out of the slot marked Guest Parking Only.

Marlene hurried off to her car.

* * *

Sullivan sighed, dragging a hand through his hair. It fell into his eyes, obstructing his vision. Just like Marlene obstructed the clarity of his thinking, he thought, leaving his office.

Taking out his car keys, Sullivan got in behind the wheel of his car. He felt unusually agitated. He'd been trying to rid his mind of Marlene all morning. It only seemed to make matters worse.

He started his car, then paused, thinking. Maybe he would take a drive over to Vesuvio's. The ambiance in the small, intimate restaurant might help to soothe him. It had been a hell of a day, and he could do with a glass of wine and a good meal in a place where there were no demands on him, no decisions to make beyond which entrée to select.

A man could be alone there with his thoughts without really being lonely.

"Vesuvio's it is," he murmured to himself, pulling out of the lot.

The Italian restaurant was his intended destination as he threaded his car onto the road. Vesuvio's, then home. Just how he wound up going south on Pacific Coast Highway rather than north he wasn't quite sure. But it was as if his car were in direct confrontation with his mind. And the car wanted to head south.

To Spyglass Hill.

To Marlene.

Though they had talked several times and he had sent over more gifts for the baby, he hadn't seen her since the night he had made love with her. His schedule, mercifully, had gotten even more demanding. Everyone seemed to want to finish up before Christmas. So he allowed himself to be taken with the tide. All but his mind, where Marlene was firmly entrenched.

He thought of her every night. And every morning. It was getting so that there was little room for anything else.

Sullivan surrendered to his instincts. He drove the winding path up to her house and hoped she would understand. He sure as hell didn't.

He knew he shouldn't do this. Whatever existed between them wasn't going to lead anywhere. There were just too many complicating factors in the way. His father expected him to obtain custody, and he was still hopeful that it could be done without the publicity of a trial. But in order to do that, what there was between Marlene and him would be destroyed.

What *was* there between him and Marlene? he questioned silently, resisting the larger picture. Only a few moments...

And a hell of a lot of emotion.

He would work on that tomorrow, too, he thought, his hands tightening on the steering wheel. Right now, he just wanted to see her.

He'd left the window on the driver's side open. The cold air whipped along his face as his mind wandered. Christmas was coming soon, and he thought of Marlene. She was probably the kind of person who made a big deal out of the holidays. So had he before he'd grown up and taken on responsibilities.

A bittersweet sadness seeped in, making him long for the boy he had been. Before he'd become his brother's keeper. And his father's right-hand man.

Damn, what was the matter with him? He'd never felt this way before. He'd just taken life in stride and did the best that he could. He'd never chafed against his role in the scheme of things. It was all the fault of a small, wide-eyed woman and her carefully planned offspring. She was to blame. She had all but uprooted his life.

Hell, she *had* uprooted it.

He didn't want to think about that. Didn't want to think about anything. He felt too tired to think. There was nothing good to fix his thoughts on.

Except for Marlene.

It was as if he were a ship, lost at sea in a fog that insisted on clinging to the waters, and she was the beacon, her light slicing through the murky cotton, guiding him to shore.

He had to be tired, he thought, bringing the car to a stop in front of Marlene's house. He was waxing poetic. He *never* waxed poetic.

He noted the lively colored Christmas wreath on her front door. The door itself was gift wrapped. He shook his head. He'd been right, she was the type to make a big deal out of Christmas. Sullivan found that rather charming.

"He sent over another gift today," Sally told Marlene. She stood with her arms crossed before her small chest, her face puckered into a frown. She watched as Marlene made strange noises at her son.

Marlene turned her head to look at Sally. She'd already noticed the new package under the tree and read the tag. "By 'he' I take it you mean Sullivan."

Sally nodded her head. "That's the one. If you ask me, he's trying to buy you."

The baby looked as if he were ready to fall asleep already. She'd only had an hour with him. With a sigh, Marlene began to rock the boy. "I wasn't asking."

Sally snorted. "That's why I volunteered the information."

Marlene rose, the baby nestled against her. The doorbell rang. "You should know me better than to think I could be bought that way."

Sally shrugged. "All right, not bought. Rented, maybe."

The bell rang again. "The door, Sally. Get the door."

"I hear it, I hear it." Sally muttered something unintelligible under her breath as she crossed to the door and opened it. "Well, speak of the devil." Sally stepped back, holding the door open, though it was obvious that she would have rather slammed it. "Now he's here in the flesh."

Marlene strode over quickly, gently elbowing the smaller woman out of the way. She smiled at him. An adolescent flutter began in her stomach. "Hi."

Sullivan felt as if he had swallowed his tongue. Marlene was standing there, barefoot and in jeans, wearing a baggy fishnet sweater that was quickly acquiring a small glob of recycled formula on one shoulder courtesy of the infant she held there.

She looked absolutely radiant.

He tried to tell himself that seeing her this way didn't excite him, but he had never learned to be an accomplished liar. Not like Derek.

He could feel Sally's glare penetrating his skin. Not, he supposed, that he really blamed her. "I was just in the neighborhood..."

Liar, Marlene thought. She began to relax. He wasn't here as an emissary. One look at his face told her that. He was here because he wanted to be. Or didn't, as the case might be. She could relate to that emotional ambivalence very well. He had her feeling as if she didn't know if she was coming or going.

"Come on in," Marlene urged, stepping back. She effectively blocked Sally with her body, forcing the woman into the background. Marlene patted Robby's back as the baby hiccuped.

The baby was trying to eat her sweater, Sullivan noticed. Reaching over, he tugged the wool out of the infant's mouth. His fingers brushed against Marlene's breast. Instantly, their eyes met and held as electricity snapped through the air between them.

He dropped his hand to his side and cleared his throat. "You're beginning to look natural that way, with a baby attached to you."

Marlene grinned as she pushed a wayward strand of hair behind one ear. "More importantly, I'm becoming very good at doing things with one hand." She gestured toward the silver-and-blue garland that wound along the staircase banister. "I did part of that with one hand."

Out of the corner of her eye, she saw Sally roll her eyes. Sally was standing to one side, staring at Sullivan like a watchful guard dog, waiting for him to make one wrong move, to say one wrong thing.

The garland sagged in places and was hardly the work of someone who'd had the time to fuss. Decorating, Sullivan thought, as it should be, reflecting love rather than expertise.

Slowly, the awkwardness slipped from him like a cloak dropping to the floor and he laughed. "It shows."

Marlene took a step back and appraised the banister critically. A frown played on her lips. He was right. "It does."

Very carefully, he smoothed out the tiny furrow between her brows with the tip of his finger. "Christmas decorating isn't supposed to look professional. That's for department stores, not families."

She shrugged. "This is just my second Christmas. I'll get better."

He doubted that. She was close to perfect now. Sullivan kept his observation to himself.

"Let me take the baby." Sally's offer came across more like a demand. She fixed her glare on Sullivan even as she took the tiny bundle from Marlene. "You two might disturb him with your talking."

As Sally left the room, she made Sullivan feel as if she were taking her charge to a haven away from him.

He nodded toward the banister, picking up the threads of their conversation. "Your father didn't celebrate Christmas?"

Her mouth curved, but it was curiously unlike a smile. "Oh, he celebrated it all right. In a big way. For show. There was always a team of professionals decorating everything that didn't move. I did that." She gestured at the ten-foot Christmas tree she had put up in the family room. The large silver star almost touched the top of the vaulted ceiling. "Not for show, but for Robby."

There was no missing the pride in her voice. Crossing to the tree, Sullivan noted that it was artificial. She was playing it safe, he thought. Real trees could burn with a speed that took a person's breath away. "I take it you didn't do that using only one hand."

"No, I did that last night while the baby was asleep. With Sally."

He couldn't visualize the small, acid-tongued woman decorating a Christmas tree.

There was a small pile of thin, rectangular boxes on the coffee table. The light caught the silver tinsel peeking out of the top box. It gleamed like small strands of fire.

"The tree isn't finished yet," she told him.

"Oh?"

She nodded. "Needs tinsel." Marlene gestured toward the boxes. "You can help me throw it."

Sullivan shoved his hands into his pockets. He couldn't remember the last time he had decorated a Christmas tree. "I'm not much at tinsel throwing."

She pretended to appraise his arm. "It doesn't take much to pitch strands." She glanced at his expression. For some reason, he didn't seem to want to decorate. Marlene shrugged. "Suit yourself." She paused, thinking. She'd just finished feeding Robby, but hadn't had time to eat herself. "Have you had dinner yet?"

He thought of the aborted attempt to drive to Vesuvio's and tried not to smile. "No, I—"

She nodded toward the kitchen. "Neither have I. C'mon, I'll make us some sandwiches."

He said, "Don't trouble yourself," but followed her into the kitchen. The mention of food had caused his stomach to pinch.

"No trouble," she promised. "Roast beef all right with you?" she asked over her shoulder as she took inventory of the refrigerator contents. "It's my favorite."

He smiled as he sat down on the stool beside the counter. "Roast beef is fine."

They brought the tray of sandwiches back into the family room. Setting it down on the coffee table, Marlene decided to have another go at him, to try to convince him to relax. Maybe if he did, then she would. Something was going on inside of her, and she wanted desperately to sort it out. And he was the key.

Perching on the arm of the sofa, she picked up half a sandwich and began to nibble slowly, studying his profile. "What are you doing here?"

He raised his eyes to hers. "I keep asking myself the same question."

Her eyes encouraged him. "And what answer did you come up with?"

He could have told her a dozen different things, debating over which reason to choose. He went with the truth. "That I like being with you."

Her smile widened. "Good answer. Keep going."

He picked up a napkin and wiped his lips. "I think I've gone further than I intended to already."

She cocked her head, trying to hear nuances in his voice. "Regrets?"

"No." He thought of his life and the narrow path he'd taken. "Well, maybe a few. But they don't have anything to do with you."

He'd said as much as he was willing to right now, she thought. She nodded at the second half of his sandwich. "Eat."

He wasn't as hungry as he had thought. At least, not for food. "I'd rather do something else."

She could feel her blood beginning to rush in anticipation. *Idiot.* "Like?"

He pulled her down from her perch, onto his lap. "Like kiss you."

His lips covered hers. Marlene laced her arms around his neck, allowing herself to go with the feeling that instantly arose at his touch.

It felt as if white lightning had been released in her veins. An urgency began to build within her, culminating in her loins. Her arms tightened around his neck. "Mmm."

His feeling exactly, he thought. His head was already swimming. With effort, he leaned his head back, grinning. "Is it me, or was that a tad more heartfelt than usual?"

"It was." Her eyes danced. "But that's because there's a trace of mayonnaise on your lips." She lightly flicked her tongue along his lips and was pleased as she felt him shiver. "I love mayonnaise."

God, she could do things to him he hadn't even imagined possible. And she did it all without knowing. "I'll have to remember that." Fire flashed through him, consuming him, needing fuel. Thoughts of today and tomorrow, of things done and things needing to be done, disappeared.

All there was, was now.

"I'm not hungry any more," he told her, vocalizing his earlier thoughts. "Not for food."

"Then for what?" Her voice was thick.

His smile was seductive as it seeped into her soul. "Guess."

"I'm very bad at guessing." Sullivan's hands played along her back. Marlene arched against him. "Why don't you show me?"

Chapter Fourteen

Marlene felt herself quickly sinking into the hot, steamy world that Sullivan seemed so adept at creating for her. All it took was the taste of his mouth, the touch of his hand along her body, and she was on the road to becoming completely lost.

And then it came to her like a message streaked across the sky.

So this is what it felt like. This was what being in love was like. Without knowing exactly when and how, she had completely lost her heart. One moment it was hers, and the next, it was not. It was surrendered without a single shot being fired, a single ounce of resistance being exerted to stem the tide.

If it was gone, she knew how to make the most of what she had. And she intended to make the most of the time she had with Sullivan. She knew that it wouldn't be forever and if that hurt, she wouldn't think of it now. There would be ample time for that later.

Feeling as if she were more than a little intoxicated, Marlene moved her mouth from Sullivan's. "You know what I'd really like?"

He ran his hands languidly along the outline of her body. None of the women he had been with had ever aroused this tender, protective feeling within him that he felt toward Marlene. Not one of them had made him actually feel sensations that transcended the pleasures of the flesh and whispered along his soul.

He smiled, confident he already knew the answer. "No, what?"

Her eyes were laughing, giving birth to doubt within him. "To see you throw tinsel." The surprised look on Sullivan's face delighted her. She'd caught him completely off guard.

His brows drew together as he studied her. "Is this some sort of kinky fantasy of yours, or are you actually being serious?"

A fantasy. Why not? "Maybe, of sorts." Her heart beat a little faster. "And for the record, I'm being very serious."

With one hand pressed against his chest to hold him back, or maybe just to mark her place, Marlene leaned over and picked up the top box of tinsel from the coffee table. She held it up to him, waiting. The strands gleamed before him like silver dreams.

"My father always insisted that everything had to be just so for his guests. That's why he had the tree professionally decorated. I doubt if he ever experienced a desire to do it himself even as a child." Marlene frowned as she remembered. "Strands had to be hung so that they 'looked like icicles, not balled up foil.'"

The quote belonged to her father. He'd sternly lectured her the time she had slipped into the room where the decorators were working and had attempted to help. She was nine and so hurt at being unceremoniously ushered from the room. Robby had taken her aside and told her not to mind. That someday he would have a tree, and then she could decorate it with him. She'd never gotten the chance, she thought now, holding back tears that suddenly threatened to emerge. Robby had died that summer.

Sullivan sensed her sharp stab of pain. "What's the matter?"

She shook her head, dismissing it. She didn't want to talk about her brother. Not yet. "Nothing."

But there *was* something wrong, something she wouldn't share. He felt shut out and called himself a fool for feeling that way. It still didn't change things.

If throwing tinsel meant that much to her, he couldn't find it in his heart to deny her something so harmless. "Okay, if that's what you want, we'll throw tinsel at the tree."

He stood up with the box of tinsel she'd given him and walked over to the tree. He looked uncertain, as if he'd never done this before. Ripping the box open, he took out a handful of strands and threw them. They all landed on one branch, settling along a blue-and-white Christmas ball like a heavy silver parenthesis.

Marlene came up beside him. She pulled strands free from the box he was still holding.

"Wimp. Is that the best you can do?" She flung a large fistful at the tree and it drizzled down, silver rain falling in slow motion.

He held the box out to her as she took more strands. "I thought the idea behind this was not to be criticized for the way you decorate."

She grinned, her eyes crinkling. "For *me* not to be criticized."

He handed her more tinsel. The box empty, Sullivan opened another and flung a few strands toward the top. "Isn't that a little bit unfair?"

"Yeah." The grin, light and airy, reached her eyes and sparkled. "But it's my tree. That lets me make the rules."

Standing on her toes, she matched him, throw for throw. Hers landed approximately at the same level as his. She looked very pleased with herself.

He found that inexplicably irresistible. Everything about the way she affected him made no logical sense. But for now, he stopped looking for answers. It was enough just to be here with her and enjoy her. He couldn't recall the last Christmas season he'd enjoyed—the last one that had meant something to him.

The tree was top-heavy in tinsel. Sullivan purposely threw the next handful toward the branches on the bottom. "Correct me if I'm wrong, but isn't that how dictatorships evolve?"

She laughed again as she threw another large handful. "Quite possibly."

They went through three boxes in approximately five minutes. Marlene picked up the last box and pulled out another fistful of silver. She held it in her hand, debating its final destination. Her eyes slanted toward Sullivan. Then, in one swift move, she threw some tinsel at him.

It landed in his hair. He brushed it off, sending it wafting down to the rug. "You missed."

"No, I didn't."

She made him feel like a kid without responsibilities. It was incredible. "If you're going to play dirty..."

There was a mischievous gleam in his eyes as he took a fistful of tinsel out of the box. Suddenly, he grabbed Marlene by the waist with his other hand. She squirmed, laughing, trying to get free as he rubbed the tinsel into her hair and along her face.

Unable to pull away, Marlene grabbed the remaining tinsel from his hand and shoved it down the front of his shirt.

Between the tinsel that had missed the tree and fallen on the floor and the heap that had just been exchanged in the minibattle, there were more strands on the rug than there were on the tree.

His hands locked around her hips, Sullivan held her comfortably against him. "You're going to have to clean this up, you know."

Marlene looked around at the shining mess. Except that it didn't really look like a mess anymore. Somewhere along the line, order had ceased to be as important as it had once been to her.

She laughed, nestling against him. She could feel his body calling to hers, wanting her. It was the most wonderful sensation she could imagine. "I know, but it was worth it."

Lightly, he passed his hand along her cheek. How had she come to mean so much to him so quickly? She truly made him feel like a kid, free to be happy. Free to do nothing at all. To laugh and throw tinsel.

Damn, he was beginning to sound sentimentally sloppy.

Tomorrow. He would stop feeling like this tomorrow. But not now. Now was for far more important things.

Shifting, his body touching hers, he saw the flash of desire in her eyes. "I meant the tinsel you deposited on me."

"That's easy enough to take care of." Her eyes on his, Marlene unbuttoned his shirt. Her fingers lightly brushed against his chest, dislodging the tinsel. It fell between them. Some reached the floor, some clung to their clothes.

The corners of his mouth lifted sensuously. "I think some of the strands got caught."

Marlene looked at the wide, smooth planes of his chest. Splaying her hand across the hard ridges, she pressed her palms against his pectorals. She could feel his heart beating faster, and she smiled.

"I don't see any."

The smile on his mouth slipped up into his eyes and down into his soul. Cupping her hips, he pulled her against him until there was no room for even a whisper. "Maybe you're not looking in the right places."

Her eyes dipped lower.

Damn, but she was sexy when she looked like that, he thought, losing the edge on his control.

"Oh."

"Yes, 'oh.'" His easy, low tone belied the desire that raged just beneath the surface. He wanted her, Lord but he wanted her. Passion drummed impatiently within him like a wild mustang pawing the ground, waiting for the gate to be flung open, allowing him the freedom to escape from his confining corral.

"Well," Marlene said loftily, her own heart beating madly in every pulse point in her body, "If that's the case, I would say we need a slightly less trafficked place to tidy you up."

He couldn't wait to get her out of her clothes and into his arms. It was all the covering he felt she needed. "My thoughts, exactly. How about your room?"

"How about my room?" she echoed, her voice husky as she hooked her arm through his. Sullivan led the way to the staircase.

Realizing that she was still holding a few strands of tinsel in her hand, she drizzled them over his head as they went up the stairs. They streaked his hair. "You know, you look good in tinsel."

He stopped on the landing. Inclining his head, he kissed her fleetingly. Anything more and the reins of control would completely slip from his hands. And he wanted this to last, to stretch through the night.

"So do you. As a matter of fact, I can envision you in tinsel. High heels and tinsel, nothing else." He rolled the image over in his mind and smiled broadly. "Now there's a fantasy."

Brazenly, falling back on the emotions that he had released within her, Marlene twined her arms around Sullivan's neck and sealed her mouth to his.

Tongues met, tangled, fueling the fire that needed no fuel to ignite. Her head fell back and she looked at him as she breathed, "Reality is much more exciting. As long as it includes you."

She completely disarmed him again. And humbled him.

Sullivan drew her into her room, shutting the door behind them. His eyes washed over her face, absorbing every detail. "You know, for someone in advertising, you're incredibly open and honest."

Which was what undid him. Deceit he was accustomed to. He knew how to deal with that, but pure honesty was something entirely different. He had no weapons at his disposal to arm himself.

Battles were lost that way. And so were wars.

She couldn't be any other way. Even if she had had the resources available to her, she couldn't lie, couldn't scheme. Especially not with him.

"Advertising's my profession, Sullivan. My career." She shrugged. "Real life is something totally different. You can't get anything worthwhile out of it if you lie or steal."

He knew exactly what she meant. She was talking about her child. The child he and his father had sought to steal out of her arms. His feelings crystalized. In that moment he became her champion. She had found precisely the right way to unravel him.

He skimmed her mouth with his own, his tongue lightly playing along her lips. Her moan of pleasure ripped into his consciousness, stirring him.

"I know what I want to get out of it. You." Slowly, he passed his lips over hers again, deepening the kiss, making it sizzle. Making both of them burn, yearning for more. "Only you."

Because she knew what was ahead, because she so desperately wanted to have reached that plateau already and yet savor the route as long as she possibly could, Marlene found herself trembling against him.

Sullivan pulled her so closely to him that the separate outlines of their bodies were blurred. "Cold?"

She moved her head from side to side, her eyes on his. "Just the opposite."

Her eyes were smoky, he thought, excitement leaping in his veins. "Funny how it grows warmer the less you have on."

"Funny," she echoed.

There was no gentle removal of clothing this time. Niceties were cast aside in their eagerness to cleave to one another.

Sullivan pulled the fishnet sweater over her head, then flung it aside. It hit the bed, then slid off. He anointed each bared shoulder with his lips as his fingers worked the clasp on the front of her bra. It popped open and her breasts, small and firm, were covered by his waiting hands.

Marlene drew in a sharp breath as she felt Sullivan's fingers pass over her nipples, hardening them until they ached so that he could caress them with his tongue. Unable to remain still, she arched and twisted against him, needing to absorb the heat of his body.

Her breathing was ragged as she felt desire throb insistently within her loins. She grasped at his shirt, almost tearing it from him.

He caught her hands, wanting to prolong this just a little longer. The eagerness with which she touched him, with which she took possession of him, annihilated his self-control. There was just the barest shred left.

"Hey, slow down."

It took her a moment to focus on the world, a moment longer to focus on his face. "Why?" she breathed.

He grinned, his mouth coming down on hers. Suddenly, he couldn't remember the reason that had been there a moment ago. "You've got me."

Did she, she wondered, her mind hazy. Did she really?

Just an expression, Marlene, don't get carried away. You only have today. Tomorrow it might be a completely different story.

But she fervently prayed that the story would repeat itself, like a treasured rerun.

And then she couldn't think at all. Her mind was filled with the sight, the taste, the feel of him and nothing more. There wasn't room for anything more.

Marlene dragged the shirt from his arms, flinging it to the floor. She was anxious to feel his chest sealed to hers. Eager to have him make love with her.

She felt him smiling against her skin. The very sensation tantalized her. "I think you ripped off a button."

Who cared about shirts or buttons, or anything else at a time like this? "I'll buy you a new one for Christmas," she promised, her voice thick. "We just landed a shirt company. I have my pick."

With each pass, her excitement rose. Her mouth scrambled along his skin, tasting, savoring the dusky flavors, heightening the passion that burned between them like an untended grass fire.

Sullivan gripped her shoulders, trying to slow her down. He could hardly keep up. "Blue."

She stopped, looking at him, confused. "Blue what?"

He dove his fingers into her hair, cupping her head. "The shirt. Make the shirt blue, like your eyes, so I can think of them when I wear it." His words whispered along her face. "So I can think of you."

They tumbled onto the bed, clinging to each other. He knew he'd said too much, exposed too much of himself. But right now, he didn't want to think about anything except the delicious sensations that were battering against his body, demanding release.

A bittersweetness wove through him, and he knew she was the source. He felt sorry that it had taken him so many years to find someone like her, sorry that it would be over much too quickly. Circumstances would see to that.

And yet, he felt happy because he had snared this moment in time.

By his own example, he knew that there were men who had so much less and would never know this kind of feeling no matter how many women they had.

He didn't have her, he reminded himself. She was only on loan. He had to be satisfied with that.

His fingers tangled in her underwear, almost tearing them aside. Sullivan ran his hands over the length of her body. She felt like ivory, like something far too precious to be real. But she was real, and for the night, she was his to adore and worship.

He worshiped freely, passionately and at length.

Marlene moaned, moving to the rhythm he created for them. His hands and mouth discovered all her secrets, all her pulse points which touched off alarms throughout her body.

Alarms that echoed within his own.

By all rights, the bed should have been on fire. Lord knew that she was. She twisted and turned, grasping the comforter and smothering the cries that leaped to her lips, begging for release as Sullivan, with his clever hands and questing mouth, brought her from one high peak to another.

How could he do this, over and over, make her climb a summit and explode into star bursts, only to begin the process again?

It didn't seem possible. And yet it was happening. Deliciously, wondrously, it was happening. Her body wasn't her own. She hovered over it, experiencing everything twofold and glorying in it.

She felt his mouth lowering wantonly, sliding along her belly. Her skin quivered as the heat from his lips burned his brand into her. Marlene thought her fingers were going to break off as she clutched the comforter, swallowing a scream.

His tongue worked magic.

Hot, sweaty, she slipped back to earth, knowing the spell was never going to be broken.

"I'm exhausted," she fairly gasped as his mouth withdrew from the core of her femininity.

His body slid up along hers. She could feel the fire flaming again. His eyes were wicked as he looked into her face. "Too tired to do it one more time?"

She might have somehow found the strength to say yes, but she knew she would have regretted it forever. One look at his face had her regaining ground.

Marlene cleaved to him, her body invitingly sealed against his. Strength suddenly came from some distant, untapped source. She silently blessed it. "What do you think?"

Sullivan ran the palm of his hand along her arm. "I think I'm going to be a hell of a tired man by morning. But I'll be happy. Very, very happy," he promised her.

Happy for perhaps the first time in his life, he thought as he rolled onto her.

He sheathed himself in her and began to move. It was a familiar place and yet so new that it was overwhelming. He'd had sex enough times to know the drill, enjoy the feelings that came and went in flashes. But making love with Marlene was different. It brought a happiness with it that was completely unknown to him.

Quick of mind, able to handle himself in any given situation, Sullivan Travis had absolutely no idea how to handle happiness.

So he allowed it to handle him.

Her hips arched up to his. The movement that caught them both in its grip was so welcomed, so intense, it took his breath away.

As did she.

If he could have had any wish in the world granted, he thought some time later, he would have wanted to remain holding her like this until the world ended.

Sullivan smiled to himself. That was a strange wish for a cynic. But then, Marlene had rubbed that edge off him. He didn't feel quite so cynical anymore. What he felt, he thought, was vulnerable.

He supposed that was the price he had to pay in exchange for the feelings that he had been showered with.

Sullivan gathered Marlene against him. "You look very pleased with yourself."

She sighed, contentment seeping through her like honey coating the side of a glass. "I guess I am. I never thought I would be, not outside the perimeter of my career. Not that I was outside the office all that much before..." She was about to say before him, but knew that placed too much pressure on Sullivan. "...the baby."

He toyed with the ends of her hair. "Why did you feel you had to work so hard?"

"To make it up to my father." Her response was automatic. "Because I wasn't Robby."

Sullivan thought of the baby. "Robby?"

She nodded, leaning her head against the crook of his arm. "My brother."

He remembered now. Curiosity and concern prodded him. "What happened to him?" he asked gently.

Marlene hesitated. Over the years she'd buried the need to mention the brother she had loved so very much. But now, she wanted to share the memory with Sullivan. Needed to share this hidden part of herself. She wanted him in her world completely, without reservations.

"He died when I was ten." She smiled sadly, remembering her brother through the haze of time. She'd adored him. "Robby was as outgoing as I was shy. He called me Mouse and tried very hard to make me feel brave." She felt Sullivan's arm tightening around her. It made her feel safe from the hurt. How could such a little thing be so terribly comforting?

"He was always there between my father and me, like a buffer. I thought he was the best brother in the whole world," she whispered with feeling.

Marlene sighed and was silent for so long, Sullivan thought she had retreated from the topic. And then she continued.

"The summer I turned ten, after my mother left us," Sullivan heard her voice quaver, "my father took the three of us to the mountains on vacation. It was a working vacation, but that didn't matter to us. Robby made everything fun.

"The first morning we were there, Robby wanted to go exploring." Her voice grew very still. "Nicole hung back and I wanted to, but Robby dared me to go with him, so I did."

She pressed her lips together as the memory suddenly grew too large to bear. She felt tears in her eyes and held them back, but they welled up in her throat.

"Robby liked to climb trees. He said that when he was in them, he felt tall enough to touch the sky. Climbing always scared me. So did watching him." She swallowed, but the lump refused to leave. "I begged him not to do it, but being Robby, he did.

"He seemed to be part squirrel. He got up high and then looked down at me. 'C'mon up, Mouse,' he called. 'The view's great.'" The words came slowly from her lips. "He lost his balance then and fell out of the tree, almost at my feet. I screamed and held him in my arms, begging him to wake up, calling for help. I held him until he died." The tears were sliding down her cheeks now, but she forced the rest of the words out. They had to get out, out of her heart and into the open. "And I held him after that, until they found us."

"Oh God, Marlene." There were no words to offer. Sullivan couldn't do anything but hold her and try to absorb her pain.

A bitter smile twisted her lips. She stared straight ahead, seeing the past. "My father said it was my fault, that Robby was showing off for me."

It was difficult for Sullivan to bridle his anger. "How could he have laid that kind of a guilt trip on a ten-year-old?" His own father had never done anything that heartless. He'd merely appointed him Derek's keeper in what he thought was everyone's best interest.

She shrugged. Her father had been what he had been. Nothing could change that. She knew. She had tried. "Probably because he didn't even know how old I was and because he was angry. That was the last time he mentioned it, though. The last time he mentioned Robby. I wanted to talk to him about it, about how much I missed Robby, about his death. But my father never let me. I knew he was hurting." She looked up at Sullivan. "He had to be. He'd lost his only son. And I tried to make it up to him." The futility burned into her soul. "I spent most of my life trying. And failing. My father was very good at pointing out how much I failed."

She realized that she was crying and brushed the tears away. She felt embarrassed. "I'm sorry. First I decorate you with tinsel, then I cry all over you..."

He kissed the top of her head, wishing there was something he could do, something he could say that would erase her pain. "It's all right. I don't mind—as long as I'm not the one who made you cry."

She let out a deep sigh that was more of a shudder. "You're not."

Marlene raised her eyes to his. There was a deep-seated need to draw closer to him, a closeness that arose from intimacy of the soul. And there were things she knew he was holding back, things that he'd bottled up inside. "Tell me about your brother."

The request caught him off guard. "There's not much to tell." But he saw that she was waiting, so he forced himself to relax and remember. If he went back to the beginning, when they'd both been very young, there were more good memories than bad. He harvested them.

"All right." He settled back, holding her against him. "Derek was tall, good-looking, with a great sense of humor." Sullivan's voice softened as the image took form. "He could have been anything he wanted to be. What he chose to be was a thorn in my father's side. He did that very well."

Sadness and anger welled up inside of him. Sullivan closed his eyes and shook his head, emitting a sigh he was unaware of. "What he was, in the end, was a jerk. He had everything going for him, and he blew it because he was angry at my father for making demands on him."

Marlene saw his rigid jaw, the feelings that were sublimated. She understood. "But you loved him."

The denial rose quickly and dissolved just as fast. For her there could be nothing but the truth. She knew it anyway.

"But I loved him." He shrugged. "Didn't help him any, and it didn't do a hell of a lot for me, either. I couldn't change him."

"But you tried. There's only so much you can do. Some people won't, or can't, change, no matter how much we love them." She brushed her hand along his cheek. "And don't knock love. Love of any kind sees you through. If I hadn't had Nicole, even though most of the time I feel responsible for her, I don't know if I'd be here today." She smiled, looking into his eyes. "Love gives you a nice warm place to go to in the middle of storms."

That's what she was to him, he thought, a nice warm place. And he wanted to go back there now.

He pressed a kiss to her temple. "Can we stop trading family histories for a while?"

Marlene could feel her pulses beginning to scramble. The past and the future disappeared, leaving just the two of them. "Sure."

Sullivan's lips slowly wove their way along the outline of her cheek. "Good, because I'd like to make love with you again."

She turned her body to his, issuing an open invitation. "That's what I like. A man who knows what he wants."

Chapter Fifteen

Osborne looked surprised to see him, but quickly took Sullivan's coat. "I would watch my step if I were you, Master Sullivan. His mood is raw this morning."

Rather than going to the office from Marlene's bed, Sullivan had decided to stop at his father's house first. They needed to talk.

"It shouldn't be." Sullivan looked toward the closed doors. Beyond them was the living room where his father liked to sit by the fire for hours, pouring over photographs of projects he had coheaded in years past. "The rains have finally stopped for a while. We might even be able to dry out and do a little construction for a change. Building always makes him happy."

Hanging the coat up, Osborne shook his head. "I'm afraid that won't help this time." Osborne gave him a knowing look as he retreated. "Good luck, sir."

Why did he feel as if he were going to need it? Taking a deep breath, Sullivan opened the double doors. The smell of scented wood, lemon polish and old cognac wafted to him. He saw the decanter on the coffee table. It was unopened. Was his father celebrating, or mourning?

"Good morning, Dad."

Oliver turned his chair so abruptly, it sent the album on his lap falling to the floor. "You weren't home last night."

Sullivan picked up the album and placed it on the table beside the decanter. "I know."

His father's eyes scrutinized him shrewdly. "I called you several times, and each time your answering machine picked up. It's not like you to stay out during the week."

Cognac wasn't just for celebrating or mourning, he realized. Sometimes, it was for taking the edge off and warming chilled bones. Such as now. Sullivan poured himself less than one finger and sipped it before answering. "It's not a school night, Dad."

"Don't get sarcastic with me, Sullivan." Oliver moved his chair so that he was directly in front of Sullivan. "That's how your brother started, and look at how he ended up."

Sullivan took another sip to wash away the bad taste in his mouth. It was all there in front of him, and the old man just couldn't see it, could he?

"Maybe *you* should take a look at how Derek ended up and change your approach."

Rage crept through the whiskers of his beard and colored Oliver's entire face. "What are you talking about?"

His father had to stop thinking that he could orchestrate everyone's life. Last night, lying beside Marlene, Sullivan had finally gotten his priorities completely in order. And he knew his father's place in the scheme of things. It wasn't at the helm.

"Marlene Bailey."

Oliver had no idea where this was leading. All he knew was that a pretty face had scrambled his son's razor-sharp mind.

"Was that where you were last night? With her?" Oliver frantically searched his son's face. No, Sullivan wouldn't just turn his back on everything. He was proceeding according to plan. That had to be it. Oliver relaxed. "Wonderful."

The shift in inflection, in manner, stunned Sullivan. He stared at his father. "I don't think I managed to jump that transition in the road with you."

The incredulousness in Sullivan's tone failed to register. Of course, it was so simple, Oliver speculated. He hadn't thought of winning the woman over with romance, but perhaps Sullivan's unorthodox methods were best.

"Of course you did," Oliver insisted. "If you wine her, dine her, get her to trust you, then we can proceed according to plan."

Sullivan sighed. He should have seen that one coming. "There isn't a plan."

Confusion mingled with annoyance rose in Oliver's gray eyes. "What are you talking about? Of course there's a plan."

Sullivan regarded his empty glass and thought of filling it, this time to the top. But alcohol wasn't the solution here, especially at this hour. There probably wasn't a solution, he thought with regret. But he had to try.

"I'm talking about leaving that boy where he is. With his mother."

It took Oliver a moment to assimilate what he was hearing. In all these years, Sullivan had never crossed him. If they'd had a difference of opinion over a project, things were always resolved rationally and quickly. This situation had the makings of something very different.

His son had changed since Derek's last folly had come to light. Changed so that he hardly recognized him.

Oliver waved a dismissive hand at Sullivan. "You're obviously not going to be any use to me. Somehow, she's turned you into her stooge. But make no mistake about this, Sullivan, I am going to sue for custody. And I'm going to win. That boy belongs in this family."

Sullivan knew that Oliver meant what he said. He'd seen that same light in his father's eyes on numerous occasions when the man had gone after something he really wanted. In the last year, that light had all but gone out. Sullivan had hoped a sense of purpose would reenter his father's life, but why did it have to be Marlene's baby? Nothing but disaster lay at the end of a custody battle. He couldn't allow him to do that to Marlene.

His hands on the wheelchair's armrests, Sullivan leaned down until he was face-to-face with his father. "Listen to me, old man. If you sue or do anything at all to threaten the unity of that family, I swear I'll oppose you with every weapon at my disposal."

"Are you crazy, Sullivan? You can't talk to me that way."

That was just it, Sullivan thought. He'd held his tongue far too long. Standing by, observing his father and brother go at each other, he'd remained silent. And Derek had died.

Straightening, Sullivan shoved his hands into his pockets and distanced himself from his father. "Somebody should have. A long time ago, somebody should have. Then maybe Derek would still be here." There was only bewildered confusion in his father's eyes. He didn't have a clue what he was saying, Sullivan thought. "You can't always get your way, Dad. You drove Derek away with your deeds. All he ever wanted was to be himself, but you weren't interested in that. You were interested in him being a younger version of you."

Oliver gripped his armrests, wishing he could stand toe to toe with this stranger he had thought was his son. He dammed the frail health that had passed this sentence of immobility on him.

"And what's so wrong with that? At his age, I'd already been running this company for five years. I was *someone,*" Oliver shouted. And then it was as if all the power, all the energy had been siphoned from his face. "Derek turned out to be a nobody." There was deep regret in his voice.

"Did it ever occur to you that maybe he failed on purpose just to show you that everything you turned your hand at didn't instantly become a success?"

Oliver's gray brows meshed into one quizzical line. "Meaning what?"

"Meaning him, your son." He saw that his father didn't comprehend. Sullivan tried again. "That you didn't raise sons very well."

"What are you talking about?" Oliver shook his head. "I raised you."

Sullivan thought of the parade of nannies after his mother's untimely death. Of the impersonal boarding schools. And of the man he'd turned out to be, one who would have gone ahead and taken a child from his mother simply because he was following edicts his father had instilled in him.

"Maybe that isn't to your credit, either. Excuse me, I need a little air." Nothing was going to be resolved here. He had to get the machinery in gear to help Marlene if he was ever going to look at himself in the mirror again.

Sullivan stormed toward the French doors and noticed for the first time that Osborne had framed the interior doorway with a silver garland. Somehow, in light of the conversation, it didn't seem appropriate.

He looked over his shoulder at his father. "And by the way, Merry Christmas."

Sullivan slammed the door in his wake.

"This is nice," Nicole whispered to Marlene over her third cup of eggnog. "Very nice."

She looked around the banquet room that Dr. Pollack had reserved for the afternoon. The restaurant was situated on the crest of a hill, and they had a clear view of the city below. Washed clean by the rains, everything looked fresh beneath the clear blue sky.

The room, decorated for the season and sporting nineteenth-century murals that gave it a Victorian flavor, had a cozy feel to it. There was even a fire burning in the brick fireplace. Nicole loved it.

Originally, Dr. Pollack had been Marlene's obstetrician. Nicole had gone to her on her sister's recommendation and remained as much because of the woman's kind, easygoing manner as her competence. She was doubly glad she did now. Nicole always loved a party.

"Do all doctors do this?" Nicole had no regular physician. Only Marlene's relentless urgings that she was endangering the baby's health had finally convinced her to see the obstetrician.

Marlene laughed. "I don't know. Maybe when they have a bumper crop."

She looked around at the women at the party. She was one of the few in the room of twenty women or so who wasn't pregnant.

"Hey, look," Nicole pointed toward a woman near the fireplace. "There's Erin."

Marlene saw a small-boned woman with a torrent of auburn hair that caught the firelight and looked almost red. She was talking to another woman, punctuating her sentences with animated gestures.

The name was vaguely familiar, but Marlene couldn't recall why. "Erin?"

Nicole looked at her sister impatiently. She'd only mentioned the woman to her three times. "You know, Erin. The woman I got into a conversation with last month. The one who offered me a job at her floral shop." She saw that Marlene still didn't remember.

This would jar her memory. Nicole leaned her head in closer to her sister, lowering her voice. "Her 'significant other' went out for the proverbial newspaper and never came back. He's been missing ever since."

"Oh, Erin," Marlene said, finally remembering. Instantly, her face clouded with sympathy. How awful to be so callously abandoned by someone you loved.

Nicole passed her hand over her abdomen. "I know it's horrid, but it made me feel as if I wasn't quite so alone in this." Craig had been gone almost six weeks now, but even before he'd died, he hadn't wanted the baby. It had made her feel isolated.

Marlene looked at Nicole. Was that how she felt? Alone? Had she gotten so wrapped up in her own problems that she had neglected her sister? Marlene threaded her arm around Nicole's slender shoulders.

"You'll never be alone, Nic," she promised. "Not as long as you have me."

"And the babies," Nicole added. "Don't forget the babies."

Just then, Nicole's baby kicked, sending a ripple through her stomach. Marlene felt it against her own ribs. She laughed, looking down at her sister's quivering abdomen. "Not likely."

"So how are you two?" Sheila Pollack came up behind them and placed a hand on either sisters' shoulder. A tall, stately blonde with emerald green eyes, she looked more suited to being in the center of a party than in the middle of an operating room. But medicine had been her passion ever since she could remember. She felt an obligation to take a personal interest in each of her patients' well-being. Inspired, she'd thrown this Christmas party at her uncle's restaurant.

"Fine," Nicole answered.

"Terrific," Marlene assured her.

Sheila smiled as she nodded, pleased. "I'm so glad you both could make it. I know how busy you are, Marlene." Sheila gestured around the room. "What do you think of my baby of the month club?"

Nicole looked at her. "Baby of the month club?" she echoed.

She nodded. "Not a free month from now until August. There's at least one or two babies due due each month. I've never had such a fertile group of patients before."

Sheila thought of the tiny life forming beneath her own heart. As of yet, she hadn't told anyone. She was determined to keep this secret to herself as long as possible. She wasn't certain if it would shake or enhance her patients' confidence to know that their doctor might deliver before they did.

Sheila smiled at Nicole. "And you're the first one up, now that your sister's had hers." She saw the cup in Nicole's hand. "How do you like the eggnog? It's nonalcoholic, but still has a kick."

"I know. This is my third one," Nicole admitted without a trace of embarrassment.

Sheila's grin widened. "Isn't science wonderful?" Tucking an arm through each of theirs, she directed them none too subtly toward a lively looking woman with dark hair. "Here, let me introduce you to some of your fellow mothers-in-waiting." Sheila winked. "Misery loves company."

Nicole shook her head. "I'm not miserable," she lied.

Sheila had her doubts. Nicole couldn't be comfortable with the weight she was carrying. She made a mental note to request another sonogram right after Christmas. The last had shown that there was only one fetus, but she wanted to be reassured. "Music to my ears, Nicole. Then you can lead the cheering section."

Nicole looked a little skeptical. "I wouldn't go that far."

Marlene laughed as she allowed Sheila to lead her away. She glanced at the way the doctor's dress fit her and noted that it was a little tight. She dismissed the observation as soon as it registered. After all, it was the holidays. Everyone tended to overeat.

"Mallory, I'd like you to meet Nicole Logan and her sister, Marlene Bailey." Sheila smiled warmly at the petite redhead. "Mallory's in real estate. She sold me the house I'm living in."

Mallory looked down at her expanding girth. "Now I just look like a house." She eyed Marlene. "Do you have any children?"

"One." It felt wonderful to say that, she thought. "A son."

"She delivered in an elevator during that big storm at the beginning of the month," Nicole chimed in. Just thinking about it still made her shiver.

Mallory looked at Marlene appreciatively. "A little more than three weeks and you look like that?" She looked up toward the sky. "Yes, Virginia, there is a Santa Claus." Taking over as Sheila moved on to other guests, Mallory directed Marlene and Nicole to a group of women at the banquet table. "C'mon, let me introduce you around. I know everyone. So, what line of work are you in?" she asked Marlene.

"Advertising."

Mallory's eyes lit up. "Really? Listen, tell me what you think of this slogan—"

Marlene let herself in and closed the door quietly behind her. The lights on the Christmas tree crept out into the hall and lit up the foyer. Nicole had remained at the Christmas party, but Marlene had been in a hurry to come home to Robby. After all, this was his first Christmas Eve.

In honor of that, and in the spirit of the season, she'd given everyone at the agency Christmas Eve Day off as well as the week between the two holidays. They'd all worked hard during the preholiday madness and more than deserved a few extra days off. Except for two people, they all had families, and now that she was in the same boat, Marlene knew what it meant to want to spend a little extra time with loved ones.

She found Sally in the kitchen, putting the finishing touches on a tray of rum balls.

Marlene picked one up and popped it into her mouth. She savored the taste for a moment. "How's my guy?" she asked.

Sally beamed. "He was a little angel while you were gone."

Robby was almost too good to be true. Marlene was infinitely grateful to the powers that be for making him so. "Glad to hear that." She debated taking a second rum ball, then decided to save them for later.

Sally nodded her head, eyeing Marlene. "Not like you."

Marlene laughed. "Thank you for sharing, Sally." She looked toward the stairs. "Is he up?"

"I put him down half an hour ago." She indicated the baby monitor on the counter. It was one of several set around the house. "He's sleeping like the baby he is."

Marlene felt disappointed. She'd left the party as soon as it was politely feasible. "I wanted to play with him tonight." It was only six o'clock, but Robby had already developed a pattern, and she knew that he would be asleep until after eleven. "Guess I'll have to wait until Christmas morning."

Sally dusted her hands on her apron. "Need some company?"

Marlene shook her head. "No, that's all right. I think I'll just have a little eggnog and watch my movie." The videotape was exactly where she had left it, in the family room on the coffee table. As she picked it up, the doorbell rang. She exchanged looks with Sally.

"Well, looks like you're going to get some company whether you want it or not." Sally shuffled out to the foyer.

Her hand on the doorknob, Sally looked through the peephole. She hesitated a moment, then stepped back as she opened the door. She looked from the man in the wheelchair to the tall, stately man standing behind him.

"Yes?"

Osborne gave the small woman a perfunctory smile. "Mr. Oliver Travis to see Ms. Marlene Bailey."

Sally gestured behind her. "Right this way."

Oh God, not tonight, Marlene thought, coming forward. The only Travis she had wanted to see was Sullivan, not his father.

"I'll take it from here, Sally." Marlene's tone was formal as she braced herself for what was coming.

Oliver looked around the house with a discerning eye, then turned his chair to face Marlene. "So, is he here?"

Marlene felt her spine stiffening. Did Travis actually think that she was just going to hand over her son to him? She looked at Osborne

"Who?"

"Sullivan." Oliver's answer surprised her, but she recovered quickly. "I know he was here last night."

She took it as an accusation and treated it as such. "Whether he was or not is none of your business, Mr. Travis."

"Everything is my business." Oliver held up a hand that had once been powerful. "I didn't come here to fight."

He was undoubtedly accustomed to having his way, with people giving in to him automatically. That wasn't going to happen tonight. "Why did you come here?"

Rendering apologies was not something he was accustomed to doing. Still, he was man enough to extend one when he was wrong. And Sullivan had helped him to realize that he had been, about some things.

"To offer a peace pipe, so to speak. You like Indians, Ms. Bailey?" He continued before she could answer. "No, they're not Indians any more, are they? These days they're Native Americans." Oliver snorted. "Everyone gets offended because they're not called by some fancy new label. In my time, things were what they were and there were rules for everything. Now, the only rule is that there aren't any rules." He looked truly saddened. "None of the old ones at any rate."

Oliver sighed. He knew that he was rambling, but the young woman had the decency to let him. Maybe he'd been wrong. Maybe he could get to like her after all. "Well, at any rate, they used to have this custom of smoking a peace pipe when making a treaty with the enemy."

She still wasn't certain she understood why he was here. Was this all just an act to throw her off, or was he serious? If he was, his choice of words left something to be desired.

"Is that what I am, the enemy?"

"I don't know what you are yet, but I intend to find out. You're my grandson's mother, and it seems that I'm going to have to learn how to live with that."

Her expression gave nothing away. "Yes, you are."

It was the first time she saw the man smile. "Spunky, aren't you?"

She hadn't heard that word in years. Slowly, a smile curved her own lips. Maybe this was a peace treaty after all. But what had suddenly brought it on? "I try to be."

Oliver nodded. "Just like Sullivan." He pursed his lips, a thoughtful expression on his face. "Talked back to me today. First time I can remember that I couldn't get him to carry out an order."

"Which was?"

"Making arrangements to take you to court," Oliver told her honestly. "Said it was my fault Derek left home." It was hard at his age to admit he was wrong, but better now than never. Mistakes were for fools. The only thing worse than a fool was someone who stubbornly refused to admit he had made a mistake when he had. "Said a lot of things that made me think." He got directly to the point. "I lost my firstborn, Ms. Bailey. I don't want to lose my first grandson."

She knew it had to have taken a lot for him to come here tonight. That he did touched her. And she had been wrong. Oliver Travis wasn't anything like her father at all.

"You won't. And it's Marlene." She smiled. "You can visit Robby any time you want."

Her answer seemed to please Oliver to no end. "Fine I'll have my lawyer draw up papers about the visitation rights tomorrow."

Did he really think that was necessary? Marlene shook her head. "It's Christmas. And we don't need papers. Just a handshake." She extended hers to the old man. "We're family."

He took her hand, enveloping it in both of his. "Yes, I suppose we are in a manner of speaking." He could see why Sullivan had sided with her against him. The lady had style. "Too bad Derek never had the opportunity to meet you. Things might have turned out differently if he had. I might have gotten a grandson in the usual manner." Oliver smiled at her knowingly. "I still might."

She had no idea what he was referring to, but let it go. They'd made enough headway today.

She glanced down at the tape in her other hand, surprised that she had held on to it throughout the conversation.

"I was just about to watch my favorite movie. It's a Christmas Eve tradition. Would you like to join me?" Her invitation took in the man with Travis as well.

Oliver thought of declining, then paused. It had been a long time since a pretty girl had asked him to spend some time with her.

"I'd love to," he told her a moment later. "For a little while."

"My name is Osborne, Miss," Osborne said to her as he followed Travis into the living room.

"Glad to meet you, Osborne." Marlene hugged the tape to her. "Very glad."

He should have gone home, Sullivan thought, but somehow, it seemed too empty a place to go to. He didn't want to be alone tonight. Instead, he made his way to Marlene's house. Where he belonged, he thought. At least for a little while.

Sullivan caught a glimpse of the car in his rearview mirror as he pulled into Marlene's driveway. His father's limousine. The long, black vehicle was disappearing down the road.

Damn that old man, he'd harassed her on Christmas Eve. Sullivan swore under his breath. How could he? Had his father become so obsessed with getting custody of Derek's son that he'd actually come to have papers served on Marlene on Christmas Eve?

It was entirely possible. Sullivan wondered what sort of extensive damage control would be required this time before things were made right. He wondered if this meant he'd gone up in the world, from cleaning up his brother's messes to smoothing over his father's.

Getting out of the car, he hurried to the front door. He didn't bother ringing the bell; he was too agitated. Instead, he knocked, hard.

When she opened the door, he saw that her eyes were red-rimmed. It was worse than he thought. Damn that old man, thinking he had a right to play God with other people's lives.

Sullivan took hold of her arms. "What did he say to you? Did he threaten you? Anything he says he can do, Marlene, I swear I'll—"

He was talking too fast. Marlene laid a finger to his lips before he could continue. "No, he was rather sweet, actually."

Dazed, he moved her hand aside. "Sweet? My father?" That didn't sound like an apt description of Oliver Travis even at his best. He eyed her dubiously. "Then why are you crying?"

Marlene threaded her fingers through his and led Sullivan into the living room. There was a black-and-white film playing on the wide-screen TV housed within the ebony entertainment center.

She gestured toward it. "I always cry when I watch *It's A Wonderful Life.*" She smiled without embarrassment. "It's a tradition."

Sullivan stared dumbly at the picture on the screen. "A movie?"

She shook her head at his choice of words, like a parent listening to her child making an elementary mistake. "Not just a movie, the best movie ever made."

Sullivan let out a sigh and dragged his hand through his hair. "You had me going for a minute." He brushed aside the remnant of a tear on her cheek with his thumb. "As a matter of fact, you've had me going since I first saw you."

She raised her face to look up into his eyes. So many things to be thankful for tonight, she thought. "Is that a good thing or a bad thing?"

That depended purely on the outcome of their situation. "You tell me."

She smiled up at him. "I vote 'good.'"

Moved beyond words, Sullivan took her into his arms. He felt as if something had been lifted from him. And it was. The last of the indecision he'd been wrestling with all the way over here disintegrated. He saw the rest of his life with clarity now. And he wanted to spend it with Marlene, because if she wasn't there, then his life had no meaning at all.

Marlene pressed her cheek against his chest. His cologne mingled with the outdoorsy scent of a cold, crisp evening. She breathed it in and felt safe.

He stroked her hair. The familiar feel seeped into his subconscious. Funny how he had gotten accustomed to so many little things so quickly. And what a huge gap not having those things in his life would create.

"You know, holding you like this makes the rest of my life look bleak, if I think of it in terms of going on alone."

She raised her head to look at his face. One last chasm to leap over, she thought. Mentally she backed up, gaining momentum. "You could always come to visit, along with your father."

He wanted more than that, much more. He was accustomed to taking risks, but never privately, never where his emotions were concerned. It was time to take a risk now.

"Could I come to stay?" He searched her face, looking for his answer.

Hope rose like a phoenix, full-bodied, with wings raised high. The chasm became smaller. "For as long as you like."

He kissed her temple. "And if I'd like forever?"

She blinked back a tear. Damn, she wasn't going to cry, not now. Not when she was happy. "It's right here, waiting for you."

Yes, he thought, it was. But he'd been too blind, too safe in his solitary world to see.

But not any more.

He kissed her lips, savoring the taste. He was the luckiest man to walk the face of the earth. And he owed it, at least in part, to Derek.

Sullivan held her against him. "I love you, Marlene. I keep waiting for these feelings I have for you to go away, but they don't. I can't seem to reason with myself or talk myself out of them."

"Why would you want to?" She touched his cheek. "Love is the greatest thing in the world. I know, because I feel it."

It was too much to hope for. "For Robby."

"Yes, for Robby. But I wasn't thinking of him just now." Some horses you not only led to water, you had to shove their faces into the trough before they drank. "I was thinking of you, you big idiot."

They were right. This was a time for miracles, Sullivan thought. "Me? You love me?"

The smile spread slowly, splitting her mouth until it encompassed her entire face. "You *have* been paying attention."

He laughed and she felt the sound rumble along his chest into hers. "I guess this means that we're going to have to change Robert's middle name."

She drew her brows together, lost. "Why?"

What had she thought he'd meant by "forever"? "Because Robert Travis Travis sounds a little redundant, don't you think?"

Marlene's mouth dropped open. "Are you...asking me to marry you?"

"In a clumsy, roundabout fashion, yes." As far as proposals went, this was a poor one. She deserved better. A romantic restaurant, violins. But he was too impatient to wait. "I don't have any practice at this."

If a person was actually capable of bursting with happiness, Marlene knew she would have. "And you're not going to get any."

"Then it's yes?"

"Of course it's yes," she cried. She blinked furiously to keep back the tears.

She loved him and she was going to marry him. He played the sentences over in his head, waiting for them to really sink in. "I intend to be a good father to Robby. The kind of father Robby deserves."

"Robby deserves you." She rose on her toes and brought her lips to his. "We both do."

"I don't know about 'deserves,' but you're getting me whether you like it or not." His lips met hers, and he lost himself in the deep, tangy flavor of her mouth.

Vaguely, a noise registered. Sullivan lifted his head. It sounded like a tiny bell tinkling in the distance. Doorbell? Telephone? Sullivan tried to place the sound. "What was that?"

Marlene pointed toward the tree without looking. "That's probably just Clarence, getting his wings. That's what usually takes place when a miracle happens." Her eyes held his. "This is the night for miracles."

Sullivan grinned broadly, his arms tightening around her. He had no idea what she was talking about. All he knew was that he'd never felt so happy in his entire life. And he suspected that he would continue to feel the same way, as long as she was his. "And I'm holding one."

Marlene slipped her hands around his face and drew it down to her. "Shut up and kiss me again."

"Yes, ma'am. With pleasure."

And it was. A great deal of pleasure. For both of them.

* * * * *

Dear Reader,

Hi, it's me again. I hope you don't mind my repeating how much I enjoy writing romance novels, because I never tire of saying it. I never tire of stopping what I'm doing and focusing on the fact that, yes, I'm a writer (finally) and people are really reading what I've written. I look at my books on the shelf and there are times when it feels as if I'm still dreaming. There is nothing more in this world that I want to be than a writer (with the exception of Charlie's wife and Nicky and Jessi's mum).

Special Editions® have a special (no pun intended) place in my heart. My first large book was a Special Edition. Writing it opened up a wonderful new world for me, one I love returning to. I am very pleased and proud to be launching my new series, The Baby of the Month Club, at this time. Each story is a mini-world where there are obstacles to be overcome, differences that are finally resolved and love waits as a final reward. It's the kind of world that I truly wish existed. I'm deeply touched that each time you pick up one of my books, you allow me to take you along, for although I would always go on writing, it's really nice to have someone to share it with. Thank you for being there.

All my very best,

Marie Ferrarella

I've taken a few liberties with the situation depicted here for the sake of my story (and hopefully your entertainment). What goes on within these pages in no way reflects what transpires in actual sperm banks. Just wanted you to know. Thank you for reading!

COMING NEXT MONTH

HUSBAND BY THE HOUR Susan Mallery

That Special Woman!

Hannah Pace needed a pretend husband and so she hired bad boy Nick Archer. He might not be her long-lost mother's dream groom for Hannah, but he was Hannah's hottest fantasy!

COWBOY'S LADY Victoria Pade

A Ranching Family

Ivey Heller had narrowly escaped marrying the wrong man, so she'd come home to Elk Creek. But within one day she'd met Cully Culhane, a single father with two adorable little girls, and he was now aiming his *considerable* charm right at Ivey!

REMEMBER ME? Jennifer Mikels

Running through the night she remembered nothing of her past. But she needed shelter. She found a cabin...and a broad-shouldered, darkly sensual stranger. Soon she wanted no yesterdays, only today and tomorrow...and this man.

MARRIAGE MATERIAL Ruth Wind

The Forrest Brothers

Lance Forrest had never known that he had a son, a son that Tamara raised as her own, but he hadn't exactly seemed father material back then. But now...now he was looking like very good father material, not to mention irresistible husband material!

RINGS, ROSES...AND ROMANCE Barbara Benedict

Darcy MacTeague had a life on the fast track of the corporate world, but she was very tempted to abandon it all for life as the mistress of sleepy Rose Arbour. Mitch Rose and his three irrepressible kids really wanted her to stay...

A DOCTOR IN THE HOUSE Ellen Tanner Marsh

Millionaire Josh Alden didn't know how to have fun anymore, until he found himself being rescued by Rebel McCade. They were worlds apart, but they couldn't get close enough!